Picture Perfect

Laurie Ellingham writes romances that centre around family and second chances, adding humour to the everyday moments of life.

Before becoming a full-time writer, Laurie studied a degree in psychology and worked in public relations in London. She now lives with her family in the Suffolk countryside, alongside a cockerpoo called Rodney, and two guinea pigs. Laurie also writes psychological suspense as Lauren North.

Readers can follow Laurie on Twitter @LaurieEllingham and Facebook, searching for Laurie Ellingham Author.

PICTURE PERFECT

Laurie Ellingham

This edition first published in Great Britain in 2023 by Orion Dash,
an imprint of The Orion Publishing Group Ltd.,
Carmelite House, 50 Victoria Embankment
London EC4Y 0DZ

A Hachette UK Company

A CIP catalogue record for this book
is available from the British Library.

ISBN (eBook) 978 1 3987 1000 9
ISBN (Paperback) 978 1 3987 1724 4

The Orion Publishing Group Ltd
Carmelite House
50 Victoria Embankment
London, EC4Y 0DZ

An Hachette UK company

www.orionbooks.co.uk

This book is dedicated to all the parents trying their best and not always getting it right. We've all been there! xx

Dear Toddler Tamer

Help!! My children are out of control. They are monsters!

Olly is eight. He's full of energy. So inquisitive about the world. He loves inventing things. But he's a magnet for trouble. He sets traps for the postman and for me. I can't walk into a room anymore without worrying I'm going to be hit by a falling bowl of water. When he's not leading his brother and sister into trouble, he's lashing out at them. Our house is a war zone!

Ben and Matilda are four. They're becoming even naughtier than Olly. Ben is scared of his own shadow but obsessed with slides. He's always trying to make a slide out of the stairs. Matilda is competitive. She's always trying to outdo her brothers and when she doesn't get her own way, she has vicious tantrums. Bedtimes are a nightmare. Mealtimes are a nightmare. Leaving the house is a nightmare. My life is a nightmare!!

I don't know what else to do. I'm completely alone. I have three children that don't listen to a word I say.

Please help me!!!

Becca x

Six hours earlier

Chapter 1

Dear Mrs Harris,

Unfortunately, we were unable to reach you on your contact details this afternoon regarding Ben and Matilda's behaviour at nursery today. We were able to reach your mother who has now collected the twins.

As I'm sure you are aware, there are now only two weeks left of term and all of us here at the pre-school feel it would be in the best interests of the twins to spend their final weeks at home preparing for the next stage in their education journey.

Regards,
Julie Whitehead
Pre-school Manager

I blink, once, twice, a dozen times. It doesn't make sense! I ignore the soft music drifting from the speakers at the front of the church, the shuffle of people moving, and continue to stare at my phone. The lines of the email don't change.

One word punches through my thoughts. No.

No! No, no, no!

This can't be happening.

Two extra weeks at home with Ben and Matilda.

Then the six-week summer holidays with Olly too. And let's not forget the two sneaky inset days tacked on either side of the summer, so it's actually closer to seven weeks, not six. It's like the way chocolate bars keep shrinking, and they think we won't notice one less bite of crunchy gooey chocolate. The devious bastards. I notice!

So that's nine weeks at home with my children. Nine weeks of mayhem, of juggling work and chores, and entertaining two four-year-olds and an eight-year-old who finds trouble quicker than Rex can find a clean basket of laundry to curl up in and cover with her black fur.

You won't be able to do it, a voice whispers in my head. It's right. I won't.

This can't be happening. No, no, no! That word again. The one I hear a hundred times a day. Screamed or shouted, launched at me, usually with a missile in tow – a cuddly toy if I'm lucky; a hard, plastic action figure if I'm not. The day they hold try-outs for an Olympic dodgeball team, it won't be the young and sporty at the front of the queue – all those lithe limbs and tight Lyra; it will be us – the harassed forty-something mums. The exhausted parents. I challenge any of those sporty types to dip, dodge, duck and dive their way past a Nerf gun attack while making packed lunches and answering emails.

But this time it is me who wants to scream 'No' at the top of my lungs; me who wants to stomp my foot and throw something.

Remember Josh has booked time off, I tell myself, clinging to the knowledge as though it's the last scrap of my sanity. One day a week. One whole day to myself, to work, to sniff fabrics and stare at beautiful colour charts. One day when Josh can see how hard it really is, when he'll understand why he comes home to a house that looks like a Lego bomb has exploded in the living room. Plus Mum will help too. It will be OK, won't it?

I love Olly, Ben and Matilda. I would kill for them. I'd fall on a thousand swords for my children, but even one day at home with them leaves me ragged, tattered. And I've still got Mrs Young's entire living room to remodel before Olly breaks up.

Two weeks. That's all Ben and Matilda had left. I've been tearful just thinking about the graduation ceremony with the little black hats and the rolled-up certificates tied in the St Helena's green ribbon. The clapping parents in the designer sunglasses. The little tea party in the garden – a final farewell before Ben and Matilda join Olly at the prep school next door.

Surely they're not saying Ben and Matilda can't attend the ceremony? The gossip will be all over St Helena's. Red heat prickles my skin. Sweat starts to form between my boobs. Why on earth did I choose a push-up bra today of all days? It's like a furnace in here.

'Becca?' Josh's voice is soft in my ear.

'Just a sec.' I jab at my phone and check my call log. Eighteen missed calls stare back at me. Sixteen from the pre-school. Oh God, what did Ben and Matilda do this time?

Surely the staff weren't stupid enough to leave the scissors in reach. Not after poor little Molly's hair incident. To be fair, she was a willing participant right up until the first lock of golden hair fell into her lap.

Another two missed calls – both from my mother, and a text.

Hello darling, I've collected Ben and Matilda from nursery and taken them to your house. I'm missing my afternoon tea with the bowls ladies. Call me! x

A pressure builds, tightening my chest, squeezing my brain. I touch my brow line, pushing my fingers into the skin, willing myself to stop frowning. Guilt burns through me. I should be there. It's a ten-minute drive to St Helena's, seven minutes at a dash. It should've been me picking them up.

Epic fail on the mother of the year award. That voice again. Ha! As if I was ever a contender!

But with that guilt comes a sizzling frustration. Why did it have to be today? The one day I'm not there. The one day I've travelled to west London to stand by my husband's side.

'Becca,' Josh hisses my name, following it with a nudge, and finally I look up to a sea of black and the pinched faces of the mourners waiting to leave the stuffy heat of the church. The line ahead is already at the door. I'm holding everyone up.

The apology is a soft mutter as I stuff my phone into my bag and walk with as much finesse as I can muster in my black leopard-print pumps, knowing full well how ridiculous I look, how my black tailored dress should be worn with pointed-toe, classic heels. Sexy but not slutty. The very shoes I bought last week for this funeral. The same shoes that disappeared into the vortex of lost things somewhere between 9 p.m. last night and 8:15 a.m. this morning when I was trying to get all three kids out the door for the school run while Josh was tutting about the M25 traffic and how his boss will notice if he's late.

'Just wear whatever. No one will notice your shoes,' he said with a final sigh, and so I grabbed the nearest shoes to black I could find. It doesn't matter now that I got up an hour early to wrestle my thick brown hair into mermaid tassels and perfect my make-up. It doesn't matter that I fake tanned my legs with an ancient bottle of fake tan I found in the back of the cupboard. Without the shoes, I feel short and dumpy, and every bit the tired mum of three that I am.

Everyone is staring.

I know I shouldn't care. A man has died. I know this, and yet all of Josh's colleagues are here and I never see them, and the pathetic truth is that I wanted them, I wanted Josh, to notice.

Outside, the early afternoon sun is beating down on the courtyard, a bright piercing yellow that makes everyone reach for their sunglasses. There's a Mediterranean heat to the day, which feels completely wrong for a funeral.

Mourners gather in huddles, shaking off their jackets, fanning themselves with the order of service, talking softly as everyone waits for the immediate family to finish their talk with the vicar and leave for the wake.

'Are you OK?' I ask Josh. His gaze is on the shell-shocked face of the widow, but it's Josh I'm looking at, and the grey pallor to his skin, the strain to his brown eyes that I've noticed more and more lately. There's a tension to him that seems to cloud the handsome features I know as well as my own, and I realise in that moment that I can't remember the last time I heard him laugh.

The truth is, Josh has barely mustered a smile for weeks. There was the Sunday last month when he disappeared into the garden for five hours to pin the creeping pink rose bushes around a wooden trellis archway he'd made. I remember him, standing back, sweaty in the heat, a streak of dirt on his forehead, grinning to himself as Matilda and Ben skipped through the arch, hand in hand, declaring themselves married.

'We were the same age,' Josh says and I know he's talking about Robert, whose smiling face stares out from the order of service in my hand. 'I heard one of the blokes who worked with him say that Robert never had so much as a cold. Never took a sick day. Then bam, his heart stops. No warning sign or anything. We joined the company the same year too. I think I only spoke to him twice. Twice in all that time.'

'You worked in different departments.' I slip my hand into his. It's hot and clammy and he quickly pulls away.

He doesn't want to be seen with you.

I try to ignore the thought, wishing I had something comforting to say, but the email from the pre-school nudges into the forefront of my mind and I can't stop myself from digging out my phone again.

'I need to send a quick email,' I tell Josh.

He nods, his focus on his own phone now, and I step away from the groups and find a corner, a square of shade against the cool stone wall of the church.

To: office@StHelenaspreschool.co.uk
From: Rebecca.Harris@RebeccaHarrisInteriors.com
Subject: Re: The Twins

Hi Julie,

   Sorry I wasn't able to answer my phone today. I did mention at drop-off that I would be out of contact at a funeral for most of the day.

   I must admit, I'm struggling to understand what you're saying. How is it in Ben and Matilda's interest not to return to pre-school to be with their friends for the final two weeks of term?

   Best wishes,
   Becca

The reply comes sixty seconds later.

To: Rebecca.Harris@RebeccaHarrisInteriors.com
From: office@StHelenaspreschool.co.uk
Subject: Re Re: The Twins

Dear Mrs Harris,

As I'm sure you're aware, we have twenty-six other pupils at the pre-school as well as the twins. We must consider what is best for all the children in our charge, and that is for Ben and Matilda not to return to us.

Your mother has collected them and all of their belongings. We will send their pre-school certificates in the post.

Regards,

Julie Whitehead

I grit my teeth. No ceremony then. No floral dress and afternoon tea. No little black hats and grinning photos for my Instagram feed. Anger and desperation swell inside me.

To: office@StHelenaspreschool.co.uk
From: Rebecca.Harris@RebeccaHarrisInteriors.com
Subject: Re Re Re: The Twins

You can't do this! They are four. You can't expel them from pre-school!! They love it. They'll be devastated.

We pay a lot of money to send the children to St Helena's!

To: Rebecca.Harris@RebeccaHarrisInteriors.com
From: office@StHelenaspreschool.co.uk
Subject: Re Re Re Re: The Twins

Dear Mrs Harris,

St Helena's does not believe in using the term 'expel'. Perhaps consider this a period of reflection prior to them moving up to the prep school. With regards to the fees, please refer to the terms and conditions you signed when enrolling the twins into the pre-school.

Regards,
Julie Whitehead

Tears sting at the edges of my eyes. They are hot, angry, selfish tears. Tears for me and tears for Ben and Matilda too. I know what they're like. Of course I do. I know the trouble they can find themselves in, but surely qualified staff – trained individuals – can manage two four-year-olds for two more weeks.

To: office@StHelenaspreschool.co.uk
From: Rebecca.Harris@RebeccaHarrisInteriors.com
Subject: Re Re Re Re Re: The Twins

Please don't do this!!! I know Ben and Matilda can be a handful but they're good children! I'll talk to them. I promise they'll behave for the next two weeks.
   Becca x

It's outright begging. It's pathetic is what it is, but right now I don't care. From the corner of my eye, I spot Josh striding towards me – cool and confident in his black suit, looking every bit the hedge fund manager. He brushes away a strand of brown hair that's dropped onto his forehead and I make a mental note to book haircuts for him and Olly.

'Have you been crying?' Josh asks as I drop my phone into my bag and dab at my eyes.

'It's . . .'

Josh's gaze is already pulling back to the other mourners and the funeral cars now crawling out of the car park. I swallow the words threatening to spill out of me. Josh already gets so angry at the mention of St Helena's. I can't bear another rant on extortionate fees and pompous teachers right now. He's right on both accounts, but you can't live a ten-minute drive away from the very best school in the county and not send your children there. Second cousins of Prince William send their children to St Helena's, not to mention one of the band members of The Falconers.

I'll get the full story from Ben and Matilda first. I'll see if I can fix it before I mention anything to Josh. 'Nothing,' I lie. 'Just funerals. We should get back. I have to collect Olly from after-school football at 4:15.'

There's a pause. A moment when Josh should agree but doesn't. He pulls a face. It's his 'I'm about to tell you something you're not going to like' face. All frown and grimace. The expression is so exaggerated, so Olly-like, that I almost laugh, except at the same time my stomach tenses. I know before he speaks that I'm not going to like whatever he's about to tell me.

'Actually,' he says, glancing my way before his gaze fixes on the gleaming black paintwork of our Range Rover. 'If you don't mind, I'm going to drop you at the nearest Tube station. I think Turnham Green is around here somewhere. I should head to the office for a few hours.'

'But I thought the office was closed today for compassionate leave?' My heart sinks. I'd been looking forward to Josh being home this evening. I'd pictured us sitting in the garden with a glass of wine while the children play. I had the Instagram post all planned out: *#CherishEveryMoment #FamilyIsEverything*

He pushes his fingers into his temples in that way he does when a headache is threatening. 'I heard Neil saying that he's going to pop in and do a few hours so now I have to. I'm sorry.'

Sorry. Another word I hear countless times a day.

Josh strides towards the car and now I'm grateful for my flat pumps and my ability to keep pace. It's going to take me hours to get home on the train. Josh is dumping me on the wrong side of London as it is.

'I can't get the train. There's no way I'll be back in time to collect Olly,' I say.

'Can't you ask one of your mum friends?'

You don't have any mum friends, remember?

Not anymore.

'Or your mum could do it,' Josh says. 'Isn't she collecting Ben and Matilda in a bit anyway.'

Except she's already been to the school once today and already has Ben and Matilda.

'We can't keep relying on my mum for everything,' I say instead. 'She already does so much. Can't you log on and work at home for a bit?'

'It'll be too noisy.'

'Fine. Leave me the car and you get the Tube.'

'Becca, I can't. It'll take ages to get into central London on the Tube from here. Look, there's something else I have to tell you,' he continues.

He has that face again.

'What?' I ask. What could be worse than dropping me at a Tube station in the arse end of London.

He's going to tell you he's working all weekend.

'Let's get in the car first,' he says, throwing a glance over his shoulder to where a group of mourners are still talking. I follow his gaze to a woman in the group – glossy black hair, young, skinny and sickeningly beautiful in that way twenty-somethings are now – all airbrushed make-up, drawn-on brows and plump lips.

She looks quickly to Josh and then back to me. Her gaze falls to my shoes and I catch the flicker of a smirk on her lips. Bloody shoes. Where the hell did my heels get to?

Chapter 2

The car is oven hot. My bare legs stick to the leather and I think, as I always do in moments like this, how much I hate this car. It's practically a bus for one thing. It's near impossible to park and it drinks petrol with the same gusto as I do my Friday night gin and tonic.

But I say nothing. It was me who went on and on about how impossible it would be to survive with three kids without a state-of-the-art, lease Range Rover, me who said our whizzy little VW Golf wouldn't cut it on the school run, completely skipping over the real reason – how convinced I was that the other mums would look down on me if I didn't have the right car.

As Josh starts the engine, cold air blasts from the vent and we follow the line of traffic inching out of the car park.

'What did you want to tell me?' I ask, my eyes straying back to the woman with the black hair.

Silence from Josh.

'Josh, what is it?' Irritation rings in my voice. I swallow it down. We should be having wistful conversations about living in the moment not bickering about the usual kids/work/money merry-go-round of fights we have.

'Look,' Josh says, eyes on the road ahead as we pull into slow moving traffic. 'Don't hate me. I never meant for this to happen.'

He's leaving you. He's finally had enough of you.

Oh God. Cold sweeps through my body. He wouldn't.

Can you blame him though? Look at what a mess you are all the time.

'I'm being sent to the New York office for two months.'

'What?' I gasp. A giddy relief sweeps over me. He's not leaving me. Not for ever anyway.

Josh shifts in his seat, a hand digging at the space between his collar and his neck. I briefly wonder if he's feeling strangled by it, and if he isn't, whether I can throttle him instead. 'I know the timing of this trip is rubbish,' he says, 'but I can't say no. You understand that, right? It's not optional.'

I lean my head against the headrest, feeling stupid. Of course Josh isn't leaving me. We've been married ten years, together fifteen. Our life is hectic, fraught some of the time, but we're happy, aren't we?

Then Josh's words sink in and somewhere in the back of my mind an alarm rings, loud and urgent. 'Timing? When do you have to go?'

'Next week.'

'Josh.' I jerk forwards. 'You cannot go to New York for two months next week. The summer holidays. The children.'

'I'm sorry.'

Frustration knots inside me. 'But you've taken a day off each week of the summer holidays to look after the kids so I can work, remember? How are you going to do that from New York? How am I supposed to keep my business going?' My voice is shrill, panicked but angry too. He can't do this to me.

He is!

'I know. I'm really sorry,' Josh says, pulling at his collar again.

'Stop saying sorry,' I hiss. 'And say what you mean – your job is more important than mine.'

'Yes, actually,' he snaps. 'Because I earn the money that pays the mortgage, for this sodding car you love so much, all the holidays, the school fees, everything. You pay for what exactly?'

His words slice – a dozen paper cuts inside my chest. 'Hey, I gave up a successful career in interior design to raise the kids. It's not been a massive picnic, in case you haven't noticed.'

I wait for his retort, the one about how he didn't ask me to do that, but it doesn't come. A crackling silence hangs between us – charged, waiting.

'I can't have this argument again.' He sighs. 'I'm sorry about the summer holidays. I know it's going to be hard for you. The company are paying a bonus. Why don't you hire a nanny?'

'A nanny? You're joking? I can't do that.'

Who would even agree to look after Olly, Ben and Matilda?

'Or don't then. You'll figure it out. You've got your mum. I'm leaving Sunday night, all right? For the record, I don't want to go, but if I don't then they'll send someone else and I'll be side-lined and I won't get the bonus that is going to pay for another year of school fees.'

'Sunday night?' I frown. 'As in, in two days' time? But . . .' My head spins with questions. 'How long have you known?'

He sighs again. It's the same way he sighs when Olly begs for a game of football or Matilda wants to drag him into one of her imaginary games. 'I'm the cafe owner. You're the customer.' My jaw clenches. It's the sound he makes when he wants to be somewhere else. Anywhere else.

'Josh. How long have you known about this?' I ask again.

'A few weeks,' he admits. 'I've been trying to tell you. It's just . . . It's a madhouse at home. We never get a moment to talk.'

'That's bullshit. We have the evenings.'

'You mean at ten o'clock when the kids finally pass out and you catch up on work or fall asleep on the sofa and I'm already thinking about how I need to be up at 5 a.m.?'

'That's what everyone does.' My tone is defensive but his comment stings. It's not always 10 p.m. before the kids go to sleep, is it? God, I always have the best intentions at the start of the day, grand plans to settle the kids early and cook something nice – a late dinner, just the two of us, sharing our days, laughing at the kids' mishaps. But the hours slide away and then something happens. Something always happens. Like last week when Olly brought his BMX into the house to ride down the stairs, and Ben and Matilda raided our wardrobe and played dressing-up with all of our clothes and I had to wash and iron all of Josh's shirts again.

Then all my intentions slip away and I throw something easy together, eating mine over the sink while the children squabble at the table, because I'm too bone-tired to wait for Josh to get home and eat with him.

'Maybe if you got home a bit earlier to help,' I say, unable to stop myself starting another of the arguments we've had countless times before. 'It's always work with you. It comes before me and before the kids – before everything. Even though you promised me it wouldn't.'

Josh says nothing. I wonder if he's thinking of those words he whispered in my ear all those years ago when we were lying on the bed together, looking at paint colours for Olly's nursery, when my stomach was a bulging watermelon, and we were so blissfully happy. So naive.

'I'll come home early at least three days a week and take over for bath time. I'll want to spend time with the baby too.'

What a joke! He barely lasted a week. But then, my promises were broken just as easily.

'I don't want us to be those parents who rely on technology to entertain our children. And absolutely no refined sugar unless it's a special occasion. It's so bad for them and so unnecessary.'

Ha! I feel like we alone are keeping Haribo sweets from going out of business.

The memory plunges me into a pool of sadness for the couple we used to be. It's natural for people to change though, right? I mean, we can't be all kisses and compliments all the time.

The ticking of the indicator shakes me from my thoughts. Ahead of us, I spot the red Tube sign for Turnham Green, and the bright colours of a flower stall outside.

'I can't believe this,' I say. The sadness is gone, elbowed out by the anger. Frustrated tears burn at the corners of my eyes. Just for a moment I wonder what would happen if I refused to get out of the car, like Matilda when it's time to leave the playground.

I'm torn. Furious he's dumped this on me now, fuming he's leaving me here like this. But if I slam the door and storm off like I want to, then Josh will drive away and be thinking about work in thirty seconds' time, no doubt forgetting about me and this argument.

'Please don't go into the office now.' I force the anger from my voice and try to sound reasonable, calm, while a tornado rages inside me. 'Come home so we can talk about this.'

'There's nothing more to say. I'm sorry.' His apology hangs in the air and, despite my anger, I know he means it. I open the door and leave without a word. Stunned. Bereft almost, which makes me feel like a cow, because my husband isn't dead. He's going, but he's coming back. He has to come back. I can't do this on my own.

As Josh pulls away, disappearing into the steady flow of traffic, I send a pleading text to my mum to collect Olly from football before making a beeline for a kiosk displaying rows of chocolate bars every bit as bright and colourful as the flowers at the stall next door. I buy a Toffee Crisp and a bottle of Diet Coke, breaking my 'no chocolate on week days' rule for the third time this week.

You're weak if you eat that!

I guess I'm weak then.

In the space of an hour, Ben and Matilda have been expelled and Josh has just told me he's leaving for two months.

This day cannot get any worse.

Chapter 3

A film of clammy sweat covers my skin as the taxi weaves through the narrow country lanes towards the village. My dress feels stiff, the fabric too thick for two Tube rides and cramming myself into a full train with broken air conditioning for an hour.

It's gone five now and my mind is on flinging off my bra, a cool shower, a large gin and tonic, and all the things I need to do before I can make that happen, like cooking dinner, and wrestling the children out of their school clothes so I can wash them. But among all the little jobs, the endless jobs, there is Ben and Matilda, and finding out what happened at pre-school today.

Whatever it is, I'm sure by Monday the staff will have calmed down and we can come to some kind of understanding. I'll volunteer to organise the Christmas fair or something. Nobody ever wants that job.

We dip into the valley and cross the river. The driver slows down and opens the windows and I hear the shouts of children splashing in paddling pools. The smell of barbecues hangs in the air, making me long for a hot dog and to sit with my feet up while someone else does the cooking.

I can't remember the last time we went to a barbecue at someone's house. We used to go. Almost every weekend there was something with the other parents. Slightly burnt burgers and bouncy castles, beers in ice buckets, the dads in one corner, the mums in the other, the children playing between them.

When did it all stop? When did the invites trickle out? It got harder when Ben and Matilda were born, especially with Matilda's reflux. When she wasn't puking, she was crying, and that set Ben off too; then Olly, who was four at the time, would feel left out. He wasn't exactly an angel before they were born, but things definitely got worse afterwards. We were outnumbered, exhausted.

My mum friends were amazing at first. Popping over with casseroles, helping me with trips to the nearby farm trail and soft play. Then it was the play date at Jessica's house. She'd had every room decorated and so, of course, she had to show it off. I remember being wrung out from lack of sleep. I remember Olly packing a little bag of his favourite dinosaurs to play with and reminding him to look after them.

We were there for an hour before it all went wrong. Matilda was asleep on me, Ben was on a playmat by my feet. All the mums were talking and I remember wishing I'd not come, wishing I was at home so I could drift off to sleep instead of listening to Sarah's work crisis that I couldn't find the energy to care about. Everyone was talking over each other and so it was a while before we noticed how quiet the children were being.

I didn't know then how much trouble silence could signify.

They all got up – Jessica and Faye, Sarah and Lisa – and even though I wanted to stay where I was, that alarm was ringing in my head. I tucked Matilda into her car seat, picked up Ben and followed behind the others, saying a silent prayer that Olly had been good.

He hadn't.

We traipsed through the house. Everything looked so white. Clinical. I would have done so much more with the spaces if only Jessica had asked me.

She didn't ask because she thought you were a mess. She was right!

There was giggling then and movement from one of the bedrooms. Jessica opened the door to her little boy Freddie's room and there they all were, playing with Olly's dinosaurs. All except Olly.

'Where's Olly?' Jessica asked before I had the chance, perhaps already sensing that something was not right.

'He didn't want to play,' Freddie said, his attention back on the dinosaurs. 'He's colouring.'

'Where?' Jessica asked, panic ringing in her voice.

'I don't know, Mummy,' Freddie said, but there was something in his eyes, something that made me think he knew exactly where Olly was. I turned then and opened the next door. A spare room – empty.

Then the next – a bathroom – also empty. It will be fine, I told myself. He's colouring. He can't get into too much trouble colouring.

And then the next bedroom. The master bedroom. Everything was white. White walls. White bedding. White curtains. White furniture. White, white, white.

Everything was white except the huge colourful scribbles at knee height on the walls and the bedding and the curtains. Red swirls, then green zig zags. A wobbly black car. A stick man. There were letters too. A big capital O around the light switch. An L, L and a Y.

I gasped, my gaze moving from the walls to my four-year-old son and the Sharpies clenched in his hands.

'Hello, Mummy,' he said, and then he grinned. 'Freddie wouldn't let me play with my dinosaurs so I found a new game.'

I can still hear Jessica's 'Oh my God' scream and the barrage of hissed swear words. I offered to pay for the room to be redecorated, of course I did, but I also gently suggested she keep Sharpie pens out of reach, which in hindsight was probably a mistake.

'Get out. Please, just go.'

So we did. Olly clutching his dinosaurs and skipping ahead down the path, oblivious to the destruction he'd caused. Ben and Matilda wailing for the feed they were due.

I sent a tentative message on the group chat a week later, suggesting we meet at my house, but they were all busy that week and the one after. My 'what's everyone up to today?' WhatsApp questions went unanswered.

And then I saw them. Jessica and Faye, Sarah and Lisa, clutching their Costa takeout cups and huddling together while the kids played in the park after school. My cheeks burned hot and I cried for most of the day, but I knew they'd dumped me and really, deep down, I couldn't blame them. In some ways, it was easier. No more begging talks with Olly about playing nicely, being kind. In one ear and out the other. No more struggling to listen to the other mums while I fed two babies.

I do miss the friendship though. The conspiratorial 'we're all in this together' feeling. It's lonely sometimes, but work helps, and there's Mum too. She's always happy to have a coffee with me.

Thank God for Mum today. She'll have collected Olly by now and she'll be doing something crafty with them. They'll be happy and calm – as calm as it's possible for my children to be anyway. She's so good with them.

Better than you are!

I know. But aren't kids always better for other people than they are for their own parents?

I say a silent prayer that Mum has put some dinner together for us too, and perhaps cleaned the kitchen.

We pass the stone church and the little row of shops – the Co-op and the post office, the tea rooms and the bakery – huddled together with their matching green awnings and hanging flower baskets. A scattering of Tudor houses and then the pub. It's busy. Every outdoor table is taken and children are running around on the long stretch of lawn. There's something quintessentially British summertime about the scene and I feel another pang of longing.

'It's a few more minutes, at the edge of the village,' I tell the driver as we pass the blue gates of the village school and the green opposite with its row of cherry trees and colourful playground equipment.

'Actually, love, can I drop you here?' he says, already stopping by the green. 'Easier to turn around.'

I'm silent for a moment. 'No,' is the word I want to say. My legs are tired, I have a blister on my right heel. I'm hot and thirsty, and paying an extortionate fee for a twenty-minute journey. All these thoughts run through my mind while I flail slightly, rushing to dig out my purse and saying, 'Oh, right, yes that's fine.'

When he's pulled away in a swift U-turn, I trudge the ten minutes home. Our house is one of two detached properties built in a deep red brick. They're new builds. Just eight years old. Tacked on at the edge of the village after a storm blew down an old oak tree, crushing the bungalow that used to sit on the land. The owners moved on and the site was snapped up by a developer.

I remember the day we first saw the house – all plain walls and freshness. Five bedrooms, two bathrooms, a huge open-plan kitchen overlooking a small, square garden that Josh always moans is too small, and a long living room, one of those rooms with the TV at one end and a cosy reading corner at the other, not that anyone ever sits in the corner.

I loved that the house was new, that it was only ours. We moved from a one-bed flat in south London when I was pregnant with Olly, and I spent those last weeks before he was born poring over fabric samples and wall colours, putting my stamp on every room. I wanted tranquillity and peace, adding black and white photos on to the walls and splashes of colour in the furnishings to make it feel like home, like a place where we would be happy.

And we were. We are, I correct with a shake of my head. It's just been a bad day, that's all.

The back of my neck is sun burnt by the time I reach the house. I can feel the skin tingling and sore. I spot a car parked on the driveway next door and feel the slow, creeping dread of what's to come. Another Airbnb booking for the weekend. Please don't let this lot bang on the front door late to complain when the kids are being noisy and won't go to bed.

Can you blame them?

It's quiet here. The noises from the pub and the gardens don't carry far. The only sound is the crickets from the grassy hedgerow on the other side of the road. I look out for Rex, wondering how many she'll catch and bring into the house tonight. Crickets and spiders are her favourite things. It could be worse – mice and birds and entrails.

Rex is a stupid name for a cat. I'm sure she hates it. It's in the despising looks she gives me – all disapproval and knowing. But two years ago, Olly was desperate for a dog. It was all he talked about. 'When we get our dog . . .' and 'I'm going to take our dog for a walk when we get it.' Ben and Matilda were only two at the time but they cottoned on quickly to Olly's plans. It became a campaign we couldn't win.

But there was no way I could cope with a dog alongside the kids.

You can't even cope with the kids.

They were far too young to take any responsibility, and with Josh out all day, it would've been me who looked after it. Another thing to fail at. It was Mum who suggested a cat, and it seemed like a good compromise.

Josh collected it on the way home one night – a little black and white kitten who should have been called Jess or Whiskers; but Rex was the name Olly had chosen for the dog, and Rex was the name he insisted on calling the cat.

There's no sign of Rex in the front garden as I make my way to the front door. That's when I hear the piercing scream. Not the joyful happy yells of the village children anymore, but the angry, screeching, blood-curdling fury of children fighting, of my children.

Chapter 4

A ball of anxiety burns in my stomach as I dash towards the front door, desperate to be inside, to stop whatever the hell is going on.

'Nooooo,' comes Matilda's unmistakable screech.

I shove my key in the lock and the door is opening and I'm already two steps into the gap before the door snags on something on the floor, and before I can stop it, before I can move out of its path, the door is flying back towards me, the wood smacking against my face.

Fuck! Pain sears across my forehead. Tears sting the backs of my eyes and I want to pull back, to drop to the ground in a flood of tears, take a breath and wait for the pain to pass, but Olly is laughing at something just inside the hall and the sound is quickly followed by Matilda. 'I'm going to kill you,' she screams, and I'm quite sure in that moment that she is.

I push the door again, slowly this time and hear the unmistakable skid of a metal Hot Wheels car rolling across the floor and hitting the skirting boards.

'Kids,' I shout before I can even see them. 'Olly, Matilda, what's going on?'

Everywhere I look is chaos. There are toy cars scattered across the wooden floor. There's a drinks tray being used as a ramp, balanced against my living room cushions – the yellow and grey polka dot ones, with the fabric I had bought from America, that took me hours to make, the ones I love so much.

And beside the cushions, tipped on its side is a Fruit Shoot bottle.

I think, and I can't be sure on this because of the noise levels around me, but I think I cry out at the sight of a purple stain growing across the cushion fabric. I move quickly, two long strides and then I'm snatching up the cushions, cradling them in my arms as I spin towards the source of the chaos – my children.

Olly, almost twice the height of his sister, is standing over Matilda, holding two Barbie dolls high in the air.

'I'm going to do it,' he laughs, a proper, giggly boy's laugh, out of place in the scene before me. He reaches his spare hand towards one of the doll's heads.

'Don't.' Matilda's screams change, anger to desperation. Her face is bright red and streaked with tears, and her dark blonde ringlets are straggly and matted. 'Muummmmyyy.'

'Hey, hey, hey,' I tuck the cushions in the living room doorway before scooping her hot, rigid body into my arms. 'Olly, put down the dolls.'

'No,' he says.

'PUT THEM DOWN,' Matilda screams in my ear.

'Make me.' Olly's grin is manic now.

'Olly, please put down your sister's dolls. You're upsetting her.' My voice is lost to Matilda's wails.

'Mummmmyy,' she sobs, before lifting her head up and eyeing me with a furious glare. 'Make him stop.' And then comes her tiny, clenched fist, flying towards my face, connecting with the side of my chin.

'Matilda,' I cry out in pain. 'No hitting, please.'

It's then, with Olly trying furiously to pull off one of the Barbie doll's heads, me fending off Matilda's pummelling arms with one hand and trying to stop Olly with the other, that Ben shouts from the top of the stairs.

'Watch me, Mummy. I've made a slide.'

I follow the sound to the top step where Ben is sitting, his lower body wrapped in a duvet. Clutched in his arms is the unmistakable black and white fur of a terrified Rex.

'Ben, don't move,' I say, my words ignored as he pushes off and bumps down the stairs with a delighted 'Weeee'.

'I want to try that,' Olly says, throwing Matilda's dolls to the floor and snatching the duvet from Ben before he's even reached the bottom step.

'No one is trying that,' I say as Rex leaps from Ben's lap and darts in the direction of the kitchen.

'That's not fair,' Olly shouts. 'Ben did it.'

'Yeah, not fair,' Matilda grumbles, her hatred for Olly forgotten as she wriggles from my arms and reaches for the duvet too.

I sigh, a headache pressing down on me. I've been home sixty seconds. 'Kids, stop.'

'Mum?' I call out.

'Granny is in the garden,' Olly sing-songs. 'She said we could play whatever we like. And I wanted to play killing Barbies, but now I want to play stair sliding.'

'Yeaaah,' Ben and Matilda chorus. 'Stair sliding.'

'But it's dangerous. You know you can't play on the stairs. Please go and watch TV while I find Granny,' I say, wishing I didn't sound so much like I'm begging.

There's a rush of movement as all three children scramble towards the living room, the prospect of TV trumping all else.

Olly jumps on the sofa, the remote lofted in his hand. I know what's coming and grab the tablets and headphones, handing them to Ben and Matilda. As the opening credits of *Scooby Doo* sounds from TV, a sense of calm descends on the house. It's tentative. A truce that could be broken at any second.

My eyes scan the mess around me, a trail of destruction that leaves me deflated.

I kick the cars to one side, step over the pile of Barbie dolls and walk into the kitchen. My heart sinks at the state of it. The breakfast dishes are still by the sink, along with a stack of other items. There's Play-Doh out of its tubs and drying on the table, more on the floor, squished into the grout between the tiles.

From the window, I see my mum lying on a lounger, her face tilted towards the sun, and for a split second I stop breathing, certain she must have died. How else could she have let this all happen?

'Mum?' There's a tremor to my voice as I rush outside.

She angles her face towards me and I breathe again. 'Hello, darling. How did it go?'

'Fine,' I say. 'What's happened here?'

'Whatever do you mean?' she asks, and I'm quite sure from the arch of her eyebrow and the half smile touching her lips that she knows exactly what I'm talking about.

'Why are you out here and the kids inside? They were about to kill each other when I came in.'

She sits up, pushing her sunglasses onto the top of her head. She has the same brown hair as mine, cut short into a stylish bob and showing far less grey than my own usually does. Her black and white sun dress is still immaculate, as is her make-up, and I remember that she was supposed to be at afternoon tea today.

'I had a headache and decided I needed to sit out here for a while,' she says.

'But the kids? The house?'

31

'I know, dear. It's a state. It always is. I asked the children to put their toys away when they were finished with them but they ignored my request.' Her tone is calm and matter of fact but I sense an edge to her comment.

'They're eight and four, Mum. They're just kids.'

There's a pause. Mum purses her lips. It's the same look she used when I missed my curfew as a teenager and was steeling herself to give me a lecture.

'This isn't going to be easy to hear, Rebecca,' she says and I find myself sinking onto the lounger beside her, wishing I could cover my ears with my hands and 'la, la, la' the way Olly does when I tell him it's time for bed. 'But it's been on my mind a long time now, and while I've tried to mind my own business, the situation has become untenable. I love you and I love my grandchildren very much, but they are, quite frankly, monsters.'

'Mum?' I half-laugh, with surprise not humour.

'They're old enough to know how to behave better than they do. Much better. You've let them run wild their entire lives and you expect everyone who takes care of them to live with the consequences.'

She's right. You're useless!

What she's saying, the voice in my head, they both sting, a sharp slice. I stare, mouth agog, unable to process her words. It's usually all 'They were angels', and baking cakes and little crafts I've never been able to get them to sit through; not this . . . this chaos. What the hell has got into everyone today?

'Your children are feral,' Mum adds.

'They are not,' I say, sounding less than convinced.

'Oh really? Do you know what Ben did when he got home today?'

I raise eyebrows but inside I'm cringing. 'I don't know.'

She pauses, dragging out the suspense like a pro. I wonder if she's been watching too many episodes of *The Chase* again. I can almost see the orange face of a game show host in my mind.

'Tonight, Becca, you've given the answer, "I don't know." Let's see if you're right . . . Oh, bad news. That's the wrong answer. I'm afraid it's time to send you home. But you won't be leaving us empty-handed. We're sending you on your way with a lifetime supply of parenting exhaustion and a generous helping of humiliation.'

Mum tilts her head to one side. 'He walked straight through the house, past your downstairs lavatory, and to the back door, which he proceeded to open . . .'

Heat creeps over my body. I know exactly what's coming now.

'He then dropped his shorts and pants, and stood there on the doorstep to your garden, urinating all over your patio.'

Oh God. A bubble of laughter threatens to pop inside me. It's not funny. It's really not funny, but if I don't laugh then I think I might cry. I clear my throat. 'Clearly, Mum, that's not allowed, though he has done that once before.' OK, it's more than once. Ever since we went to the park that time and he needed to go, and Olly showed him how to go behind a tree, Ben has taken a liking to weeing outdoors. 'I do tell him off.'

'No, you don't.'

'I do,' I protest. 'I spend my life telling them off.'

'That simply isn't true, Rebecca. You tell them not to do something, but you never shout at them and there's certainly no discipline in this house. There are never any consequences to their bad behaviour. I'm sorry. I know it's not easy to hear but after having to cancel my plans today, and drive back and forth to that God-awful school twice, I've quite frankly had enough. You have let them run wild for too long. They have no manners. They don't listen to a word anyone says. They are out of control.'

'I'm sorry.' Tears well in my eyes and roll in two lines down my cheeks. 'Thank you for collecting them and Olly today. I didn't mean for you to have to cancel your plans. It's so typical it happens on the one day I leave the village. I'll make it up to you. Why don't you come for a barbecue on Sunday?' I swallow back a lump of emotion, thinking of Sunday, of Josh leaving for New York, of wishing this day would end. 'You won't believe what's happened,' I say.

'I'm sure I won't and while I'd love to hear it, darling, I really must get going. I need to pack.'

'Pack? Are you going away for the weekend? You didn't mention anything to me.'

Mum laughs as she stands, smoothing out the non-existent creases in her dress. 'It's more than just the weekend. I'm going on my cruise tomorrow, remember, darling? I told you about it last month.'

'Cruise? What cruise? You didn't tell me you were going on a cruise.'

'I did, darling.'

'You mentioned you were thinking of booking a cruise.' Desperation creeps into my voice as I try to remember Mum's exact words. The memory is fuzzy. I remember having a coffee with Mum in the kitchen and her showing me a glossy cruise brochure. But I also remember Matilda skipping into the room, a tooth proffered in her outstretched hand, her smile gappy and wide, a trail of blood dripping onto the tiled floor because she and Ben had both had a wobbly tooth and she had been so desperate to be first to lose the tooth that she had pulled it out.

34

'I was thinking about it and then I did it,' Mum continues. 'Six weeks around the Mediterranean.'

'Six weeks!' My voice is a squeak. 'Who are you going with?'

'No one, darling. Just me. I'm sure I'll make friends on board. It's adults only. And I'll have plenty of books to read.'

My head is spinning. There are too many things to process. Mum's harsh comments about the children are shoved aside. Six weeks. Six weeks? 'But . . . but,' I stammer as the shock fades and realisation hits with the same force as Matilda's fist on my chin. 'It's the summer holidays coming up. I thought you'd be around to help.'

Mum sighs, her face a picture of sympathy and something else. Is she wavering? Could I convince her to postpone her trip until September? I have the sudden desire to throw myself at her feet in a full-blown Matilda meltdown and beg her not to go. But I can't do it. I swallow back the emotion forming a lump in my throat, the panic fighting to be set free.

'But a cruise sounds wonderful,' I add. 'I'm sure you'll have a wonderful time.'

Mum's posture relaxes. She's off the hook and we both know it. 'Thank you, darling,' she says before moving towards the house, leaving me to trail wordlessly behind as she collects her handbag, kisses each of the children goodbye, and heads for the front door.

It doesn't feel real. This is my mum. The same mum who stayed over on weekdays for a month when Josh's paternity leave finished and I had two tiny babies and a pre-schooler to care for. The same mum who dotes on the children, and me; who says things like, 'It's never any trouble,' when I ask for her help.

'Have a lovely summer,' she says, and then seeing something on my face, she steps forward and pulls me into a hug

'You too,' I manage to say.

'Thank you. I'm sure I will.' She holds me at arm's length, staring at my face, and for one hopeful minute I think she's going to tell me it's all a joke or that she's changed her mind. 'Now, Rebecca, do you think it's time to get a bit of Botox?'

I stand speechless for the second time in as many minutes, my fingers moving automatically to my forehead, pushing at the skin between my eyebrows.

'Something to think about over the summer.' She smiles, waves her hand in the air and with a final, 'Bye for now,' she's gone.

Leaving just like Josh. No one can stand to be around you.

Is that true? I want to protest, but Mum's words stick in my thoughts: 'Your children are feral.'

Every fibre in my being wills me to sink to the floor and cry and cry, but first I need to find out what happened at pre-school today. Without Josh or my mum, I'm completely alone, completely outnumbered, and I need to fix it, even if it only buys me two weeks before the summer holidays.

Chapter 5

I can't fix it. The thought flashes like a bright blue siren in my mind. I try to comprehend what Ben and Matilda are telling me in their jumble of words and half-comments as they stare resolutely at the colourful cartoons on their tablets.

'So.' I shift position on the living room floor so I'm sitting between them. 'I want to make sure I understand. The teachers all went into the art cupboard to get some paintbrushes and paper, and while they were in there . . .'

'I shut the door,' Ben says as though four words can explain everything.

'And I locked it,' Matilda's eyes are still on the screen of her tablet but she gives a delighted giggle.

'You locked all the teachers in the cupboard?' Oh God! Say no. Just say I've got this wrong. Please!

'Yes. It was easy,' Ben says in the same tone Josh uses when he's showing me the correct way to stack the dishwasher again, because apparently there is only one way; because it does matter if bowls go on the bottom instead of the top; because it's not about whether everything gets clean – how stupid of me to have thought that – it's about proper stacking.

Ben lifts his large brown eyes from his screen to shoot me a 'How are you not getting this?' look that makes me snort an exhale of surprise. How has my four-year-old baby boy cultivated this look with such precision?

It's hard to believe that my beautiful boy can be so daring sometimes – locking teachers in cupboards, sliding down stairs or banisters or whatever vertical slopes he can find; and other times, so terrified, scaring himself into sobbing fits when we visit new places. He once screamed so much he wet himself because I popped into Sainsbury's instead of Tesco. My boy who can't sleep in his bed without a night light that casts white stars across the ceiling, and even then still finds his way into our bed at some point during the night, squishing in between me and Josh, and elbowing me in the back at 4 a.m..

'And then we got to play whatever we wanted,' Matilda sings.

'I played squirting all the paint on the floor and making a skidding slide,' Ben says, holding up his forearms to show the faded remnants of purply-brown streaks.

'I played Barbies.'

'You *always* play Barbies,' Ben says, trying to mimic Olly's scornful tone but falling short. Ben adores Matilda. He is Robin to her Batman and always plays the role of soother when she falls out with Olly, something she does on an hourly basis most days.

'But I didn't have to share.' Matilda gives a gleeful grin.

'And no one was looking after you while the teachers were in the cupboard?' I ask, pressing my fingers to my forehead again and smoothing out the frown. I'm still reeling from my mum's Botox bombshell. Is that why she always looks so fresh at sixty-four? Even with Ben and Matilda's story unfolding before me, I can't stop the desire to wail at the injustice of it. All those times I'd told my former mum friends that I'll never need Botox because I take after my mum and have great genes. God, I was a smug bitch about it.

No wonder they ditched you.

Ben shakes his head, drawing me back to their story. 'The teachers were banging on the door but we didn't let them out. But then Luca's mummy came to take him to the dentist and unlocked the door. She ruined all our fun.'

'When's dinner, Mummy? I'm starving. I want pasta.' Matilda says.

'Soon,' I lie. 'Ben, Matilda, I want you to listen to this.' They lift their heads dutifully, almost angelically, if I didn't know better. 'What you did today was very wrong and very naughty. The teachers are very cross with you and we've all decided that you won't be going back to the pre-school anymore.'

'Never?' Matilda asks, her eyes growing wide.

'No,' I confirm.

Ben frowns, looking from his sister back to me. 'Where will we go?'

'You'll stay home for the last two weeks. Then it will be the summer holidays. And then you'll join Olly at the prep school.'

There's pause, a breath during which I can see them taking it in, and I prepare myself for the tears and the fall-out. But it doesn't come. Instead, Ben whoops, fist-pumping the air and Matilda hisses a long 'Yesssssss'.

'Aren't you upset?' I ask.

They shake their heads in unison.

'I hate it there,' Ben says. 'The teachers are stinky poo brains.'

'Ben, that's not very nice.' My admonishment is weak and ignored.

'I hate it too,' Matilda adds. 'Mummy, is dinner ready yet?'

'I'll do it now.' I pull myself up and make my way to the kitchen.

My twins. My little team of two that came along after so many years of longing and trying and failing, when I thought Olly was destined to be an only child. I can't believe what they did.

Yes you can. They're monsters, and it's all your fault.

I turn on the oven to preheat for Olly's pizza, and step into the garden, gulping in great mouthfuls of warm summery air, wishing I could ignore my own thoughts, wishing there was someone else to blame, but Josh is hardly ever here. It really is just me who has created this mess.

Ben and Matilda locked all the staff at the pre-school in a craft cupboard and wouldn't let them out. No wonder they were expelled.

There's a question in the back of mind as to why all three staff members, including the pre-school manager, would go into a cupboard at the same time, but deep down I see there's no amount of pleading that will undo this. No coming back from this humiliation. They'd rather cut us loose than admit any failing on their part.

I spy the sun lounger ahead of me, bathing in the early evening sun and think of my mum out here, enjoying some peace. For a moment, I think about flopping onto the lounger too. I think of crying ugly, fat tears of despair and asking over and over WTF has happened to my life today – first Josh tells me he's leaving for New York for two months, and then Mum practically runs out the door to hop on a cruise for the summer.

I'm all alone in this. I sigh and spot Rex's little face poking out from beneath the rattan garden set on the patio – a sofa seat and three armchairs positioned around a table with a glass top. All in dark grey. The original cushions were light grey but I made my own in a fabric of faded rainbow print, adding a splash of colour to our small stretch of garden.

'Hey.' I crouch down and hold out my hand but Rex remains where she is. She shoots me a 'How dare you let Ben slide me down the stairs' look, which I probably deserve.

I ignore the desire to flop onto the lounger and turn to walk back to the kitchen. I pick up all the toys, scrape the Play-Doh into the bin. I put the duvet back upstairs and I sponge the stain on my cushion.

Only when the house is tidy and I've cooked frozen pizza and peas for Olly, plain pasta and sweetcorn for Matilda, and chicken nuggets, French fries and broccoli for Ben, and given in to their whines and let them sit on the rug in the living room, eyes glued to the *Beethoven* movie for the tenth time this week, only then do I climb the stairs, strip off my clothes and have a shower.

The cool water slips over my skin, washing away the sweat of the commute and grime of the Tube. When I'm done, I pull my hair into a high ponytail. The ends are wet and tickle my neck and dampen the old t-shirt of Josh's that I throw on with a pair of shorts.

Downstairs, the children are still hypnotised by the TV so I fix myself a strong gin and tonic, taking two long gulps before remembering to add the slice of lime. The hit of alcohol is instant, and, like the shower water on my skin, helps to wash the day away.

I tell myself it's going to OK. I shush my panic at the weeks ahead of me with three children and no Josh, and no Mum. Just me. I drink.

When the glass is empty and my head is buzzing in that 'Everything will be alright', floaty way, I pick up my phone and open Instagram. It's a whole other kind

41

of hit I'm looking for now, and I lose myself in scrolling until I've seen hundreds of photos. New bedroom designs, bathrooms, living rooms, mixed in with shots of sunny gardens, barbecues and drinks held in front of the camera. *#FridayFeeling* dominates my newsfeed.

I fix myself a fresh glass before stepping into the garden to add my own posed shot of my drink, Rex stretched in a patch of sun in the background. I add a filter that makes the grass a vibrant green, and a dozen hashtags before posting.

The likes are instant. A dozen. Then fifty of my ten thousand two hundred followers.

I breathe in, long and deep, until the summer air hits the bottom of my lungs. It feels like my first proper breath in hours. Has it really only been hours since Josh dumped his New York trip on me? It feels like days have passed.

I'm about to keep on scrolling when a window opens from somewhere above me. I spin around, arms already up to protect myself from whatever Olly is about to fire in my direction. But it's not my house, it's next door.

My gaze lands on the open window where a topless man is standing. We stare at each other in a stunned moment. I take in the ruffled mess of black hair, the tanned naked torso.

The second passes and then he's ducking out of sight and I groan. I thought the snooty hikers were bad. Now it's bloody nudists.

I hurry inside, wishing like I always do that our old neighbours, our lovely quiet, no trouble neighbours, Greg and Glynis, hadn't run off to Spain to live with their son, leaving their house as an Airbnb rental.

What happened to poor Lola was terrible, but did they really have to leave? It was a tragic accident. It was nobody's fault. Least of all Olly's, no matter what they thought.

That cat had a death wish. I lost count of the times I'd found her sleeping behind the back wheel of my car. Her favourite game was to dash out in front of passing cars, making them screech to a halt or swerve into the bushes, scratching their paintwork.

It was only a matter of time before one of them actually hit her. And just bad luck that after getting a knock, she wandered into our garden instead of her own before collapsing in her favourite spot beneath the rose bushes. Olly saw that she was poorly, so he scooped her gently into his arms and carried her to Greg and Glynis's front door.

I still remember Glynis's scream. Her shaking, pointed finger, accusing Olly of hurting Lola. It didn't matter that the vet confirmed Lola's injuries were consistent with a car accident, or that there was nothing anyone could've done; Glynis blamed Olly.

The next week their property popped up on Airbnb and we've had a variety of visitors come and go. The occasional hen do – although out here, it's always a tame affair. Inflatable willies in the window is as raucous as it gets. For the most part, it's couples and ramblers, exploring the countryside.

I once made the mistake of reading the reviews on the Airbnb website.

3 stars

A lovely property. Beautiful village location. Shame about the noisy kids next door.

1 star

DO NOT GO HERE! I'm sorry to give this lovely house such a poor review but I feel I must warn you about the horrid children who live next door. We were having our breakfast on the patio when the first foam bullet hit us. We laughed of course, assuming it was a stray, but then the machine gun fire started. My poor wife got hit right in the eye. Thank God she wears glasses.

Then we found bird seed all over our car. It was covered in scratches, pecks and bird crap.

2 stars

The price is good. Although you'll realise why the second you arrive. It sounds like a chainsaw massacre is going on next door all night with those shouting kids. Terrible parenting!

Just thinking about those reviews causes my cheeks to burn with shame. I take a long gulp of my drink and turn back to Instagram just as a scream pierces the quiet of the kitchen. The noise is followed by the sound of china hitting something hard. Dread seeps over me, pushing away the buzz from the gin. My phone is still in my hand as I rush into the living room. The next post on my feed catches my eye. They are simple questions asked in swirly pink on a white background and, just like that, everything changes.

Chapter 6

'Olly hit me,' Matilda screams as I take in the scene before me. There's food everywhere. Pasta on the carpet, a splatter of ketchup on my Farrow & Ball Ammonite wall. Why, why, why did I let them talk me into eating in the living room?

Because you're a pushover! A terrible parent just like the reviews said. Like everyone says.

The peace I craved no longer seems worth it.

'You threw a chip at me first,' Olly retorts with a gleeful smile before all three children start shouting.

I grit my teeth. 'STOP FIGHTING.' My voice is loud and as angry as Olly's.

'NO,' comes Matilda's reply before she scrambles onto the sofa and launches herself at Olly.

'ST—' My voice is lost to the shouts, the flail of limbs, the 'oomphs', and 'ows' and angry growls.

'I WANT TO WATCH THE FILM,' Ben screams, before bursting into noisy sobs.

'Matilda, Olly, please stop fighting.' My own anger is petrol to the flames of their fury, and I will myself to calm down. I grab the remote and pause the film, dodging a kick from Matilda who is staring at me with narrowed eyes, cheeks blazing red.

'I was WATCHING that.' Another kick flies in my direction.

'No, Matilda,' I say. 'I've just paused it so we can sort this mess out. I'll press play in a minute when you've all calmed down and can actually hear it again.'

'PLAY NOW. PLAY NOW. PLAY NOW.'

My jaw tightens another notch as tears threaten behind my eyes. This is so hard. Why won't my children listen to me?

Ben leaps up and I lurch away from him, but he's heading for the stairs. A moment later he reappears, holding Matilda's favourite soft toy – a red tartan beanbag frog with dangling legs and a missing eye. She clutches it to her chest but continues to scream, her focus torn between wanting to watch the film and continuing her fight with Olly. She chooses the latter and before I can shout at them to stop, Olly and Matilda are fighting again.

I step over the dinner plates to grab hold of her, lifting her away from Olly. Her arms and legs fly out at me. She's like a wind-up toy picked up too soon, flapping and moving in every direction. A foot connects with my knee and I yelp in pain.

'Stop, Matilda. Stop. Everyone, just stop, please,' I shout.

There's a pause then. Ben has restarted the film and, from the TV, the dad is having his own meltdown at the huge St Bernard lying on a muddy bed. I take a breath, but as I'm about to put Matilda down on the sofa and begin sorting out the chaos, something moves in the corner of my eye. I turn just in time to see a slice of pizza flying out of Olly's hand. It hits me square in the face, soggy and cold.

The children freeze and before I can grapple with the fury stampeding through my body, they burst into fits of laughter. A switch flicks and they're no longer enemies but united against me.

Matilda shakes in my arms and Olly is howling from the other side of the room. Ben tips onto his back, laughing too hard to stay up right. I'd like to say I laughed too. That I found the soggy pizza on my face and down my t-shirt funny, that all of a sudden, the ketchup on my beautifully painted wall and the pasta trodden into the rug didn't matter anymore, but it did. It mattered.

The swirling pink writing of the Instagram post pummels my mind.

> *Are you a parent struggling to cope?*
> *Are your children out of control?*

I clean the living room and then the kitchen and I put the kids to bed, reading them story after story, kissing them each goodnight, tucking Olly into bed in his green dinosaur room and then Ben and Matilda in their cosmic bedroom of stars and planets, hushing Ben's sudden fears of monsters beneath the bed.

All three are up before I've made it to the kitchen, a little stampede of feet on the landing, giggling.

With a fresh gin and tonic in one hand, and my phone in the other, I drop onto the sofa in the corner of the kitchen and pretend not to hear them. There's something about the hours after bedtime that makes all three children play nicely together, as though they know they're on borrowed time. Stolen time. In an hour, they'll have burnt themselves out and I'll tuck them in again and go to bed too.

Alcohol swims through my body as I open Instagram again and find the post. That swirling writing cries out at me.

> *Are you a parent struggling to cope?*

'Yes,' I say to the empty kitchen, taking another long gulp of my drink.

Are your children out of control?

'Yes.' Tears sting my eyes. I hate that I find this so hard. That I'm so terrible at being a mother when I love my children so much.

@TheToddlerTamer is here to help!
I guarantee to tame any behavioural problems!

I click on the account and scroll through hundreds of photos. Screaming children then smiling children. Videos of crying parents and tantrums followed by a family laughing around a dinner table. Picture perfect.

I swallow hard. Josh's words from earlier drift into my thoughts. 'Hire a nanny.'

The idea was ludicrous. It *is* ludicrous. Mary Poppins wouldn't last five minutes with Olly, Ben and Matilda, but this person is offering a guarantee. Any behavioural problems!

I click through to a website and more glossy photos. But it's the words I focus on.

Out of control.
Tantrums.
Fighting.
Lashing out.

Tears slide onto my cheeks. This woman gets it. She can help me.

I click to the reviews page.

I'm a single parent with five children who were out of control. They never lifted a finger to help me. All we did was shout at each other. I was at rock bottom when I contacted The Toddler Tamer. She got straight to work and things got better immediately. It wasn't always easy but it's worth it now. We are the happy family I always wished we could be and it's all thanks to Saffron!

I search through the website, devouring the reviews and the promises, drinking them in as fast as the gin and tonic in my hand. The fees page makes me gasp, but it's not the thing I stumble on.

When signing a contract with The Toddler Tamer, you agree to photographs and videos of you and your family being used on social media.

I draw in my lower lip, biting down, wondering if I can do it. If I can let the entire world see the truth.

I tap back to Instagram, feeling the familiar lure of the pictures, the filters, the beautiful lives of those I follow, but it's not their accounts I click on, it's my own.

My profile picture is my company logo – my name in white writing on a navy background. It's simple but effective. I scroll through the photos of my work – the four individually designed bedrooms in the boutique hotel up the road; the airy orangery I did for Mr and Mrs Chapman, countless living rooms, tasteful and fresh. The images are interspersed with family shots. Josh, Olly and Ben playing catch, Matilda running between them, piggy in the middle. A brief moment of happiness caught forever in a shiny filter.

Then I remember how a second after the photo was taken, Josh's phone rang and he stepped away and Olly threw the ball too hard at Ben, hitting him on the head, and all hell broke loose.

Another photo. This one Matilda. It's a black and white shot. Her eyes are wide and watery, her hair falling around her face, and she's staring straight down the lens. Angelic, beautiful and in complete contrast to the screaming fit she had for an hour before the photo was taken because the Amazon delivery driver didn't bring the new Barbie she wanted.

We all do it, don't we? Present our best selves, glossy and filtered. When I look at the photos of my friends, I know their lives aren't as perfect as they seem. But to rip away the Ginghams and Clarendons, the Willows and Nashvilles. I . . . I don't think I can.

A scream from upstairs shatters my thoughts. Matilda. Always Matilda. Overtired now. I hurry upstairs and spend an hour coaxing them all into bed. Matilda and Ben shout and cry and sob until they finally crash in my bed. I'll move them later before Josh comes home.

It's late by the time I finally make it back to the kitchen. My head is throbbing from alcohol and exhaustion. I flop onto the sofa, dragging a hand through my hair and fight back a fresh wave of tears.

It's ridiculous. I have three beautiful, healthy children. A husband who, yes, works hard a lot of the time, but is also a wonderful dad. This gorgeous house – my dream home. Plus, I love running my little interior design company.

I have everything I've ever wanted. I'm living the dream. And yet, it's all so . . . so hard. So bloody exhausting.

I gulp back the dregs of my drink and before I can overthink it or talk myself out of it, I snatch up my phone and send a pleading message to The Toddler Tamer.

She won't be able to help you. No one can. Remember what your mum said? The kids are feral. Monsters!

It said she can help anyone.

You're completely alone in this.

The thought sinks down inside me as I finish cleaning the kitchen and drag myself upstairs to move Ben and Matilda and go to bed.

Chapter 7

I'm jolted awake by a punch to the small of my back and turn to find Ben spread-eagled beside me, Matilda on his other side. No Josh. I check the time with bleary eyes and find it's nearly six. My mouth is dry, my stomach queasy.

Ben shifts position, worming across the mattress towards me and I open my arms so he can snuggle against me, half asleep, warm, filling me with unquantifiable love. The events of the yesterday pull into focus. The funeral. Josh. New York. Mum. The kids squabbling. I bite back a groan as I remember the message I sent to The Toddler Tamer. What was I thinking?

I wasn't, I tell myself. It was too much gin on a bad day, that's all. Oh God, I called them monsters. I brush the soft ends of Ben's strawberry blond hair. 'You're not a monster,' I whisper. 'You're perfect.'

'So are you, Mummy,' he says with a sleepy smile.

I stare adoringly at my twins, admiring their long eyelashes, their button noses, drinking them in. Matilda's eyes open as though she's sensed my gaze. There's no slow awakening, no snuggly cuddle and whispers, just a switch being flicked from off to on. Delight dances across her face, and I wish I could summon even a fraction of her excitement for the weekend stretching ahead of us.

'Morning, baby,' I whisper.

She jumps up and scrambles over Ben, then me, a foot landing painfully on my knee as she tumbles down, snuggling into the crook of my arm.

'What's going on here then?' Josh asks from the doorway, a smile on his lips.

'Daddyyyyyy,' Ben and Matilda squeal in unison.

Josh's hair is ruffled with sleep; or lack of sleep, I think, noticing the smudges beneath his eyes. Too much work. It's always too much work with Josh. I would normally feel a stab of sympathy for him, but yesterday's anger is lying hot and itchy on my skin.

'What . . .' Josh starts in mock anger, voice hard, but eyes mischievous, 'are you two monkeys doing sleeping in my bed?'

'My covers were itchy,' Ben says. 'And I thought there was an alien under my bed.'

'And he wouldn't go onto the landing without me,' Matilda chips in.

'That's not what happened. You woke up.'

'You woke me up.'

I zone out of Ben and Matilda's soft bickering and I look up and meet Josh's gaze. A dozen silent things are said between us in that stare. I'm telling him I'm still pissed. Pissed at New York, and pissed too at how he told me, when he told me. Dropping a bombshell before practically kicking me out of the car at a random Tube station.

His look is apologetic and pleading. I know he's asking for us not to fight, to have one nice weekend before he leaves for New York. Pity slices through my anger. He didn't ask to be sent away.

But he didn't say no either. He wants to get away from you.

I look at my beautiful children and then I squash down all the anger I still feel, all the hurt, and I smile, because of course I will do this for him, for our family. We can argue tonight. The children deserve a happy weekend with their daddy.

Josh grins. 'Did someone order a mummy sandwich hug?'

'Yessssss,' come two replies, and then Josh is on the bed, wrapping his arms around all three of us. Ben and Matilda's little hands stretch out too, and I yelp a giggle as one of them tickles across my stomach.

Olly appears in the doorway, rubbing his eyes with the back of his hand. He's wearing his favourite Scooby Doo pjs. The faded green material stops two inches before his wrists and his ankles, reminding me how quickly he is growing.

'Dadddy,' he says. 'Can I show you my new invention. It's a Lego light switch. It's really cool.'

'In a sec, Olly boy. We need to give mummy her hug sandwich.'

Another snaking hand tickles my side. 'No, Olly,' I gasp. 'Help me. They've got me.'

'I'll save you, Mummy,' he shouts, taking a running jump and landing across us. Josh gives an 'oomph' of pain over the sound of the children laughing.

Josh pulls up the duvet and wraps it around all four of us. 'You're mine now,' he laughs.

Olly giggles and squirms his way out before leaping on Josh's back. Ben and Matilda grab an ankle each, wrestling him onto the bed.

'OK, OK, I give up,' Josh calls out. 'I give up. Ouch.'

'We win, we win,' they chorus. The children flop down beside us, grinning and red faced.

'Well done,' I laugh. 'Let's get some breakfast.'

'No,' Olly says. 'I want to keep fighting Daddy.'

'I think I'm beat,' Josh says.

'Fight.' Olly is no longer laughing, and there's sudden tension in the air that I know will end in tears or shouting if I don't step in.

'Who wants pancakes?' I sing-song and, to my relief, all three children give a whooping yes.

'I will help you make them, Mummy,' Matilda announces, bossy and proud, and I keep the smile on my face and try not to think about the mess Matilda will make and the time it will take to clean up afterwards.

'Can I show you my invention now, Daddy?' Olly asks, tugging on Josh's arm.

'In a sec,' he says and I know from the faraway tone of his voice that when I turn to look, he'll have his phone in his hand. 'Go down for breakfast. I need to send a quick email and then I'm all yours.'

I watch Olly's shoulders sag and feel his disappointment as keenly as if it were my own. 'Come on,' I smile at Olly. 'You can show me. And we can all make breakfast together.'

'No,' Olly snaps. 'It was stupid anyway.' He runs out of the room, the twins tailing behind him and, a moment later, I hear the familiar voices of a cartoon carry from the living room.

I climb out of bed, pull my hair up into a messy bun – an actual messy bun not the stylish kind that takes forever to perfect – and turn to Josh. His face is lost to his screen, tight with concentration. My anger bubbles up, incinerating my resolve for a nice weekend.

'Would it have killed you to spend twenty seconds looking at Olly's invention?'

'Umm?' he says.

'Josh,' my tone is harsh, jolting him from his thoughts. He looks up, an eyebrow raised in surprise and question.

55

'Would it have killed you to look at Olly's invention? He wanted to show you.'

'I can see it later.'

'It's always later with you. And then it's too late, and you're gone again. Except this time, you're going for two months. It's always work with you. Is it too much to ask that you show the children a little bit of attention while you're here?'

'Is it too much to ask that I have a bed to sleep in at night?' he asks in return, his voice as cutting as mine.

'I don't know. Is it too much to ask to have a husband who comes home in time to see his family before bed?'

He breathes out a long sigh, dropping his phone on to the bed. His expression changes. He looks crestfallen, beaten. For a weird moment, I think he's going to cry. His Adam's apple bobs up then down as he swallows. 'Can we please not argue?' he says eventually. 'I'm exhausted. I don't want to go to New York. It's not a holiday. It's going to be long hours and back-to-back meetings. I just . . . it's not what I want, OK?'

I bite back a 'you started it' huff, grit my teeth and force a calm into my voice that I do not feel. 'I get that you're tired. But, as you can imagine, I'm still upset that you're leaving for two months and only told me yesterday.'

'I know. I'm sorry. I handled it badly, but there is nothing I can do about that now. New York is happening. My flight is tomorrow night.'

'So, you're leaving tomorrow afternoon, then?' I ask. 'We don't even get the weekend with you.'

'We've got today.' He gives a defeated shrug.

'Only if you can tear yourself away from your phone and work.' I turn on my heels and head downstairs to start breakfast. Josh appears a few minutes later and, without a word, sets the table and rallies the kids.

56

We limp through the day like this. A merry pretence of happy families. We take the children to their swimming lessons together in the morning and let them play in the paddling pool in the afternoon while Josh potters around the garden, pruning and weeding, then inspecting the roses, leaning so close that from my position at the kitchen window, it looks like he's talking to each and every one of them. I want to ask him why he's bothering when we have a gardener to do it, but I know the question will land all wrong and really the garden is the only place where the tension seems to release from Josh's shoulders.

For a moment, I think of joining them all and sitting on a lounger in the sun, but then I turn away and throw myself into cleaning the house.

On Sunday afternoon, we gather in the hall to say goodbye to Josh. Ben and Matilda are jumping around, eager to get back to their tablets, oblivious to what's happening. Two months is a time scale they can't wrap their minds around yet.

Olly is quiet with a watchful fury. The day has been a fractious one. Josh has been distracted, wandering into the garden and staring at the roses before coming back in to pack something else. He's not himself, but there's no time to think about it.

The dark cloud of Josh's mood has rubbed off on us – Olly most of all, who has done everything he can to upset Matilda, pushing her into tantrums and tears. Three times I told him to go to his room. Three times he refused and we ended up in a screaming match that has left me exhausted, weary.

Was it only Friday when I couldn't see how I would cope without Josh? Yet it's a relief when he pecks my cheek and walks down the path to the waiting taxi. I herd the children into the garden for an ice cream and breathe a sigh of relief. Surely nine weeks alone is better than nine weeks with Josh and his dark cloud and the distracted way he does everything with us as though he always has one foot out the door on his way to somewhere else.

You've driven him away. You and your terrible parenting.

I crush the thought. It's going to take everything I have to get through this summer alone with the children, I can't be worrying about Josh.

I cannot think about Josh or our marriage.

The one he seemed so keen to run away from.

Maybe that's true, but right now the children have to be my only focus. An image of Olly, Ben and Matilda dressed in their cadmium green blazers and striped ties springs into my thoughts. Them running into their classrooms for the day. It feels as far away and dreamlike to me as the day when I'll wave them off to university or backpacking around the world.

Chapter 8

The knock at the door comes as I'm begging Olly to put his school shoes on and threatening to make him go to school barefoot if he doesn't just listen to me for one second and do as he's told. We're both one breath away from screaming at each other, one breath away from bursting into 'it's not fair' tears. I can feel the emotion pressing behind my eyes, clawing at my chest.

The strange relief I felt yesterday at saying goodbye to Josh, waving off that misery, that dark mood, his constant distraction, his inability to spend more than twenty seconds looking up from his work emails, has hardened into a grey numbness, in total contrast to the bright warm sunshine and clearest of July skies.

Matilda and Ben are sitting in the living room, still in their pjs, looking more than a little smug at not being wrestled into their pre-school uniform of shirts and shorts, and asking over and over again if we can go to the beach. A fact that has not been lost on Olly. He's never been keen to leave for school each morning, but it's worse today. I've told him we're not going to the beach. In fact, I'm dragging the twins with me to meet Mrs Young, my favourite, if rather reluctant client, who wants her entire house remodelled but, at the same time, isn't ready to let go of the past. The thought of taking the twins with me fills me with dread, and yet even the prospect of meetings appeals more to Olly than school.

It's one of those days when I wonder to myself how it's possible to not want to change a thing, to not regret a single choice I've made that's led me here, but also to feel wild jealousy of those who made different choices. The kind of day when I spend too long staring at the Instagram posts of the designers I went to college with, the ones without children who are living completely different lives, the life I thought I'd have, right up until I met Josh.

Guilt swims through me, bustling along beside my frustration at Olly and his refusal to get ready for school. Maybe it's Josh's departure, affecting Olly more than I realise. He idolises his dad.

Or maybe it's you. Maybe you're the problem.

I sigh at the tap of knuckles on wood and throw open the front door, finding myself face to face with next door's naked torso – the one I saw from my garden on Friday night. Except he's not naked this time. He's wearing khaki shorts, a white polo shirt and a sheepish grin, and I realise that with Josh home and the weekend of swimming, games, cleaning, cooking and wrangling, I had completely forgotten about the new nudist neighbour.

'Hi,' he says, raking a hand through a thick mess of wavy black hair. From behind me I hear Olly scrambling gleefully up the stairs. Something sinks inside me. We're going to be late for school again. It'll be another 'signing the late register in front of the snooty receptionist' day. 'Is this a bad time?'

I pull a face. 'Eight twenty on a Monday morning. I'm guessing you don't have children?'

'Er . . . no. Sorry,' He gives an apologetic shrug before pushing the rim of his glasses closer to his face. I follow the movement and take in the black stubble, and matching dark eyes. He looks like a grown-up version of the nerdy one from *The O.C..* What was his name? Seth. That's it. God, I loved that show. I loved Sunday morning re-runs when I didn't have anything to do or anywhere to be.

'I just er . . .' he begins. 'I wanted to apologise for my . . . er . . . well, I shouldn't have opened the window straight after my shower on Friday. It was just hot . . . and I didn't mean to scare you. I'm not a flasher or anything. That's what I wanted to say.' He gives me an awkward smile, ruffling his hair again and I notice a smudge of blue ink on his left index finger.

'Don't worry.' I wave away his concern. 'It's not like I thought we had a nudist staying next door or anything,' I lie. 'I didn't actually know you were naked. I thought you just had your top off because you're hot.' Oh no! Did I just say that? 'I mean, it was hot. Not you're hot.' Heat burns my cheeks and I don't need to glance in the hallway mirror to know my face is glowing red.

'Well, I'm glad we cleared that up then,' he says, laughter in his tone. Then he smiles. It's a mischievous, amused kind of smile where his lips pinch together and his eyes narrow, like he's trying to stop himself from laughing. And there's something about it that makes me feel like I know this man from somewhere.

I search his face, trying to attach that lingering sense of familiarity to a memory, like a cryptic version of pin the tail on the donkey.

'Rebecca?' he says, head tilting a little.

'How did you . . . ?' I start.

'Rebecca Double. It is you,' he declares, the smile now a broad grin.

I give an exhale of a laugh, surprise more than humour at the use of my maiden name. 'Yes, although it's been a long time since anyone has called me that. I'm Rebecca Harris now. Becca actually.'

'You don't remember me, do you?' He grins, eyes twinkling behind his glasses.

It's just out of reach – a name, a memory. On the tip of my tongue, but I shake my head. 'No,' I confess.

'Matthew Short?' he says as though his name is a question. 'Well Matt really. We sat next to each other in biology and chemistry in Year 9. I was the puny boy with the glasses and, God, I still can't believe this – a briefcase for a school bag. We did a peanut experiment together and you set fire to the desk.'

I clasp my hand over my mouth and laugh. 'Oh God. I remember that.' The memories of school are fuzzy, more a feeling of belonging and fun, standing with friends, heavy school bags and rolled up skirts, than anything specific, but I remember the desk fire and the short, nerdy boy who made me laugh and reluctantly let me take charge.

'Do I need to take a step back?' Matt grins, holding his arms out in an 'I come in peace' gesture. 'Are you still Double Trouble?' he asks, using a nickname I've not heard for at least twenty years.

'Not me.' I shake my head, thinking of Olly, Ben and Matilda. My triple trouble gang.

'It's good to see you,' Matt says. 'You look exactly the same. I did wonder if I'd bump into anyone from the old days, but I never expected to move next door to *the* Rebecca Double.'

'You make me sound notorious,' I laugh. 'Which is slightly rich coming from briefcase boy.'

'Don't remind me. Still, it's nothing compared to you. I bet there are Facebook groups dedicated to your exploits. All those 'true crime junkie' types obsessing over potential sightings.'

'I was not a master criminal, you know. I was just—'

'Completely fierce?'

'I was going to say reckless.'

'No. You weren't.' Matt's grin widens. 'You were someone who stood up to everyone, for everyone, and never took any nonsense. It wasn't reckless. It was brave. This is going to make me sound like some weirdo stalker, but I'm a writer now and the main character in my books is a female detective, who's a bit like you.' He adds, heat creeping into his cheeks.

'Comics,' I blurt out the word as the memory surfaces. 'You used to make those comic books, didn't you? They were really funny. Teachers who were aliens, the school thug who was a secret ballerina.'

'That one got me quite a few beatings.' He rubs ruefully at the side of his head as though the bruise is still there.

'I bet. Are you a children's author?'

'Crime,' he says. 'The gritty, serial killer, murder and gore stuff, I'm afraid. I still think about those comics though.'

'My boy Olly is eight and he'd have loved them. He's not a great reader . . .' I trail off, feeling awkward at the mention of Olly. As though for the briefest of moments Matt and I were fourteen again and chatting behind our science books and I've just ruined it by mentioning my children.

'Some kids just aren't,' Matt continues, oblivious. 'I hated reading. That's why I created my own comics back in the day. I always liked my stories better.'

I smile at that. 'What brings you back to the village?' I ask.

'Ah.' Matt shifts on his feet as though I've touched a nerve. 'Well, I live in south London now. It's full of the distractions of my life and I'm in serious danger of missing the deadline of my next book, so I found this little bolthole house on Airbnb and I've rented it out for the summer. A good excuse to see my mum, sister and little brother a bit more as well. Mum and my sister still live in the village, and Liam lives in the next one, just down the road.'

'You're here the whole summer?' I ask, failing to keep the horror from my tone.

'Yep.' His smile drops. 'Why? That's not going to be a problem, is it?'

'No. Of course not. It's just . . .' I wave my hands back into the house. 'I have three children. It's not exactly going to be peaceful.'

'I don't mind noise. It's my friends and . . .' He pauses, looking uncomfortable again. 'Anyway, while I'm here, I was in the garden yesterday—'

'I'm sorry,' I blurt out. 'The Nerf bullets can really sting. I'll tell Olly you're one of the good guys.'

'Like mother like son, hey?' Matt chuckles, and the sound is so weirdly familiar. I never would have guessed for a moment that I had that sound stored away in the back of my memories somewhere, but hearing it transports me back to those wobbly, uncomfortable wooden stools and the rubbery orange tubes of the Bunsen burners, the smell of gas and chalk in the air.

'I have got some stray bullets here,' he continues, 'but it was this actually that brought me round.' He holds up a pair of shoes. My shoes. My black patent, three-inch-heeled shoes that I was supposed to wear to the funeral on Friday.

'My shoes,' I exclaim, taking it from him. 'Where did you find them?'

'There are a few other bits as well. I've put them in a bag. I thought you might have a dog who likes to hide things. I'm a sucker for pointless Facebook videos and I saw this dog once who stole everything and hid it behind the sofa.'

'I saw that,' I laugh. 'With the—'

'Car keys,' we say together.

I look down at the bag in my hands, already opening the handles.

'You don't need to open it now,' he says, his voice suddenly urgent. But it's too late. I'm already staring at a pile of items. There's a lost library book on top, dirty and frayed at the edges. A scattering of Nerf bullets, a tea towel, and . . . oh crap. Crap. Crap. Crap. Knickers. My knickers. My black lace knickers.

Heat floods my cheeks. Is it bad that he's seen these knickers – the sexy ones I only wear on my rare nights out? But would my big, comfortable, 'never ride up into unwanted places' knickers have been worse?

'Well, see you around, Double Trouble.'

I say a distracted goodbye and close the front door, leaning against the wood and letting the wave of embarrassment wash over me. Then I smile and huff a laugh. Double Trouble. I'd forgotten that nickname. That confidence I had. I've always thought I was a bit wayward, a bit naughty – that's certainly how Mum paints it – but now I think about it, maybe Matt was right. I remember this one teacher – Mrs Devonshire – who seemed to hate all students. She wouldn't rest until she'd made someone in the class cry, and I was forever being sent out of class for sticking up for whichever victim she'd selected that day.

I feel buoyed by the memory. Not just the memory, but the feeling too. That sense of being unstoppable. I push away from the door, grab my car keys and shout up the stairs. 'Anyone not ready and in the car in the next two minutes won't be getting a doughnut after school.'

There's a scramble of feet and movement from the living room as Ben and Matilda rush towards me.

'Krispy Kreme?' Olly's voice shouts back.

'With the chocolate filling,' I confirm.

I know it's bribery. I know it's going to make tomorrow harder and the day after that and the day after that. But, just this once, I feel a little whisper of that Rebecca Double inside me.

Chapter 9

A clammy sweat clings to my palms as I sip from Mrs Young's bone china teacup. The tea is weak. Milk and water. I have a vision of the teabag waving at the cup from across the kitchen in a socially distanced, 'don't come to near to me' fashion. An elbow bump instead of a full-on bear hug.

Ben and Matilda are at my feet, sipping strong squash from plastic cups and doing a very good job of appearing sweet and innocent. My pulse is racing in my chest. I'm flustered. Trying to chat normally to Mrs Young and watch for any sign of movement from the twins.

Mrs Young is telling me, not for the first time, how excited she is by my visit and the prospect of a new interior, but that she's not quite ready to start. Soon, but not yet. If she hadn't paid a deposit, if she wasn't so lovely, then I'd think she was wasting my time, but I can see how torn she is. This is the house she lived in with her husband, the house they raised their children in. And now it is just her.

We're in the conservatory at the back of the house. The windows are open and it's hot, the air still. The furniture is white wicker with under-stuffed pale blue cushions. The wall into the house is painted a bright yellow and covered with small oil paintings of the countryside.

I love Mrs Young's house. It's nothing special on the outside. A red-brick property, built in the 1950s, in a little cul-de-sac of ten matching houses. But the interior is where my heart lies. The entire property, top to bottom, hasn't been updated since it was built. Not one lick of paint or strip of wallpaper, not one new carpet or tile. The bathroom suite is avocado green, the kitchen is white wood and pale worktops. Net curtains hang over every window, and the surfaces are filled with photographs of children and grandchildren, and Mr and Mrs Young in their heyday.

The entire house screams potential, and on every other visit here – and there have been quite a few – my stomach has danced with delight and a desperation to get started. My notebook is already filled with ideas. Simple and fresh designs. Classic. My biggest project so far. An entire house. I've spent hours on the designs.

From below me, Ben stretches out a leg, knocking it against a coffee table filled with framed photographs. I let out a gasp and touch my hand to his shoulder. They've been promised ice creams if we can just get through this.

'Be careful with your drink, Ben,' I say, before shooting Mrs Young an apologetic look. 'I'm so sorry I had to bring Ben and Matilda with me this time. Their pre-school closed early for the summer,' I lie. 'Nine weeks of summer holidays, here we come,' I add with a panic barely disguised as chipper.

'It's no problem, Rebecca. I love children and yours are so good. My grandson Thomas is the same age.'

Matilda beams at Mrs Young with a toothy innocence that causes a fresh prickling of sweat to break out beneath my blouse. It doesn't help that it it's eleven billion degrees in this room. Another glance to the children. The edges of their hair are damp, their cheeks flushed. They fidget on their bottoms, ignoring the little rucksack of toys they'd promised me faithfully they'd play with if they can have two flakes in their ice creams.

'I've got some ideas I want to share with you for your bedroom,' I say, forcing myself to look up at Mrs Young's expectant face. 'If that's still the room you'd like to start in.'

She hesitates and takes a sip from her teacup. 'I think so.' Her tone is uncertain. We've been doing this dance together since she called me last month, all guns blazing about redecorating her entire house. 'Top to bottom,' she said before waving a healthy budget in front of my eyes and going on to explain that Mr Young passed away over a year ago and it was time for a change. 'I don't want to move. This is my home, the house I shared with Stan for fifty-nine years, the place my children come back to every Christmas. But I don't want to feel like I'm living in a shrine to him and to us. It really does need some freshness. Nothing whacky though. No leopard print, you understand. I hope you're not going to be like that man off the TV.'

She meant Laurence Llewelyn-Bowen, the eccentric designer from *Changing Rooms* that has left a zebra-print zany mark on my profession.

But after that first phone call, it has been a series of hesitant visits. All my questions have been met with a 'I really don't know, dear. Perhaps ask me next week.'

'This wallpaper,' I say, pressing on, determined to make progress today as I pull out my sample with a flourish, hoping to waft away her uncertainty, 'would be perfect for a concept wall opposite your bed. Imagine waking up to this.' I say, fingering the delicate humming birds and white blossom on a duck-egg blue finish.

My phone buzzes with an email as Mrs Young takes the wallpaper sample in her hands. Hope balloons and I glance quickly at my phone, wondering if the pre-school have had a change of heart, but it's not them, it's a reply from The Toddler Tamer. I scan the words quickly:

I was delighted to receive your application . . . Planning meeting . . .

Monday, 25 July, 10 a.m. . . . Reply to this email if you are unable to . . .

I cringe inwardly. I still can't believe I contacted her. I stuff my phone back into my bag. I'll reply later. Tell her I've made a mistake. It must happen all the time. I mean, surely she should just ignore any email sent to her on a Friday evening after 6 p.m.?

'This is beautiful,' Mrs Young says, sending a bolt of triumph right through my centre. There is no better feeling in the world to me than understanding a brief and finding that perfect thing my client will love.

'I wonder if—' Mrs Young begins before Ben cuts in.

'Mummy,' he says. 'I need the toilet.' His eyes move from me to the back door and the garden beyond.

'Right, em . . . Mrs Young, would you mind if I take Ben to use your facilities?'

'Of course. You know where it is. Up the stairs and first door on the right. I'm sure he's old enough to go on his own, isn't he? What wall colour did you have in mind for the rest of the bedroom?'

Ben leaps up. 'I'm OK, Mummy. I can go on my own.' He walks quickly out of the room, his hand reaching for his crotch. I stare after him, torn between an urge to follow him, to make sure he doesn't find his way into bother in the two minutes he's out of my sight, and wanting to stay and show Mrs Young the almond white paint sample that will offset the wallpaper so perfectly. It's the first question she's asked about the designs and I'm desperate to leap on it.

I say a silent prayer that Ben makes it to the bathroom before finding a plant pot to relieve himself in. I have a horrible feeling that grown-up Ben is going to be the type of man who, after five pints on a Saturday night, mistakes the washing machine for the toilet.

Mrs Young runs a finger over the wallpaper sample that is sitting on her lap beside the paint card. She's looking wistful, but there's a smile on her face. 'Yes,' she nods. 'Yes, I think this will work well. What about the curtains?'

'I've got just the thing,' I say, reaching into my holdall for one of my fabric sample books. But before I can I open the folder there's a shout from the hall.

'Mummy, watch me,' Ben says with a high-pitched giggle that makes my stomach drop.

Matilda jumps to her feet, rushing in search of the fun Ben has found.

'Ben,' I call out, chasing after Matilda and sensing Mrs Young on my heels.

Matilda stops suddenly at the bottom of the stairs, looking up with delight on her face. I follow her gaze to where Ben is straddled backwards on the banister, his grinning face twisted round to his audience.

'Watch me,' he sings.

'Oh my,' Mrs Young says with a mix of horror and sadness in her voice.

'Ben, get down now please.' My voice comes out low and firm through my gritted teeth.

'OK, Mummy,' Ben giggles. 'I'm coming down.' And before I can correct him, tell him 'no,' he lets go and flies with alarming speed down the polished wood.

Matilda screams with delight, a war cry to follow her brother, but I grab her in my arms before she can reach the second step and watch helplessly as Ben follows the twist of the banister and falls off the end, landing on his

71

feet. The momentum causes him to stagger back and crash into Mrs Young's hallway table.

Ben's expression moves from glee to 'Oh no' as his eyes grow wide and his mouth drops open. There's a collective pause in the hallway and then Mrs Young and I both reach for the photo frame on the table as it wobbles precariously and topples to the floor.

Mrs Young snatches it into her hands and turns it over. The glass is cracked. One slicing line right down the middle of her wedding photo with Mr Young.

'I'm sorry,' I gasp, tightening my hold on Matilda as she fights to wriggle free. 'I'll replace it, of course.'

'Sorry, Mummy,' Ben says meekly.

'It's OK,' Mrs Young says, although it clearly isn't. 'I think . . . perhaps,' she looks from me to Ben and then Matilda before our eyes meet again, 'perhaps now isn't the best time, after all.'

She's firing you. She can see what kind of woman you really are now!

I want to plead. I want to coax Mrs Young back to the living room and our watery tea. I want to show her the ideas I have for her kitchen and the sofas I think she'll love, but Ben has fat tears leaking down his face and Matilda is hot with rage at being stopped from having her turn on the banister, and suddenly I'm fighting back tears too. Frustrated tears at seeing this project die when I could have done so much with the house and for Mrs Young.

You've failed. It's over. You're a crap mother and now you can't even keep your clients.

'Of course. I completely understand. I'll get my things,' I say.

Ten minutes later we're back in the car on our way home, the children silent in their car seats. Even Matilda's temper has dissolved.

'Can we get the paddling pool out when we get home?' Matilda asks.

I nod and find myself wondering, of all things, if the gardener has been yet to cut the grass.

A hollow emptiness takes hold of me. My business, my designs and projects, they are what make me me. The one thing I have that is completely mine and not shared with Josh or the children. When I'm working, I am not harassed mum to three out-of-control children, frustrated wife to a man who is barely home. I am Rebecca Harris, interior designer. It's what keeps me sane most days.

It was ludicrous of me to think that without Josh and my mum I'd be able to work at all this summer. Nine weeks of just me and the children. I'm not sure how much of me will be left at the end of it.

Three weeks later

Chapter 10

Me:

Hey, Any idea why the gardener hasn't turned up for two weeks? Can you chase? I don't have his number and the lawn currently resembles a jungle! xx

Josh:

I cancelled the gardener last month. I thought I told you. x

Me:

Please tell me you're joking. You know I can't work the old petrol mower you insisted on buying!!!!!

Josh:

I did it because looking after the garden is one of the few joys I actually have in my life and I wanted to do it myself and save us the extortionate fees we've been paying those rip off merchants.

Me:

Few joys? I assume you mean as well as spending time with your family!!!! Who is supposed to look after the garden while you're away? In case you haven't noticed, you're never here! FFS! You could've talked to me about this!!

Josh:

I'm coming home for the weekend soon. I will sort the garden out then.

Me:

And spend time with your children!!!!! Presumably you're not coming home just to see your rose bushes?!

Josh:

Obviously I want to see you and the children. I have a meeting now. I need to go.

Chapter 11

I pull onto the driveway and glance at Olly, Ben and Matilda, all asleep in the back. The twins are on either side of Olly. Matilda on the left, with a ring of Mr Whippy ice cream around her rosebud lips. She's wearing her favourite wellies despite the heat. They are green, with little frog eyes at the end where her toes sit. They're a size too big and she clomps around in them everywhere we go – the only shoes she'll agree to wear, no matter where we're going. They used to be mine. Decades ago. God knows why Mum kept them, but she did, bringing them around to the house one day for Ben but it was Matilda who fell in love with them.

On Olly's other side, Ben is clutching a bucket half-filled with shells and, based on his unwillingness to put the bucket in the boot, I have a sneaking suspicion it may also contain a kidnapped crab.

Olly is in the middle. His brown hair plastered to his forehead, he looks peaceful in sleep in a way he never does when he's awake. Despite all my efforts to wash away the sand, his long legs are covered in it.

I cut the engine and rest my head against the seat. I have sixty seconds before the lingering air conditioning is swallowed by the hot afternoon sun glaring through the windscreen. Sixty seconds before the children stir.

The list of jobs I need to do runs through my head. Unpack the boot. Put the beach things away. Wash the

79

sand from the kids. Put a supermarket delivery order in for tomorrow. Cook dinner. Wash the two sets of soggy beach clothes all three children went through despite their promises that they wouldn't get wet again. But still I sit. Breathing in the hot calm.

It's nearly 4 p.m. on Sunday. I have survived the weeks at home with Ben and Matilda. Weeks of coaxing, dragging and bribing Olly into school. And here I am, surviving the first weekend of the summer holidays and a trip to the beach on my own with three children. I glance out of the window, wondering where my fanfare is, my medal.

Exhaustion sweeps over me, adding to the pounding headache of dehydration and a day in the sunshine alongside every other family in the South East of England.

The gridlock traffic on the way home was the cherry on top of my exhaustion. All three kids whined and bickered until they eventually fell asleep. Any whisper of hope that they might go to bed earlier than usual tonight has since disappeared and I close my eyes for a moment and fight the desire to cry.

I have survived, but it's been hard. Every step, every minute has been a battle I've fought and rarely won. The week ahead looms in my thoughts. I can't do this for another six days let alone six weeks.

There's movement behind me and I force open my eyes.

'Mummy?' Olly says in a sleep voice. 'Ben's had an accident.'

I turn in my seat, looking first at Olly and then at Ben who is still fast asleep but now has a wet patch spreading across his shorts. He promised me he didn't need to go before we got in the car. Hand on heart promised. *Bollocks,* I think, adding cleaning the car seat to my list of jobs.

'That's OK,' I tell Olly. 'Let's get out. Matilda, Ben, time to wake up. We're home. Everyone in the garden for de-sanding. No one in the house until they're clean.'

Arms loaded with bags and buckets, wet towels and a deflated beach ball, we trudge through the back gate, dumping everything in a pile on the patio.

'Everyone jump in paddling pool,' I shout.

Olly goes first, stripping naked before plonking himself in the little inflatable pool, then jumping out and running into the house before I can hand him a towel. At least he's not sandy, I console myself, ignoring the damp footprints he's trodden across the floors.

'We'll have a proper bath later,' I shout out.

The twins do the same and disappear inside, and when I peak in through the living room window, all three are dressed in underwear and tucked on the sofa watching TV, Matilda and Ben cuddling their matching panda teddies in a way that makes my heart leap. How are they old enough to be going to school next month?

It's only when I turn back to empty the beach bags that I notice the garden looks different. Tidy. The lawn is trimmed and neat, the edges cut too. I experience a burst of warmth for Josh that cuts through the daily annoyance I feel that he hasn't called once in the weeks he's been away. We've shared texts and 'How was your days?' but every time I've picked up the phone, he's rushing into a meeting or the time zone is out and he's in bed, too tired to talk.

Or maybe he just doesn't want to talk to you.

I swallow back the comment and send him a text:

Thanks for rehiring the gardeners!! xx

His reply comes a minute later:

No need to be sarcastic! I told you we don't need them.
I'm going to do it when I'm back!

I stare, disbelieving, at his text. He didn't rehire the gardener. He thinks my text is a petty dig. So, who cut the grass? I step to the fence and peek over to Matt's garden and smile as I take in his matching neat lawn.

I've seen Matt most days in the last few weeks. We've shared 'Hellos' and 'How's your day going?' chats over the fence or on the front paths as one of us has been leaving and the other just arriving. Polite and friendly. Normal neighbours keeping to their own little worlds. The only reminder of our doorstep reminiscing is the knowing smile that stretches so easily across his face, the feeling that at any moment he's going to start laughing.

Anytime I'm in the garden now, I find myself looking for the open back door that tells me he's home. I see him sometimes, hunched over a laptop at the kitchen table, surrounded by notebooks and coffee cups. He pops his head out when he hears us and gives a wave. It's nice to see a friendly face, another adult.

I try not to think about what Matt must hear in the evenings – all the time, actually. Like yesterday when Olly set up a trap above the kitchen door, balancing a plastic bowl filled with water on top so that when I pushed open the door, the bowl would topple and soak me through. Except it wasn't me who walked through first. It was Matilda, carrying a colouring she'd just completed. The paper was soaked, the colours running like the angry tears spilling down her face. She ignored all my efforts to comfort her, and screamed and raged for five very long minutes, only stopping when she'd stomped upstairs and thrown one of Olly's Lego creations out the window, setting him off too.

'I hope you don't mind,' Matt says, appearing at his back door and striding towards me in another 'shorts and polo shirt' combination that shows off his long, tanned limbs.

'You did this?' I wave a hand at my garden and Matt nods.

'I said to . . . Greg, is it, the owner? That I'd happily do the lawn over the summer to save them the gardening fees. I quite like it. Bit of a novelty to have a garden, and then I noticed your lawn was—'

'Looking like a jungle.'

Matt smiles. 'I just thought, with your husband . . .' he pauses, just for a second, as though considering his next word, 'away, you might need the help.'

'Thank you. You're a lifesaver.'

'That's a relief.' He ruffles his hair. It's curlier today, the curls springing back into place the moment his hand moves. 'I wasn't sure if you were growing it for a special purpose.'

'What kind of special purpose might that be?' I raise an eyebrow.

'Longest lawn in the village award?' He gives me a teasing smile.

I laugh. 'Most scruffiest garden of the year more like. I've already got the worst neighbour award in the bag.'

'Nah, you've got nothing on the curtain twitchers down the road.' Matt's eyes find mine. His gaze is intense as though he's looking not at me but into me, and even though he's still smiling, there's something else in that look that makes me shuffle back and fiddle with my hair, pulling it out of its ponytail and retying it.

'It's really great,' I say. 'Thank you. We usually have a gardener but Josh cancelled him last month.'

'Why?' Matt asks.

I sigh. 'I don't know. I think he wanted to do it himself but then got sent to New York for two months.'

'And left you to deal with it.'

'And the rest.' I give a rueful smile. It feels surprisingly good to get my annoyance at Josh out of my head.

'If you need a hand with the garden again, or anything else, just ask.' Matt steps forward, leaning on the fence, his eyes never leaving mine.

'Thanks, but I'm OK. Josh is back at the weekend for a flying visit.'

'Are you really OK?' He stops smiling and his eyes fill with a concern that makes me want to cry.

A lump forms in my throat and all I want to do is shake my head and tell Matt the truth, that I'm not OK. I'm a crap mum. I have no friends, no husband right now, no family either. I'm all alone. I press the thought down into the darkest of corners and paste on a smile. 'Yep. Absolutely. How's the writing going?'

Matt groans. 'Not great.'

'Like trying to get school shoes on an eight-year-old who doesn't want to go to school?'

Matt laughs. 'Exactly. The strange thing is, I don't know why I'm having so much trouble with this book. It's the fifth one in the series. I know the characters inside out. I know the story I'm trying to write, and yet the words don't want to come.'

'Have a break and stop thinking about it. I don't know anything about writing, but when I'm trying to find the right colour scheme for a room and I stare at my colour boards until my eyes blur, I never get anywhere. But the minute I go take a shower . . .'

'Inspiration strikes.'

'For me anyway.'

'You're a designer?' he asks.

I nod. 'Trying to be. I have my own interior design business.'

'That's cool. And not at all surprising. I remember your epic doodles on the front cover of your science book.'

'I'd forgotten about that.' I smile. 'I got a detention for that.'

'Seems like you've forgotten quite lot, Double Trouble.' Matt pushes away from the fence.

'Maybe,' I reply, wondering if he's right. 'So, how are you finding village life after London?'

Matt stops to think for a moment. 'I think to answer that I'm going to need a drink. This grass cutting is thirsty work.'

'Of course.' I step back, feeling strangely disappointed that our chat is coming to an end. 'I didn't mean to keep you.'

Idiot!

'Actually, I wondered if you wanted a drink too? A chat without a fence between us.' A tinge of pink colours his cheeks. He pulls a silly face that makes me smile. 'I could pop over for ten minutes. If you're not too busy, that is?'

'That would be great.' My answer is quick and I could kick myself. 'Come round. I'll put the kettle on.'

'I was thinking something stronger actually.'

I laugh. 'Something stronger coming up.'

'Great. Give me a few minutes to power down my laptop.' Matt disappears into the house and I spin around, scooping up wet, sandy clothes and flinging them into the washing machine. My beach t-shirt is smeared with sun cream and I swap it for my favourite summer outfit – a simple black maxi dress. I dowse myself in deodorant before running back down stairs.

I kick the buckets and spades to one side and try to ignore the list of jobs I was going to do before dinner. I fix a tray of snacks for the kids, buying myself extra time. They don't look up as I come in to living room. They are lost to technology and after a whole day playing in the sun, I decide that's OK, and maybe I deserve to sit and talk to another adult over a glass of wine.

Chapter 12

Matt steps through the back gate and into garden just as I'm placing a cooler and a bottle of white wine on the outside table. He takes the glasses and pours the wine, handing me a glass as I drop onto the chair opposite him.

The t-shirt has been replaced with a white cotton shirt and Matt looks fresh and youthful, despite the fact we're the same age. Something squirms in my insides. I know the feeling. All mothers do. It's guilt. And, on the surface, I understand it. I'm sitting alone in my garden on a late Sunday afternoon, drinking wine with an attractive man, while my husband is away. But that's not what this is. This is two old friends catching up. It's adult company we both need. Crave. Nothing more.

I take a gulp of wine and wash the guilt away. The wine is cold, crisp and buttery, and I relish the feel of it sliding down my throat.

'So, village life,' I say. 'You were going to tell me how you're finding it?'

He drags a hand through his hair again. It's his go-to move when he's thinking, I realise. 'Ah, yes. It's pretty weird to be honest. A proper 'the grass is always greener' thing. I thought I'd love the countryside and the change of scene but I can't get used to the quiet. I'm used to hearing drunken arguments from the street at one in the morning, sirens at all hours, car horns, life. Any time I got stuck or frustrated with my work, I'd go out for a pint with a mate. In London, there's always someone you know you can grab a drink with.'

'It's lonely here,' I admit.

'Yes,' he says. 'That's it. And I knew it would be. I thought that was what I wanted. To be alone, to sort my head out and get this book written, but I wonder now if it's distractions that keep me focused. Does that sound really stupid?'

'Not at all. It's whatever works.'

'I've found myself popping in for a cup of tea to Mum's or Liam's every day this week, just to talk to someone.'

'Your mum must be pleased to see you.'

'She is, but she's got my sister's kids there most of the time and I feel like I'm getting in the way.'

'Well, you can always pop over here for a cup of tea, or something stronger.' I raise my glass.

He grins, his face lighting up. 'Thanks. I'm going to hold you to that.'

'Are you thinking of going back to London earlier than planned? If you're not enjoying it here, I mean.' I find myself holding my breath as I wait for the answer.

A sudden sadness crosses Matt's face and I can't help but feel like I've asked the wrong question. I'm about to take it back and apologise, when he answers. 'I've got nowhere to go back to right now. I was in a relationship,' he sighs, taking a long sip of wine. 'It was pretty serious. We were living together and I thought we'd go the distance, but then we stopped getting on, I guess, and she ended it.'

'Oh, I'm so sorry,' I blurt out. There is pain in Matt's eyes and, without thinking, I reach my hand across the table and take his. 'That must have been really awful.'

He nods, taking another a sip of wine. I move my hand, picking up the bottle and topping up our glasses.

'I'm OK. It's just painful, you know? Trying to unpick a life you've built with someone. Lisa – that's my ex – is still in the flat. We were renting and our contract is up in September so we'll split all our stuff then. Hence why I'm here.'

'How long were you together?'

'Six years,' he sighs. 'I keep going over it and I just . . . I don't know what happened. Why it went so wrong. It just did. Everything we had that made us right in the beginning seemed to disappear. We used to love staying up until midnight, vegging on the sofa, eating crisps and watching zombie films. But then Lisa started wanting to go to the gym all the time and out for dinner. She thought I was lazy and introverted because I didn't want to do those things. It feels like she changed, or she wanted me to change. Then, one day, it was like she'd just had enough of me and wanted to end it.' Matt pulls a face. 'Sorry, that's a lot to dump on you.'

'I don't mind. That must have been awful. Was there someone else?'

'I don't know. Maybe. Who knows. You sound like you're talking from experience,' Matt says, looking at me with a mix of pity and curiosity.

'Oh, no,' I'm quick to say. 'Josh is . . . No. He wouldn't. I mean, I don't think he would. He's away a lot and works long hours but . . .' I trail off from my spluttering ramble, face hot and uncomfortable. Josh wouldn't cheat on me.

Would he?

'That must be hard, with the kids and everything,' Matt continues.

'It is. But he's flying back this weekend to see us so that will break the time up.'

We fall into a companionable silence and I sip my wine and feel the early evening sun on my face.

'Hey, remember that teacher?' Matt says, sitting up a little straighter. 'Mr Block, the maths teacher?'

'Blocky, you mean?' I grin.

'I saw him the other day. He lives in the same village as Liam.'

'Noooo. I can't believe he's still alive. He was ancient twenty years ago.'

'He looked exactly the same. Not a day older,' Matt grins.

We launch into a scathing discussion about old teachers and laugh at the torture we put them through, and before I know it, the bottle of wine is empty.

'Mummy?' Olly says, hands on his hips as he appears beside us, looking suspiciously at Matt. 'We're hungry.'

I look at the time and gasp. It's seven o'clock. I leap up. 'Ah, sorry, Olly. I lost track of time. Ten minutes, OK?' Thank goodness I made a massive bolognaise yesterday. 'This is my friend Matt, from next door,' I say, waving a hand at Matt who makes no move to stand. 'Matt, this is Olly.'

'I went to school with your mummy,' Matt says, winking at Olly. 'Would you like to know what she was like?'

Olly grins and gives a fierce nod.

'I'm sorry,' I say to Matt. 'I need to cook dinner.' I gesture towards the kitchen. 'You're welcome to stay.'

'I'd love to, thank you. If you're sure it's no trouble.'

'None at all,' I smile. 'It's only pasta bolognaise though. It's the only thing all three of the children will eat.'

'We eat it nearly every night,' Olly says, like he's talking about ice cream for dinner.

'I bet it's going to be a lot tastier than the beans on toast I was planning to eat tonight.'

Dinner is a fun affair. With Matt regaling us all with stories of our school days, the children don't protest at sitting at the table. There is more wine, more food, ice cream and laughter. Matt tells the kids about the desk I set on fire, the girl I stood up for whose name we can't remember. I remember the bully though. Lara Williams. I remember how pushy she was with everyone. Always poking at us, looking for weaknesses. I hated her. I couldn't stand how she made so many of my classmates cower. And, one day, I stood my ground and I told her to stop threatening to punch everyone and get on with it. I was right there, ready for her. I'd forgotten all about it, but as Matt retold the story, I remember how my heart had pounded in my chest, waiting for the first smack to hit my face.

It didn't come. Lara backed away and, while she continued to be a first-class bitch, she didn't threaten anyone while I was in ear shot again.

'And Matt used to draw these really funny comics,' I say, as I clear the table of our pudding bowls. 'You'd have loved them, Olly.'

'Can I read one?' he asks, looking at Matt as though he's going to whip one out from his back pocket.

'Sure,' Matt says. 'They're in my mum's loft. I'll dig them out.'

'Oh, wow,' I say, 'that's really kind. Thank you.'

He shrugs. 'It's nothing.'

It's gone nine by the time dinner is over. I send the children to get ready for bed. They whine and plead but Matt stands to go and, without him, they scurry upstairs.

'Thank you for a wonderful evening,' Matt says at the front door. He leans forward and kisses my cheek. I catch the scent of his aftershave – a woody, masculine smell, as unfamiliar as it is nice.

It's a friendly peck, that's all. The same way I used to kiss the husbands of my mum friends at barbecues. And yet it feels nice. Human contact. I wonder about Josh. Whether he is lonely or if he's found some friends.

'It was good fun,' I smile. 'We'll have to do it again.'

'I'd like that. Well, I'd better go take the shower I meant to have four hours ago.'

'Me too,' I smile. Matt's lips twitch, his left eyebrow raising in a question and I feel my face flush. 'In my own bathroom, I mean.' God, why did I just say that? Of course, in my bathroom. It did *not* need to be clarified, and the fact that I felt a need to do so makes it seem like I was thinking of us showering together.

Idiot!

'That's a shame.' He laughs and turns around, striding down the path. Only when he's at his own front door does he flash me a smile over his shoulder and wave goodbye. I find myself rooted to the spot. Did Matt just say what I think he said? It was a joke, I tell myself. Why would someone like Matt be interested in me? A married mother of three, exhausted, wrung-out and . . . lost. The final word hits me like a slap. I don't know where it came from, but I push it aside and hurry upstairs to run a bath for the children.

Chapter 13

'. . . get it,' Olly's voice screeches from the living room as I step back into the kitchen and pull out a fresh bin liner.

'Get what?' I call back, sounding grumpier than I mean to. Boredom is a sludge through my veins. I'm tired, hot and sweaty. Last night with Matt was fun. A break from the day in, day out, but all the jobs I didn't do last night have mounted up for me to do today. Plus, I tried to call Josh late last night when I thought he might be back at the hotel, and he didn't answer.

He doesn't want to talk to you. Who can blame him?

The jobs from yesterday, Josh, the kids around my ankles desperate to play Ludo but giving up halfway through, getting the Lego out and then changing their minds, bickering and playing and bickering again. It curdles inside me until I'm grumpy. Beaten.

We should be having a picnic today, enjoying the July heatwave, but my mood is too sour to brave a trip out with Olly, Ben and Matilda, and so I've spent the morning cleaning. There is no magic cleaning fairy here. Not even a husband to swoop in and help. It's me doing *everything*.

Matilda is in the foulest of moods too. Whining and crying, stomping her little feet at me every few minutes when I won't let her have another biscuit. She's tired. Olly and Ben are too. Another late night. I tried after Matt left. I really tried to get them to bed, but they were

93

wired, bouncing off the walls, and I gave up and hid in the kitchen as they played pirates and crocodiles in the living room, pulling out every toy from the toy box, every cushion, every blanket, every teddy – a heap that took me an hour to put away.

It was gone eleven before they finally crashed, all falling asleep in my bed, leaving me to lie awake in Olly's room with Rex doing everything she could to sleep on my head, and all the while there was a feeling nipping at my ankles that no matter what I do, how I do it, I'm doing everything wrong. Why don't they listen to me? Why does nobody listen to me?

I sigh, sinking onto one of the stools that sit around the island in the centre of the kitchen. I'm aware of Olly chatting away to Ben or Matilda in the hallway, talking at a hundred miles an hour about something. I have about sixty seconds before he says or does something that elicits a scream. Sixty seconds to myself, to get my shit together and cheer up before I make some lunch and herd the kids out to the park or maybe the cinema if I can bear to sit through whatever all-singing, all-dancing monstrosity of a kids' film is playing this week. At least the cinema will have air conditioning.

I reach for my phone and open Instagram, losing myself to the photos and reels. My finger pauses at a photo of a shop-front window. A London boutique clothes store. It's a mint green display. Everything the same colour. Shoes and sunglasses, handbags and clutches, a dress, a top, all mint green and suspended from invisible wire that makes it look as though the suitcase on the ground has exploded and the photo has captured the moment when everything is flying through the air. It's ingenious. It will make every passer-by stop and stare. The photo is from Office17, the interior design agency I used to work for, and staring at it causes a pang of acute longing that makes me want to run upstairs to the study, barricade myself in and design something. Anything. I wonder about calling Mrs Young and begging her to reconsider.

But I can't. Because I have three children who need me, who I love even more than I love designing. And so, I take a photo of my tidy kitchen with the sun gleaming through the windows and bouncing on the worktops, and my copper pots hanging above the island, each one angled just so. I add a caption: *My happy place!* and twenty or so hashtags on interior design before posting.

For a moment, I think about editing the caption. Adding something real.

The definition of crazy is doing the same thing over and over and expecting a different result. #cleaningday #mumlife

I read that saying on a birthday card someone sent Josh once. There was a cartoon picture of a man in colourful golf clothes whacking a ball into a bunker. Josh doesn't even play golf. But I think about that saying every time I clean the house, every time I spend hours putting the toys back one by one into the correct toy box.

I leave the caption as it is. My Instagram is about calm, tranquillity and order. It's an illusion and certainly doesn't exist in my real life, and while I'm sure every one of my 10,000 followers knows it's fake, I don't want to spoil it, for myself more than them.

The noise of the front door shutting jolts me from my thoughts. Olly's 'get it' shout clicks into place. The doorbell must have rung while I was putting the rubbish out. Who the hell has he been talking to for the last few minutes? I dash towards the hallway, already fearing what I'll find – an Amazon delivery driver held prisoner with a sling shot. A charity sales worker soaked by a water-bomb.

But it's neither of these things. Instead, there's a woman in the hallway. She's wearing a smart trouser suit and a pink blouse, the colour of a cold glass of pale rosé. She's neat as a pin, as my old design teacher would say. Her blonde hair is swept into a bun and she's gleaming with health and vitality in that way women in their twenties do so effortlessly. Just standing beside her in my cleaning joggers and vest top makes me feel haggard.

'You must be Becca.' She smiles warmly, taking my hand and giving it a firm shake.

There's something familiar about the woman. I recognise her face. Is it the school? Christ, did I miss an email about a home visit from Ben and Matilda's reception teacher?

'Hi.' My smile betrays my uncertainty.

'I'm Saffron. Saffron Thomas,' she says as though that should explain everything; and then, 'the Toddler Tamer.'

'Oh.' My face burns crimson as I remember my drunken plea for help. Why, why, why did I send that message? And why is she here now? And then I remember the email that arrived while I was with Mrs Young. Something about a visit. A date and a time. I'd planned to reply with a polite 'No thanks', but then Ben and the banister and the broken picture frame and all those hours on Mrs Young's house wasted. I completely forgot.

And now the Toddler Tamer is standing in my hallway, a polite smile on her lips, waiting for me to welcome her into my home, but there is only one question spinning in my thoughts – how quickly can I get rid of this woman?

Chapter 14

The silence drags out for a moment more than is comfortable. Olly hops between us like an excited puppy. I wouldn't be surprised if he started to lick her hand.

'Shall we go into the kitchen?' Saffron says in a way that is more suggestive than questioning. She looks to Olly first and he leads the way as though he is the host, as though Saffron is here for him. A yip of a laugh escapes my mouth at the sight of him waving at her to follow. It's shock, I think, as I dip my head and follow behind.

She thinks you're an idiot.

Saffron steps to the island and pulls out a stool. I watch her eyes travelling around the kitchen. My beautiful, clean, 'everything in its place' kitchen. I wait for her look of approval, of envy, the same look everyone has when they walk into this space for the first time. But it doesn't come. There is no smile, no eyebrow raise, no outward signal to indicate what she is thinking, leaving me feeling wrong-footed.

'Shall we have a cup of coffee while we talk?' she suggests as she pulls out a notebook and pen from her bag and places them on the counter.

I cringe inwardly. I should have offered. I need to say something. This has gone too far already, but the words won't come. I've not said a thing since my surprised 'Hi' five minutes ago. She tucks her large shoulder bag beside the stool and I can't help wonder what else she has in there, my mind springing to that moment in *Mary Poppins* when she unpacks her bag, and a lamp and a plant come out. Except this woman is not Mary Poppins, she is an Instagram influencer who will humiliate me online for thousands to see and probably won't even help.

I feel suddenly so very foolish to have bought into the photos of happy families on her feed. It's all for show, just like my own account. She probably doesn't know the first thing about children.

'Becca, is everything alright?' Saffron asks.

The question spurs me into action. 'Yes, of course. I'll make us coffee,' I say, busying myself with making the drinks. I want this woman to leave, and yet I can't kick her out. She might badmouth me on Instagram or turn into one of those trolls set on ruining the innocent lives of those they've never met. I give Saffron a sideways glance as I flap around the kitchen, forgetting where the cups are kept, dropping the teaspoon, and all the while Saffron chats to Olly like they're old friends. She doesn't look like the trolling type, I'll give her that.

'What's your favourite *Scooby Doo* episode?' She listens intently to his reply before telling him hers. They share a joke about Shaggy that I don't get, and yet I laugh along too, more flustered than I care to admit.

What was I thinking? The question screams in my mind.

It was Friday night. I was drunk. I wasn't thinking.

When Saffron's hands are wrapped around the mug of hot coffee I've spent a full five minutes making; when I'm sat opposite, trying desperately to sip from my own cup; when the silence in the kitchen stretches out and even Olly is staring at me expectantly; I take a breath and I force myself to speak.

'Um . . . thanks for coming.' I try to smile, then stop when I'm sure the look on my face is more constipated than welcoming. 'The thing is, I shouldn't have sent you that email. I was having a bad day. A really bad day. I'd had a gin and tonic, I wasn't thinking clearly, but things are OK here, as you can see, and now just isn't a good time to try to change the routine.'

'When would be a good time?' she asks without missing a beat. There is no hint of sarcasm or mirth in her tone. It's a genuine question. Her eyes stare into mine as she waits for my reply and I drop my gaze and stare at the immaculate baby-pink nail varnish coating her nails.

'I . . . don't know,' I reply, when really I mean, I don't know what you want me to say. I don't know how I can get out of this conversation.

'That's because there is never a good time to face up to your problems.' Each word is slow and delivered with an absolute certainty that makes me nod my head, even though I don't agree, . . . do I?

Then her words sink in. Problems! That stings and I feel myself prickle. Who does this woman think she is? She can't be older than twenty-three. What experience of children can she have? What right does she have to talk to me about problems?

'Why don't I tell you both a little about myself?' Saffron says, looking to Olly who nods again, jumping onto the stool beside her. I bite the skin on my lip, wishing I was anywhere but here.

'I'm the oldest of seven children,' she says.

'Seven?' Olly says, eyes growing wide.

'Yep,' Saffron grins. 'You're eight, right?'

'Eight and a half.'

'Of course. Eight and a half. Well, that makes you six months older than Sully. He's the youngest. I have three other brothers, and two sisters. I grew up helping my mum look after my siblings. I have a degree in child psychology and a Master's in child behavioural therapies.'

OK, so maybe she does know something about children. But not my children.

'I set up the Toddler Tamer as a way to help mums and dads.'

'Have you come to help my mum?' Olly asks.

'I hope so.' She flicks a glance at me before turning back to Olly. 'Do you think she needs help?'

The coffee I'm halfway through swallowing sticks in my throat and I cough, unable to jump in, to answer for Olly, to tell her that I'm fine. We're fine. I really don't need any help.

Olly gives a guffaw of a laugh before he answers with a surprisingly confident, 'Yes.'

'Why do you think that?' Saffron asks, like I'm not there.

My jaw tightens. 'I do not need help.' The words leave my mouth with more force than I intend. I'm about to add something softer – a joke to lighten the mood – when a squeal of Matilda's laughter carries through the house.

'That's my sister,' Olly says.

'Come back.' Ben's shout follows Matilda's screams of delight.

'And that's my brother. They're twins and they're four.'

'That must be a lot of work,' Saffron says, and Olly nods earnestly.

'They're not very good at listening,' he says.

I bark a laugh at Olly's audacity.

'They do listen, Olly,' I say, ignoring the confusion that crosses his face. 'They've been playing dressing-up in their room,' I say with more than a little smugness. 'So, as you can see, we're all fine.'

I stand up, placing my mug by the sink in a clear indication that we're done here, and so my back is turned as Matilda races into the kitchen, Ben right behind her, the pair of them giggling and laughing at something Ben is holding in his hand and trying to get Matilda with.

'Stop,' she giggles. 'Mummy, make him stop.'

There's a scraping of stools and the thud of little hands knocking into cupboards as they race around and around the island. One of them nudges my leg and only then do I spot the smudge of orange on the floor. It looks like . . . leftover sauce? Or a felt tip pen. But I've just washed the floors. It doesn't make sense.

'Mummy,' Olly says as I'm still peering at the floor. 'Something smells funny.'

A whiff of tropical coconut hits my senses. It's that pungent, slightly off smell, like . . . like . . . fake tan. Reality hits with a dawning nausea as Ben charges past me, his orange hands outstretched.

Matilda screams as he approaches and I spot orange streaks coating her blonde hair. Everywhere I look, there are now orange splodges and smudges and streaks and blobs.

I stare, gob smacked, unmoving at the chaos now charging around the island. I don't know what's worse – the children or the mess of my just cleaned kitchen and, no doubt, the bathroom, the stairs. Hours of cleaning gone in seconds. Bollocks!

Matilda stops and so does Ben, both dancing at each end of the island, waiting to see who will run first, and it's then I see the full horror of their game. Their faces are covered in dark orange. Their hands, their legs, their clothes, their hair, it's everywhere and darkening with every minute that passes.

'Matilda, Ben,' I gasp. 'Don't move.'

They ignore me, their game starting again as they sprint around the kitchen and it's no longer clear who is chasing who. Despite the chaos and the growing realisation that my children have got enough fake tan on themselves to pass for pumpkins, I'm aware of Saffron's cool gaze on the scene and the phone in her hand. Is she recording this? I feel my face grow hot with humiliation and anger.

'Stop,' I shout again, my voice screeching with desperation. My demand is lost to the screams of Ben and Matilda.

Saffron stands and for a moment I think she's going to walk out, to give up on us, and there's a part of me that's glad and another part of me, a stronger part, that doesn't care that she's seeing this, filming this, a part of me that wants to throw myself at her feet and beg her to help.

She places her phone in a small black stand, positioned on one of the counters, and then turns and claps her hands together once. 'When I clap my hands again, everyone is going to freeze. No one move. Let's see who can be a statue for the longest.' Her voice isn't loud but it's commanding and when she claps again even I keep myself still.

'Now, Ben and Matilda, my name is Saffron Thomas. It's nice to meet you. I'd shake your hands, but you are a bit messy at the moment. I'm here to help your mummy and right now, we all need to help Mummy get you clean because you are covered in fake tan, which looks rather silly and is making a big mess around the house. So, when I clap my hands again, you are going to walk up the stairs like robots.' She does an impression of walking with stiff arms and legs. 'Robots don't wave their hands about, do they? They don't rub their hands on their bodies or touch the walls as they pass. They walk very carefully and slowly. You are going to walk like robots to the bathroom and let Mummy clean you up and when you're clean, you can help to magic away all the mess.'

A bubble of laughter pushes up inside me. Oh, the naivety of this woman. Does she really think my children will listen to her?

'What do I do?' Olly asks.

'You are going to show me where the cloths and cleaning products are kept. We're going to play detectives and track down every last bit of fake tan we can find in the kitchen.'

'Yessss,' Olly grins at me, eyes glistening in a way I don't recognise. Where is the tantrum? The 'no I won't', the 'you can't make me'. It can't really be this simple, can it?

It's just you they don't listen to. You that fails.

'Do you have any lemon juice?' Saffron asks me.

'Er . . . I think so.' My cheeks smart as the taunting voice fills my head. I open the cupboard and reach for the bottle, handing it to her.

'It's for you. For their skin,' she explains. 'It will help get the fake tan off.'

'I want to play detectives too,' Matilda says. I recognise the set of her face and sense the tantrum coming.

'Me too,' Ben says with a huff.

And before Saffron or I can say another word, they are off again around the kitchen, this time pointing and shouting at every orange smudge, completely unaware that with every footstep they are adding to the mess.

'Matilda, Ben,' Saffron says and they stop and look at this stranger in our home. 'Of course you can play detectives. I bet there is loads of orange upstairs and in the hall that only detectives of your height will be able to find.'

They give furtive bobs of their heads, already stepping towards the hall.

'But,' Saffron says, 'you need to be clean first like Olly is and like I am. OK?'

They pause. I can see them think. Saffron doesn't give them a chance to reply. She claps her hands. 'Like robots,' she says and it's as though her words are a lightning bolt. Ben and Matilda freeze, their bodies turning rigid, and they walk robotically upstairs, me trailing behind, wondering what just happened and how exactly this woman has got through to my children in two minutes flat.

The failure I feel at Saffron's success is far greater than the humiliation of the scene that Saffron has just captured on camera for her many followers to see. In five minutes, this 'neat as a pin' woman, this Toddler Tamer, has got through to my children in a way I'm rarely able to. It's what I wanted, isn't it? Help. Or did I just want validation that I'm not the one to blame for their behaviour?

And that's when I realise that in the five minutes that Saffron has been here, I've gone from wanting her to leave, to wanting to beg her to stay.

Chapter 15

Saffron slides the contract towards me as I return from scrubbing the twins. Matilda's hair still has an odd tinge to it, their faces a rather healthy glow, but they are no longer orange, and nor is the kitchen after Saffron and Olly's detective work.

'Thank you,' I say. The threat of tears burns behind my eyes.

She smiles, wide and genuine. 'You're welcome,' she says before giving a cloth to Matilda and Ben, and telling them to search the stairs and any other places for smudges of orange. They run off with the same excitement levels as though Saffron had given them a new toy to play with.

'We can start tomorrow,' Saffron says. 'I call it "rules and observations" day. I'll film a few scenes of things going wrong and then lots of things going right. I'll make notes but I won't begin stepping in until we've had a parent meeting and discussed the behavioural issues in more detail.'

I nod, barely listening as I skim the paperwork in front of me.

Tomorrow. Less than twenty-four hours away. This woman will be in my home, caring for my children. Not just caring, guiding them, teaching them, showing them how to behave in a way I've never managed. And I'll be free. Those hours will be mine. A giddiness skips through my veins. I think about climbing into my car and escaping or tucking myself away in my little office with my fabrics and designs.

I feel like someone has thrown me a life raft. I was drowning and now I've been saved.

Drama queen.

'I'm sure you understand that my business relies on Instagram for referrals,' Saffron continues. 'And new content is essential for my feed. But I want to reassure you that it's not as constant as people think. It won't be all the time and I don't tag you in the posts.'

A whisper of relief unfolds in my thoughts. Even if Saffron's tens of thousands of followers see what a crap mother I am, my calm and perfect Instagram life is safe.

Everyone will be judging you. Laughing at you. Everyone will know what a failure you are as a mother.

I bite my lip and hesitate, glancing up to see Olly now helping the twins hunt for more orange marks. All three of my children are happy and calm. I doubt I'll be in any of the videos anyway. It'll be Saffron and the kids, not me.

I take a breath and sign my name.

Saffron scoops up the contract and tucks it into a hot-pink folder. There are tabs and labels, everything organised and in its place, and there is something reassuring about that. Then, barely an hour after she arrived, Saffron waves us all goodbye and we close the door, and Olly and Ben and Matilda stare at each other and me, with the best WTF faces, and I laugh because I feel it too, as though none of us can quite believe what just happened.

'Is she a witch?' Ben whispers.

I laugh and Olly joins in but Ben's face is serious until I reassure him. It's only later when the house descends back into chaos – the slow-motion collapse of a building being demolished – that I find myself wondering if Ben is right. Was there some kind of sorcery involved? A spell. That's the only way to describe it – the power she had over all of us.

By bedtime, Olly and Matilda are fighting again, Ben is crying and I'm shouting, but instead of despair, I feel hope. And it's only as it settles over me that I realise how long it's been since I've felt hopeful about anything. I slide into bed, daydreaming about my freedom, planning what I'll do tomorrow while Saffron takes care of my children. Even a trip to the supermarket alone would feel like a lottery win.

Chapter 16

The following morning, the doorbell rings at exactly 9 a.m. I'm ready for Saffron this time and rush to open it, beckoning her straight into the kitchen with a welcoming smile. Today, I'm the excited puppy who wants to bounce around her, hug her even. This woman is my life jacket.

Saffron is wearing another suit with a white silk top beneath it. It's not the kind of outfit I'd have expected for looking after children, but Saffron is clearly not a normal type of nanny; she's proved that already. Her make-up is celebrity flawless right down to the touch of bronzer on her cheek bones.

I feel a wobble when Saffron pulls out two black stands and starts clipping cameras on to them. But I remind myself that it will be fine. I won't be tagged in the posts. I won't even be here.

Olly, Ben and Matilda appear at the top of the stairs before running down to greet Saffron. She takes her time to say hello to each of them in turn as I make the coffee.

'What shall we do?' Olly asks her. Matilda gives a nod beside him, hands on hips. Only Ben hovers in the doorway, still wondering if Saffron is perhaps a witch.

'Well,' she begins. 'I noticed as I came in that there are lots of toys out in the living room. That must make it really hard to play when it's such a mess.'

Olly bobs his head up and down as she talks.

'I was going to suggest playing a game, but it's too messy in there.'

'Yeah,' Matilda says, shooting a dagger-look at me as though I've made the mess, as though it's my fault.

'Who normally tidies up?' Saffron asks.

'Mummy,' all three say in unison.

Saffron tilts her head to one side. 'And who makes the mess?'

The children look at each other for a moment before Olly says, 'We do.'

'I won't tidy it,' Ben says, crossing his arms.

'Me neither,' Matilda says.

'OK,' Saffron says. 'So, we'll close the living room for now.'

'What do you mean?' Ben asks.

'I mean, we can't go in there when it's so messy. So, let's close the door and no one will go in there until you're ready to tidy it.'

'But what if I want to watch TV?' Olly asks and at the same time Matilda cries out about needing her Barbie dolls.

'So, you do want to tidy it?' Saffron asks.

'Let's pretend we're detectives again,' Olly says, pushing the twins towards the door. 'We've got to find a clue but it's hidden.'

'Yeah,' Matilda says, and I bite back a gasp.

'Good idea,' Saffron smiles. 'If you three tidy your toys, that will be a really big help to Mummy and to me. And I'll chat to your mum and we'll make a plan of action for today.' She claps her hands just like yesterday and I notice that it's not a normal, palms-together clap, but the back of the fingers slapping the other palm. Three chirpy, 'Let's do this' claps that spur the children into action, eager to please in a way they never are with me.

'So,' Saffron begins, as she settles herself once again at

the island, a coffee in her hands and one of the small digital cameras balanced on a pod in front of us.

Everyone will be laughing. They'll see the truth. They'll see what a bad mother you are.

I take a sip of coffee, swallowing back the nerves. Just get through this bit, I tell myself, and then Saffron will take over and she'll work her magic on the kids and there will be nothing embarrassing to see.

'Becca, let's talk about what house rules you have in place,' she continues, a notebook in front of her. Pen poised on a blank page. It's a different pen today. A pink thing with a feather at the end. Very *Legally Blonde*.

'Yes, sure,' I say, racking my brains for rules I can tell her about. There are plenty, of course – no running on the stairs, bedtime at 8 p.m., eat all your vegetables, tidy up after yourself, don't be mean to anyone.

Except the rules are broken so often that they are flimsy instead of rigid. 'Um . . . before we get to all that,' I reply. 'May I ask what hours you work? I'm an interior designer so I can work around you. But if you can stay for dinner times, that would be useful.' I swallow, hoping my voice isn't betraying the desperation I feel inside.

There's a shout from the living room. 'I'll do that,' Olly says. Then Ben, 'I'll do this bit.'

I exhale – half laugh, half 'I can't believe my children are tidying'; willingly tidying; in fact, happily tidying.

'Today, I'll be here until bedtime so I can observe and get a full sense of your routine, or lack of one,' Saffron explains. 'I'll put some strategies in place, which we can talk over tomorrow and get started. I don't work at the weekends, but during the week, I'll do a mix of mornings and afternoons for several weeks by which time I'm sure you'll be ready to say goodbye to me.'

I snort. 'I don't think I'll ever be ready for that.'

'You will.' Saffron smiles knowingly.

'So, when you say you're just observing today?'

'I'll be watching,' she confirms. 'Making notes and videos on how you do things. Getting to know you and the kids.'

'But what actual hours will you be here for after today?'

'It's going to depend a lot on you and your family situation.'

'So, I can ask for more?' A worm of uncertainty begins to wriggle through me. Why is Saffron being so cryptic? Has she changed her mind about becoming our nanny? I really should have read the contract and information folder Saffron left for me yesterday.

She tilts her head from side to side. 'It's not so much an ask as a need.'

'I need all the hours,' I laugh.

The smile on Saffron's face freezes and I feel shitty at my comment. A bad mother. I remember the camera is on, and my face flames.

'I just meant,' I say, 'that I'd like to be able to work every day for at least four hours.'

'That's not a problem.' Saffron nods and makes a note. 'I can come at the times you're not working.'

I give a nervous laugh, my gaze flicking to the lens of the camera and then back to Saffron. 'Surely you mean you'll come when I *am* working? To look after the kids. That's the point of it, isn't it?'

'No,' Saffron says, matter of fact, giving a shake of her head. Her hair is in a bun again, not a hair out of place. 'That's not why I'm here. Did you read any of the paperwork I left?'

'I skimmed it,' I lie.

'Becca,' Saffron says, leaning forward on the counter, her eyes fixed on mine. 'You do understand what this is, don't you? I'm not here to look after your children,' she says, her words slow as though I'm a child myself.

'What?' The word flies out. The freedom I've been clinging to for the last twenty-four hours starts to feel slippery in my grasp. How is this woman a nanny and not going to look after my children? 'But—'

'I'm not here to look after Olly, Matilda or Ben. I'm not here to teach them how to behave,' she continues.

My head moves up and down as though I understand even though I don't. Not even close. 'I do get that this is more than just being a nanny, because you specialise in . . . er . . . behavioural issues, but you will be looking after the children, won't you?'

Saffron shakes her head and I try not to cringe at the pity in her eyes. 'No.'

'But . . . why are you here then?' I say at last when I can think of no other way to phrase the question. Panic circles inside me. What the hell have I signed up for?

She smiles and I have the sense that I've asked the right question. 'I'm here to teach you how to behave.'

'Me?' A bubble of laughter escapes, popping instantly at the sight of Saffron's calm features. She isn't laughing. She isn't even smiling now. Without her saying a word, I feel scolded.

'Why didn't Ben and Matilda stop running around the table yesterday when you told them to?' she asks.

'I don't know.' Something deflates inside me. 'They never listen to me. They never listen to anyone.'

'They listened to me.'

I give a reluctant nod. She's got me there.

'Children are not born naughty or bad.' Saffron's voice has taken on a lecturing quality. All the warmth I felt towards her when I flung open the door this morning evaporates. I seethe quietly at my error, the freedom I thought I would have that has been snatched away. 'We – adults, parents – we teach it to them, and now you and I need to unteach them behaviours which are causing problems for them and for you.'

'I do get that, but I'm trying. I don't know what I'm doing wrong all the time.' Emotion carries in my voice. Hot tears burn in my eyes. I feel got at, attacked, and utterly shit because I know she's right.

She's saying you're a terrible mother. And she's right.

'Becca . . .' Saffron reaches across the counter and places a warm hand on mine. 'The very last thing I'm saying here is that you aren't a good mother,' she says as though reading my mind. 'In fact, it's very clear to me that you are a wonderful mother; it's very clear that you love your children and they love you.'

Her words tip tearful to crying. Emotion pushes through me. I'm failing at something that's supposed to come naturally. I'm a failure.

Saffron falls silent, allowing me a moment to pull myself together. I sniff and wipe my eyes. 'I do try to keep their behaviour in check.'

'I know, and part of why I'm here is to get to the bottom of why they don't listen to you.'

'It's not the kids' fault. No one listens to me. It's a thing. I'm invisible. I have been for years.' The words spill out, as though coming from a place I didn't know existed inside me. I jolt as though I'm surprised and yet it was me who said it. 'I just want what's best for them.' I swallow a lump in my throat, fighting back the urge to sob. I've got to get myself together.

It's the shock of stupidly thinking Saffron was here to look after the kids, to give me a little time to myself. I need to get a grip. Thanks to Ben and his ability to make a slide out of anything, Mrs Young's house is now on hold, probably indefinitely, and however much I love the design work, at least I don't have to juggle it with the children this summer.

'Of course you do,' Saffron soothes. 'And, right now, what is best for them?

'This,' I whisper. 'You helping me.'

She gives a satisfied nod.

'Do I get a gold star sticker?' I ask, trying to lighten the mood.

It works. Saffron tips back her head and laughs. 'Absolutely.' She reaches into her bag and, the next thing I know, she's walking around the island, tapping a sticker onto the top of my t-shirt and enveloping me in a hug that should feel weird. This woman is practically a stranger to me, and yet it's nice. Comforting.

I wipe my eyes and whisper, 'Thank you.'

We spend nearly an hour talking about routines and the times I find the children's behaviour most challenging. By the time we're done, I'm exhausted and emotional, but there's something else circling my body – relief. For so long, I've told my mum, Josh and myself that the kids are fine, that our lives are fine. The kids are mischievous, but aren't all kids? The reason we don't go out to dinner or even to the park, the reason our lives have shrunk to school, the house and swimming lessons is that Ben and Matilda are at a difficult age and with Olly too – we're outnumbered.

But deep down I knew things were out of control. That 'mischievous' was the understatement of the century. Admitting it to Saffron and myself feels like a shaky first step and, as Saffron stands, smoothing out her suit, I allow myself to wonder if this could be the start of a new way of life for us.

'So, bedtimes and mealtimes and activities out of the house are when you feel you struggle the most.'

I nod before pulling a pained expression. 'Doesn't leave much, does it?'

'When women become mothers, their worlds often shrink as they put their careers on hold and their lives change astronomically overnight. On top of that, there is the huge weight of expectation that's placed on all mothers to have that instant love and bond, to know exactly what to do and to do it willingly and happily. It's pretty insane when you think about it. What other job can you think of that throws someone so far into the deep end without any training and very little support? The expectation is that mothers will do it all, and they'll do most of it alone. Hundreds of years ago, there would have been village elders, women who'd been through it, there to help. It's tough now, more so than ever before.'

The desire to cry wells up inside me again. My warmth towards Saffron returns and I fight the desire to hug her once more.

Saffron gives me a final sympathetic smile and I find myself staring back at her, wondering how this woman, this girl really – who is so young, who doesn't have children of her own – who has spent all of two hours with me, has summed up my life so completely.

A silence draws out between us. I struggle to find the words, any words actually. I'm saved by Ben whose piercing scream shatters the peace. It's followed by a yell from Matilda and I realise observation day has begun.

Chapter 17

By the time 8 p.m. rolls around and Saffron packs her camera into her bag and wishes us all goodnight, I am ten steps, and then some, beyond exhaustion. Having Saffron watch our every move has put me on edge.

The weight of her judgement has been constant. I made the mistake of asking her what I should do when Olly started throwing Matilda's Barbies out of the window, aiming for the paddling pool, and I told him to stop, only to find him back at his window two minutes later throwing my clothes out. Saffron shook her head and told me to do whatever I would normally do.

I snatched my clothes from the lawn, screaming up at Olly to stop, threatening to ban him from the TV, to take away his toys. On and on it went until I was near tears with frustration. Saffron stood and watched, capturing snippets on one of the cameras and sometimes on her phone. Her face showed neutral acceptance, but that judgement was there anyway, lurking just beneath the surface of her smile.

'Are you putting them to bed soon,' she asked at ten to eight, making a point of looking at her watch.

I shrugged, too tired to defend myself. And anyway, what excuse do I have? Of course they should be in bed, but they're playing Peter Pan in Olly's room and I'm too tired, too weak to do anything about it. Her disapproval was palpable.

'Don't you want some down-time, to have the evenings to yourself?'

I laughed at that. 'Yes,' was all I could say before shrugging.

She hugged me. A tight embrace. 'I believe in you, Becca,' she said. 'I'm going to help you to believe in yourself.' Then she picked up her bag and opened the front door. 'Tomorrow is going to be very hard,' she warned before disappearing into the evening, and I couldn't tell in that moment whether I wanted to beg her to stay or scream at her never to come back.

I drop onto the sofa and call Josh. It rings five times before he answers. My heart lifts. I'm desperate to tell him everything, to unburden the horror of this day.

'Hey,' I smile for what feels like the first time in hours. 'How's New York?'

'Hello?' It's a woman's voice, and even though she has the twang of an American accent, I pull the phone away from my ear and check in my exhausted state that it is Josh I've called.

'Hello?' she says again. 'Josh's phone.'

She sounds young and peppy, and I hate her already.

'Is Josh available please?' I say at last, aware of how clipped my voice sounds, how polite. How British. Inside, my heart is hammering in my chest. Blood roaring in my ears. Why is this woman answering his phone?

Isn't it obvious? He's probably having an affair. Who could blame him?

'He's just stepped away from his desk,' she says. 'Can I take a message?'

Yes, is what I think. Yes, you bloody well can. And the message is — tell him his wife wants to know why this young, hot (OK, I don't know she's hot, but she sounds hot) woman knows you well enough to presume to answer your phone?

Who even does that?

She must have looked at the display and seen my name, must've known it wasn't work related. Bitch. Bitch. Bitch.

Exhausted tears build in my eyes and spill onto my cheeks and I brush them away.

You're a mess. No wonder Josh is looking elsewhere.

'No,' I say. 'No, thank you. I'll call back.'

'OK then. Bye.'

She hangs up and I stare at my blank screen for a long time, willing Josh to call me, to tell me about his day, to pop every single one of the doubts I have bubbling in my mind. The jealousy knots in my stomach and I hate it as much as I hate that woman for answering Josh's phone.

It's just tiredness and my imagination running wild, dragging my emotions with it. And talking to Matt the other day about whether his girlfriend might be having an affair; it's planted a rotten seed in my unconscious. That's what I tell myself.

I trust Josh. I've always trusted Josh.

I try to think of a happy memory, something – anything to distract me. And yet there's nothing but the constant hollow loneliness I feel day after day after day, and the weight of his absence and the knowledge that his job will always, always come before the children, before me.

Come on, I tell myself. There must be something. It's bad enough Josh is away, I can't allow myself to think about all the what-ifs. I close my eyes and think of Josh's warm, firm hand squeezing mine.

The memory comes then. The hospital. The bed. The gel on my stomach. Staring at that black and white screen. Waiting.

How nervous we both were. It took so long to get pregnant the second time around. Olly had been easy. We barely tried. Naively, I thought it would be the same again.

Except it wasn't. We tried for years. We tried until all the fun had gone out of it, and it was ovulation calendars and month after month of that slicing disappointment when that single line appeared, when my period came.

Lying on that bed, Josh on one side, the sonographer on the other, I don't think either of us really believed it was happening. And then, there they were – not one perfect baby on the screen, but two. Two heads. Two sets of legs. Two beating heats. Two miracles.

Josh burst into tears, shoulders heaving, laughing too. I just stared at that screen, stunned, happy, terrified. And then Josh looked at my face and it was like he saw every emotion, every single worry running through my thoughts. He wrapped his arms around me, held me close, tight. He told me how perfect it would be. How lucky we were. How complete our family would be. He said all the right things. Made all the right promises.

I take a long breath, drawing the air into my lungs slowly, blowing out through pursed lips so it's almost a whistle. The memory has eased the tightness in my chest. I want to say I'm fine now, the call with that woman was nothing. Except there's that doubt again, that Gollum-like voice.

He has been so distant for months now. He's been working later too. And there was that night last month when he didn't come home at all, calling the next day to say he'd missed the last train and slept in the office.

My heart starts to pound in my chest and I shake the thoughts away again, willing myself to step back from the rabbit hole my thoughts are dragging me towards. I pick up my phone and text Josh.

Hey, How's it going in NY? Got time to call the kids this week?

I hired a nanny (sort of). She's going to help the kids'
behaviour. I hope!!
x
PS Who was the woman who answered your phone?

Three rolling dots appear, telling me that Josh is typing a reply. A minute passes and then nothing. The dots disappear and no message arrives. I wonder if he's been called into a meeting or if just can't be bothered to explain, and now I wish I'd not texted him at all.

I think fleetingly of Matt and the hurt radiating from him when he talked about his ex-girlfriend. I wonder if he knew things were ending. Maybe I'll ask him if we get to know each other a little more. The thought is comforting and I pick up my phone and lose myself to my Instagram feed, until I feel calmer, more together.

Then I click on to Saffron's Toddler Tamer profile. She's added a photo from today. It's the garden in chaos, toys and clothes scattered across the lawn where Olly threw them out of the window. There's a blur of Olly, Ben and Matilda in the background. Even out of focus, you can see the fury on Matilda's face, the taunting stance of Olly.

The text reads: *Observation day on a brand-new family. I can't wait to help them!*

I can't wait either.

I close the app, feeling deflated all over again. Am I really ready to have my life played out on Instagram – my real life, warts and all? Am I really going to be able to do this? Saffron can say she believes in me as much as she wants, but it's just words. I know deep down that I'll never be a good-enough mother.

Chapter 18

There's the thud of feet above me, a shout of delight, a yell, a giggle. I pull myself out of my stupor and up from the sofa, and even though I know I should go upstairs and try to calm the children, I walk into the garden instead. Another twenty minutes won't make any difference. The sun is sinking below the horizon, the sky pink then purple, like an explosion of candy floss. Two strips of white mist from an aeroplane cross the sky, making me long for a holiday, a pool, cocktails, that delicious heat that is so welcome abroad, when there are no clothes to wash or chores to do, just a sun lounger and a book.

I think of my mum. I miss her. I miss her help with the kids, but I miss her company more. If she weren't on holiday right now, I'd be calling her. Chatting about nonsense stuff, telling her about what the kids have done. I almost text her then to tell her about Saffron, but she'll be having a wonderful time on her cruise and doesn't need me reminding her of home and my messy life.

I'm reaching to scoop up a pile of discarded My Little Ponies when a male voice says, 'Hi'.

I jump, yelping as I spin around.

'Oh God, I'm sorry.' Matt is leaning on the fence a metre away from me, the smile fading into alarm. 'Did I scare you?'

'A bit,' I admit, stepping to my own side of the fence. 'It's my fault. I was miles away.'

'Anywhere nice?'

'A sun lounger by a pool,' I say with a wistful smile. 'A cocktail in my hand.'

'That sounds—'

'Far away from my current reality,' I cut in with a shrug.

'I saw you out there and I wanted to give you these.' He holds out a stack of paper in his hands. 'My old comics. For Olly.'

'Oh wow, you found them.' The paper is crumbled and aged, but the colours are still bright, a medley of pinks and greens. The top one has a cartoon drawing on the front of a round-faced boy wearing a pink leotard. His pimpled face is set in an angry scowl but somehow Matt has made his body, his pirouette, look graceful.

I laugh at the image as the memory of the boy it was based on pops into my head. 'I'd forgotten how talented you were,' I say. 'And brave.'

'Um, well I also uncovered several school reports and apparently I wasn't quite the studious boy I remember. "Must try harder" was a regular feature, alongside, "not as clever as he thinks he is",' Matt adds with a smirk before running a hand through his hair and leaving it looking windswept and wild.

He catches my eye and smiles. It's warm and kind, and makes me smile too.

'I decided to take a quick peak to make sure they're appropriate and I ended up reading them all afternoon. I even started jotting down some ideas for extended versions, proper kids' books, before I remembered I'm not a children's author.'

'Can't gritty crime writers also write children's books?'

'Maybe, but I'm not sure I'm talented enough to do both.' Something changes in Matt's face and I see a glimpse of vulnerability. It makes him look younger for that one moment; more like the boy I remember who used to let me copy his science homework three minutes before the start of class.

'We'll be your testers if you like. If we think you're talented, then you can write them.'

'OK,' Matt grins. 'Deal. As long as you tell me if it's naff too.'

'You can count on it,' I say and we both laugh.

'I'm guessing they are appropriate if you're giving them to me?' I say, gesturing at the comics in my hand.

'Surprisingly, yes. There's a bit of smooching in the second one when Geek Boy kisses the most popular girl in school right after they defeat the alien head teacher.'

I laugh at that but when I look up, Matt's cheeks are flushed, his gaze intense and I find myself wondering if Matt used to have a crush on me. The thought makes me laugh again and I tell myself not to be so stupid. I was well liked in school but I was never popular.

I'm about to ask how Matt's crime book is coming along when Olly appears in the garden, calling out a delighted 'Matt', before racing over to the fence. 'We're playing Peter Pan and I'm Peter.' He thrusts his hands onto his hips as though proving his point.

'I'm Hook, arrggh,' comes Matilda's voice as she trails after Olly, wearing one of my red going-out dresses. The material drags on the floor, stretching and tugging as she trips over herself. I feel a pang of sadness for the dress, as though it is a living thing, once much admired, much coveted by all who saw it. To be plucked from the rail and warn to dinners and dancing, living its life to the fullest, until being relegated to the back of a dark wardrobe, forgotten and discarded, only to resurface as a dressing-up outfit. Oh, how the mighty have fallen.

I go to protest at the outfit, but Matilda is grinning from ear to ear and it's not as though I'm going anywhere that I could wear a dress like that. Why did I even keep it? Wishful thinking, I guess. As if any amount of dieting is going to shrink my hips back to the size of my pre-children days.

'And who is Ben?' Matt asks.

'The crocodile,' Olly and Matilda say in unison. 'Mum is Wendy,' Olly adds.

'I've come to capture her,' Matilda grins, attaching herself to my leg.

'Mummy is actually pretty tired,' I say. 'And doesn't want to be captured. I actually think it's bedtime. And look what Matt has lent us.'

'What?' Olly says, standing on his tiptoes to nose at the stapled paper in my hands.

'These are the comics he talked about at dinner the other night. They're really funny.'

'Can we read them now?' Matilda asks.

'Yes,' I agree. 'But in bed.'

'But, Mummy,' Ben says, 'we're not tired.' The whine in his voice tells a different story. Guilt pricks, a dozen needles to the pit of my stomach. I should have put them to bed hours ago. They are still so young. Even Olly should be in bed.

Another thought comes unbidden to my thoughts – if I had put them to bed, Matt and I could have kept on talking.

A flush creeps up my neck as I think again of the intensity in his eyes just now and how much better it made me feel after that woman answered Josh's phone.

'I should be going to bed too,' Matt says with an exaggerated yawn.

'You?' Olly says, his eyes growing wide. 'But you're a grown-up. You can stay up really late.'

'Ah, but then I'd be too tired tomorrow to have fun.'

Olly cocks his head, clearly thinking over Matt's words. He gives a small nod and doesn't protest when I shoo them into the house, Olly carrying the comics as though they are as precious as the crown jewels, and me with Matilda resting on one hip and my hands full of toys to be put away.

'Good night,' Matt calls from his back door.

'Night,' I say, and just before he disappears, our eyes meet again and I feel a flash of joy at our friendship, at thinking of myself as he sees me – Double Trouble – that fierce girl who is completely lost to me.

Later, much later, thanks to Matt's comic, which even I didn't want to stop reading with the children, I lie in bed and wonder again about the girl I used to be. I feel like a different person now, but doesn't everyone look back at themselves and roll their eyes or shake their head? Don't we all change?

I don't know what made me so fierce. Maybe it was not having a dad around. Or because I grew up watching *Thelma and Louise* when I was too young to understand it, *Pretty Woman* and *Supergirl* – the original 80s version. It gave me this inflated belief that I could be anything, over-power anyone. When did that feeling die? It faded I guess, under the weight of revising for exams, the hit of puberty and boys, and girls for that matter, how mean they could be. It dulled me. And maybe that's how it should be, but when the hell did I become the type of person who'll tell the waiter the food is lovely when they ask, even if it's a cold, stodgy mess? The kind of person who doesn't protest when a taxi drops me off in the wrong place?

I close my eyes and a single tear slides onto the pillow and I turn over and fall into a fitful sleep.

Chapter 19

The clock in the kitchen inches towards 9 a.m. as I will my coffee to cool down so I can drink it. It's my third one this morning, but the caffeine has yet to hit me. I hold the cup close to my mouth, hoping the steam might contain a smidgen of extra boost I can inhale.

At 5 a.m. Ben kicked me awake. And 2 a.m. and 3 am. By six, all three children were awake and bleary-eyed in front of the TV while I showered and applied a careful layer of make-up, as though eyeliner and extra foundation will make me feel more human. As if it will protect me from whatever Saffron has in store for us today. Her first proper day.

Saffron's warning swims in my head. 'Tomorrow is going to be hard.' Harder than having someone stand over you, watching you fail while the cameras are rolling.

The kids are playing a game now. They've dragged the little rug out with its roads and houses, a little town to drive their toy cars on. There's a low-level squabbling to their play that I sense will escalate into a full-blown argument any second, but there's no time to worry about it now.

I scroll through Saffron's Instagram feed while I wait for her to arrive. She's already uploaded three videos of us. The first is of the twins and the fake-tan moment. The second is a short clip from our meeting. Thankfully she cut the misunderstanding over who would be looking after the children, but it's still hard to watch. I'm surprised at the emotion on my face, the hollow desperation as I talk about our routines and rules, and lack of both.

The third video is from observation day. It already has 60,000 views. I tap play and watch a giggling Olly throw my clothes out of the window, quickly followed by me telling him to stop. My voice is shrill, a shriek more than a shout. I look desperate and upset but what strikes me most is how out of control I seem.

60,000 people have watched this. It doesn't seem real.

Everyone can see the truth now – you're a terrible mother.

My face flames pink and I close down my Instagram, feeling none of the usual calm from my scrolling. There's a knock at the door. My eyes flick to the clock. It's one minute to nine. My clock must be slow, I think as I step down the hall. Rex shoots by, heading for the back door as if sensing the chaos that's about to ensue. A jittery energy pulses through me, leaving me breathless and feeling a little sick at what the day might hold.

'Morning,' Saffron sings, gliding into the house with a wide grin as I open the door. I look back at the empty path before I close the door. I don't know what I expect to see. A broomstick? A dozen forest animals, dancing and singing? But all I spot is Saffron's baby-pink mini parked outside the house.

Olly and Matilda appear in the hall, greeting Saffron like a long-lost friend and skittering around her as she walks into the kitchen

'What are we doing today?'

'What's your favourite colour?'

'How long are you staying for?

The questions ping, ping, ping. I check on Ben who is building a Lego garage for the Hot Wheels cars he's lined up at the edge of the rug. He's lost in his game, but his eyes are puffy and he looks as tired as I feel. Guilt hits like a Nerf bullet to my insides. It's my fault he's so tired. It's me who can't convince him that there is no monster beneath his bed, nothing to be scared of in the room he shares with Matilda.

'Today,' Saffron says, with the same clap, clap, clap of her hands that she seems to love so much, 'we need to undo bad habits and put some boundaries in place.'

Olly and Matilda grin up at her, nodding as though she's suggested a trip for ice cream, and I wonder how hard today will be for them.

Saffron's clothes are more casual today. The suit has gone and in its place, is a pair of long denim shorts and a black t-shirt. She catches me looking and smiles. 'It's more hands-on for all of us today,' she says, before clapping again. 'Right, Olly and Matilda, I need to speak to Mummy before we do anything. Are you able to carry on playing? It looks like you've got a very fun game going on in the living room.'

Olly turns to leave just as Matilda shakes her head. 'I want to do painting,' she says, making her way to the craft cupboard. Dread seeps through me at the thought of the mess. The faff of getting it all out and then cleaning it all up for three paintings of splodges. I try to rally myself. This is not the mother I wanted to be.

It's Saffron who stops us both. 'Hang on,' she says. 'Matilda, you're in the middle of a game in the living room. If the game is finished, then we should tidy it away. But now isn't the best time for crafts. Mummy hasn't set anything up and that's going to take some time.'

'Painting now,' she says with narrowed eyes, and even though I know it's wrong, there's a part of me that's pleased she isn't as willing as Olly to listen to Saffron, that it isn't just me who Matilda ignores.

'We're not painting now,' Saffron says again, her voice silky smooth. 'I have a super-fun craft activity planned this afternoon but Mummy and I need time to organise it. If you paint now, we won't be able to do the fun painting activity I've planned for later.'

Matilda stares at Saffron for another beat. She's going to protest again. I can see it in the set of her face. But just as she opens her mouth to say something, Ben shouts out, 'Hey, that's mine,' and her attention is pulled back to the living room and she turns on her heel and is gone.

I make us fresh coffee as Saffron sets up the camera stands. My hands shake as we settle at the island. Caffeine and nerves in equal measure. From the living room, the low hum of squabbling begins again. I catch another whine from Ben.

'Today, we're introducing the reflection step.'

I bark a laugh, despite my nerves. 'Is that like the naughty step?'

She smiles. 'That's not the term I like to use. I think it's too negative. You see, when a child misbehaves, two things need to happen. They need to calm down and they need to understand that there are consequences to their behaviour, which helps to ensure it doesn't happen again.'

'Right,' I nod. 'Reflection step. Got it.'

'Give one warning, and then if they don't listen, it's straight to the step. Keep your voice firm,' she says, using the tone herself. I find myself sitting up a little straighter. 'Don't be emotional, don't shout.' Images of my shrill cries to 'Stop' in the video spring into my mind.

I can do this, I tell myself. Stay calm.

No you can't!

I'm going to try.

'Take the child to the reflection step with as little fuss as possible. Explain why you've put them there and set a two-minute timer.' She stops talking, pulling an egg timer out from her bag. It's purple and pink, and has a logo of The Toddler Tamer written in white.

'For you,' she says, sliding it across the counter.

'Thanks.' I hold it in my hands, fiddling with the edges and wondering how on earth this one device is going to change my life.

'If they sit for—' she stops talking as the timer in my hands explodes in a loud buzzing. I jump at the noise, dropping it to the counter where it buzzes at me like an annoying fly. I grab it in my hands and stop the noise.

'Sorry,' I mumble, feeling stupid. Maybe I'll be the first to try out the reflection step.

'Everyone does that,' she grins. 'If they sit for the two minutes, then you go back, you repeat why they were on the reflection step and then it's a hug and an apology, and off they go to play again.'

The laughter escapes. It suddenly all feels so ridiculous. So outrageous. Like she's asking the children to cook a gourmet meal on *MasterChef*. Olly can barely sit still for two minutes when there's a reward for him. No way will he sit for two minutes as a punishment. 'Off they go? Just like that?'

Saffron doesn't smile or laugh. 'You'll be surprised how quickly children adapt to the reflection step.'

'And if they don't sit for the full two minutes?' I ask, because of course they won't.

'Then you put them back and you start the timer again. No need to say anything this time. The less attention you give them during this process, the better.'

The amusement I felt moments ago morphs into a burst of fluttering panic. It's slowly dawning on me that today is not going to be hard at all, it's going to be impossible.

Saffron leans down to her magic bag, pulling out a Ziploc pack filled with colourful pieces of paper and glittery stickers. 'Reward charts,' she says. 'Just as behaviour we don't want should be stopped, good behaviour should be encouraged. Ben, Olly and Matilda can make their own charts. Children love doing this and it will really get them involved in the process.'

Saffron continues her explanations – her lecture, it feels like – and I nod along, but I'm only half listening now. From the living room, there is the unmistakable scrape of Lego bricks being tipped. It's followed by a 'Not fair' from Olly and a scream from Matilda.

I start to stand and Saffron grins. 'Show time,' she says, before hustling over to my side of the counter and giving my arm a squeeze. 'You've got this.'

Yeah right!

'Remember,' she says as we make our way to the living room, 'be firm but don't shout. Always set clear boundaries. Give one warning for behaviour you want to stop, but plenty of warnings if you want them to do something. In ten minutes we're leaving, or in five minutes, I'm going to ask you to get dressed for school.'

'Mummy!,' Ben shouts as I reach the doorway, my head spinning with all of Saffron's advice. 'Matilda put her Barbie in my Lego house and it broke.' His bottom lip juts out, wobbling under the pressure of his emotions.

'Matilda,' I admonish. 'Say sorry to Ben. Maybe you could help him fix it.'

She gives an insincere 'Sorry' before continuing to play with her Barbie.

Saffron launches into an explanation of the reflection step and rewards charts. I watch the children's faces light up. They are nodding eagerly, lapping up her every word.

'And Saffron has brought some crafts to do,' I sing-song, trying to sound as peppy as Saffron. 'You get to make your own reward charts and you get a sticker when you do something good.'

'Yaayyyy.' Ben jumps up, dancing around my legs, his Lego house forgotten. Olly and Matilda are right behind him. I feel bolstered, like maybe this won't be so bad. That is until I glance at Saffron and she nods at the toys, an eyebrow raised. 'Tidy up first,' she says.

'Right, yes.' I turn around, feeling the burning lens of one of the cameras Saffron has set up in here. My pulse quickens as I stare down at the expectant faces of Olly, Ben and Matilda. My first test. I know I'm going to fail. 'Kids, you need to tidy away your toys before we do any crafts.'

There's a collective groan, but to my surprise, they turn back. Olly drops to his knees and starts throwing the cars into their toy box. Matilda, seeing the fun of throwing, picks up a Lego brick, but instead of aiming for the container, she flings it across the room and it hits the wall.

'Matilda,' I say, trying desperately to mimic Saffron's firm tones, but sounding more like I'm putting on a man's voice. 'Please stop throwing the Lego. You need to tidy up your toys before we can do something fun.'

'Give her a warning,' Saffron says.

'This is your warning,' I add. 'If you don't start tidying, you're going to have a time-out on the reflection step.'

'No.' Matilda's grin is wide and assured in a way that threatens to break me. She follows it up with a kick of her leg that sends Lego bricks skidding across the floor.

I'm aware of Olly and Ben watching me now, too. They're still tidying, moving their toys with comical slowness into the toy boxes, as their gaze remains fixed on me, waiting to see just how I'll react.

'Is Matilda going on the reflection step?' Olly asks. 'She had her warning.' There's something in his voice. I'd expect glee, the one-up-ness of seeing a sibling in trouble, but it's not glee at all, it's disbelief, as though even Olly, at eight years old, knows I'll never be able to do this.

My eyes flick from a grinning Matilda, to Olly, to Saffron. Olly's question is hanging in the air and I'm faltering. Saffron gives a small nod and mouths, 'You've got this,' which has to be the overstatement of the century. Whatever 'this' is, I do not have it!

And yet that disbelief from Olly is like the smallest of paper cuts against my insides. I might not believe in myself, but I can't bear it that Olly doesn't believe in me. I have to do this.

'Let's go, Matilda,' I say, pointing to the stairs.

She doesn't move and so I step to pick her up. She screams, a piercing caterwaul of a noise, and as I reach out to her, she lashes out flailing arms and legs, kicking and hitting. A foot catches me in the shin, sending a bolt of pain up my leg.

You're failing before you've even begun!

Saffron knows it. All those people watching will know it. Your own children know it.

But Olly and Ben are still tidying their toys. If I don't follow through now, they'll all stop, and I'll be left to do it later. I'll be left to do it for the rest of my life.

I scoop up Matilda's writhing body and carry her to the bottom step of the stairs. 'I'm putting you here because you've refused to help tidy up,' I say. 'You need to stay

133

here for two minutes.' I set the timer and place it by her feet, but before I've stood up, Matilda is scrambling back to the living room, giggling and gleeful with her victory. She snatches a toy from the box and throws it on the floor.

'Get to the reflection step,' Olly shouts, and the fury in his voice surprises me. I catch a raised eyebrow from Saffron before I dart back into the room and pick Matilda up again.

'No,' she shouts. 'No, no, no.'

She wriggles in my arms and I'm so focused on keeping hold of her, on getting her back to the step, on Saffron and her camera watching me, that I don't see where I'm stepping. My left foot touches the floor and a split second later a sharp pain shoots out from my foot.

My face contorts. A 'No' forms on my lips. Realisation punches into my thoughts. I've stepped on a Lego brick and the pain is excruciating. A dozen swear words ricochet through my mind. 'No,' I shout, hopping across the floor, barely clinging onto Matilda who at least has stopped trying to escape as I half-stumble forwards.

It hurts. It really hurts. Why, why, why did I have to step on a piece of Lego now? And why, the mother of all fucks, is it so painful? One tiny piece of plastic and it feels more like a shard of glass is slicing into my foot. Tears sting my eyes from the pain.

But with the pain, comes a burst of frustration, that makes me grit my teeth and keep going. I may be a massive failure, a terrible mother, stupid, vain and all the rest, but now, in this moment with Matilda, I will not be defeated.

I limp towards the stairs and place Matilda back on her spot, determined this time that she will stay there, and yet before I've even turned around, she's off again, running into the kitchen and then out to the garden.

'Go after her,' Saffron says, voice gentle and encouraging.

So I do. I chase her around the garden in the glaring sun.

Back and forth we go to the stairs. I lose count of how many times she runs away, to the garden or upstairs to slither on her belly under her bed.

Tears are stinging the backs of my eyes. Fury is burning through my body. It's impossible. I'm wasting my time.

Again, I place Matilda back on the step, arms poised for her to run again, but she doesn't. I set the timer. I step away. Still she sits. Calmly, patiently, humming a little tune to herself.

My mouth gapes open and I turn away, helping Ben and Olly put the last of the toy boxes back in place. A sticky sweat coats my skin. I'm thirsty and I'm tired and I could weep with relief.

When the timer starts to buzz, I move back to the stairs, Saffron behind me. 'Remind her what she did,' Saffron prompts.

'Matilda, I put you on the reflection step because—' my mind blanks. I can't even remember the reason I started all this.

'She wouldn't help tidy up,' Olly says.

'That's right. Matilda – you didn't help to tidy up.'

'She's only sitting there now because it's finished.' Olly huffs. I take in the tidy living room and then look back to Matilda, who is grinning with such triumph I want to cry all over again.

'Can we make our reward charts now?' Matilda asks.

I nod, grateful to Saffron for taking over the project and helping the children to create their charts while I gulp back a pint of water and make the lunch.

Most of the day is taken up with reward charts. When they're done, Saffron moves to stick them on the fridge door and I yelp a sudden 'No'.

She gives me a quizzical look. I don't want to tell her that the kitchen is my space, my beautiful, perfect space, and that I can't stand the thought of glittery pieces of paper cluttering it up. Even in my head it sounds selfish. What kind of mother won't display their children's artwork in pride of place on the fridge?

'I . . . think they'd look better on the back of the kitchen door,' I say. 'There's more space.' There isn't, of course, but the children don't seem to mind, and so I try not to cringe at the spray of glitter that falls to my tiled floor every time the door is opened or closed.

It will get easier, won't it? It can't possibly get any harder.

Chapter 20

Later, when the three children disappear into their cartoons, I drop onto the stool in the kitchen and stare at the rain pattering against the windows. The heatwave broke at lunchtime. Blue skies replaced with a cool wind and rain that falls in sheets. Two loads of washing are still hanging on the line and I contemplate dashing out there, but it's already soaked. I might as well wait for the rain to stop.

Saffron pulls out a stool and sits beside me. The island has become our meeting place, for pep talks and telling offs. But I'm too frazzled for anything more today — I'm a sweaty heap of a human being — and I drop my head into my hands, avoiding her gaze and how fresh she still looks, make-up perfect, hair so neat. Saffron is supposed to be helping but all I've felt today is a failure.

'Let's have a chat.' Saffron's voice is light but firm and already I know I'm not going to like what she has to say.

I groan. 'I need a minute.'

'You've done brilliantly today,' she says.

The praise seems to sting as much as the failure. More, I think. Tears form a wall in my eyes but I lift my head to look at her. 'You are joking? Did you not see Matilda earlier?'

'She did her two minutes in the end. That's what matters.'

'Only because the tidying had all been done and she'd got her way and hadn't had to help.'

'And next time, you'll leave something for her to do.'

I nod, but don't feel any better.

'And when you gave Olly a warning for teasing Matilda, what did he do?'

'He stopped,' I admit.

'Exactly. You need to give yourself a big pat on the back.'

Saffron smiles at me, her face expectant, like she actually wants me to pat myself on the back.

'Could a pat on the back be a glass of wine?' I ask. 'Do I get a reward chart too?'

Saffron laughs. 'Now that's a good idea.' She pauses a beat before her hands clap together. Clap, clap, clap. Always a burst of three, like she's punctuating her speech. 'So,' she says, and I have a sudden flash of desire to run upstairs and hide under my bed just as Matilda did earlier. 'I'd like to get to the bottom of how things have got so out of control for you. I sense there's still a barrier up, Becca.'

I feel myself bristle. She's giving me the shit sandwich. Praise, then criticism, then praise again, no doubt. 'What do you mean?' I ask. 'I did everything you told me to today.'

'You did,' she agrees. 'But without any conviction. It's like you've already decided you're going to fail.'

'That's not true.' My protest is automatic, but of course she's right. I did think I would fail. I have failed. Saffron might be painting today as a success, but I'm not.

'You're a good mother, Becca.'

The tears fall in two lines down my face. I shake my head. 'You don't have to say that. I'm crap at this. I always have been. Whatever parenting book every other mother read when they were pregnant, I missed out.'

'You're not crap at all,' Saffron cries out. 'You have three happy and healthy children. The behavioural challenges you're facing can be straightened out. And believe it or not, the problems you're facing are because you love your children.'

'What?' I pull a face.

'You love them and you want them to be happy all of the time, and so you constantly give in and appease. You're trying to be their mum, their dad, their friend, their play-mate, but in trying to be all these things and show them all the love you have for them, you've stopped being what they need, which is a parent – a guide. Someone who can give them boundaries and structure alongside the love. Children thrive on stability and rules.'

'I've tried.' I give a half-sob.

'I know you have. But when it was hard, when they didn't do as you wanted, you didn't persevere. You gave in time and time again and now you're practically a hostage in this house.'

I go to protest but Saffron gets there first.

'You told me this week that taking them out anywhere feels impossible because of how they behave.'

'I know, but I still go out. We went to the beach the other day.'

'And that's great, but wouldn't it be nice to go out more than just occasionally? To go out and it not feel like a really big deal that leaves you exhausted afterwards? You need to believe in yourself, Becca. You need to believe you're a good mother and you need to believe that your children will listen to you. How do you expect them to respect you when you don't respect yourself? It's easy to lose your confidence as a mother. And if you don't have confidence, you start to second guess yourself and that comes across in your parenting, giving mixed messages to the children on what is acceptable behaviour. And you, Becca, have no confidence in yourself at all.'

We fall silent. Saffron waits for me to respond, but I don't. What is there to say? I close my eyes, blinking away more tears and think again of the Double Trouble girl Matt remembers.

I sigh. 'What do I do? Just tell me what to do.'

'So, there are two things I think we need to work on and they're both connected. The first is building your confidence.'

'Oh right. That sounds easy,' I reply, voice dripping with sarcasm.

'Nothing worth doing is ever easy,' she says, sounding so much like a fortune cookie that I don't know whether to laugh or cry.

'It would be easy if you could tell the voice in my head to shut up.'

'Voice?' Saffron tilts her head, looking at me curiously.

I shrug, feeling stupid, wishing I'd kept my mouth shut. 'It's nothing.'

'It's something.'

'I just . . .' I shrug. 'It's like there's this voice in my head telling me how stupid I am and how I'm doing everything wrong.'

'That must be hard.'

Another shrug. My face is hot. I've never told anyone this stuff before. Not even Josh. Especially not Josh. He's so confident, so together. He's always got everything worked out. He'd never understand the voice I hear or how I feel so much of the time.

'I'm not a psychologist,' Saffron says. 'And I don't pretend to be anything close, but I do think positive reinforcement is a really powerful tool, and so is negative reinforcement. So, if you are constantly telling yourself that you're getting things wrong, then you're going to constantly feel like you're failing.

'Next time you hear yourself being negative, I want you to tell yourself to shut up. Then I want you to say something positive instead. Say it out loud three times.'

'Am I in *The Wizard of Oz* now or something?'

'I know it sounds stupid, but what have you got to lose? Just try it for me.'

'OK,' I concede, feeling the last of my energy drain away. I can't imagine chanting positive 'You can do it' comments to myself, and yet I'm quickly learning, it's easier to agree with Saffron.

My eyes stray to the clock. I have two hours before I need to cook the dinner and pry Olly, Ben and Matilda away from the TV. All I want to do is lock myself in a dark room and close my eyes, but Saffron is still looking at me with an eager determination and I sense we're nowhere near to being done.

Chapter 21

I frown, rubbing at the lines pinching between my brows. Thoughts of my mum flash in my mind. Despite my disappointment that she's not here to help me this summer, I am glad she's gone away. It took her years after Dad died to join some local clubs and learn to do things just for her. I really hope she's having a nice time.

I picture her stretched out on a sun lounger with a cocktail and book, and feel a stab of jealousy. But there's something else too – that whisper of determination. How good would it feel to have well-behaved children when she returns? For her not to see me as a weak pushover.

A lottery win seems more doable!

I clench my jaw and push the thought away. I'm not about to start saying things out loud, but I get what Saffron is telling me about listening to that voice. If only it wasn't so loud, so constant, it would be easier to ignore.

'So, your confidence is one thing to work on,' Saffron continues. 'And the other thing is your body language towards the children.'

'What do you mean?'

'When you were talking to Matilda on the reflection step earlier, you were standing up and she was sitting on the step. Next time, try getting down to her level, maintaining eye contact when you talk to her.'

'OK. I can do that.' Finally, something that feels easy.

'I know you can. Eye contact, be on their level, be open with them. Show them you're listening.'

I nod again. 'Is that it?' I ask as my eyes drag back to the clock.

Saffron exhales a laugh. 'Come on, Becca. We're only talking here. Tell me a bit more about you.'

I shift on the stool, suddenly uncomfortable. 'There's nothing more to tell. You've seen what my life is like. Josh works long hours or is away like he is right now. I run around like a headless chicken every day, trying to put out fires.'

'There you go, putting yourself down when I know there's more to you than that. I can see from your Instagram posts that you're a talented designer.'

A smile touches my lips. Saffron's comment releases a burst of warmth inside me. 'I love interior design.'

'It shows.' Saffron gestures to the kitchen and I feel a well of pride that she's noticed.

'And what do you do for fun?'

'Er . . . what do you mean?' I know what's she asking, but I'm stalling, playing for time on the inevitable answer.

'What do you do for you? Where do you go? Dinner with friends, hobbies?'

'I told you. I love interior design. That's what I do for fun. I work.'

'That's your job.'

I laugh then. A short huff. Surprised to hear Rebecca Harris Interiors referred to as my job. It is, and yet, Josh doesn't see it that way. He thinks it's a hobby. And even though I shouldn't let his opinion cloud my judgement, it does. I love my interior design work and when Matilda and Ben go to school in September, I know I'll throw myself into it again, that it's something I can grow over the next few years.

'It still feels like it's the thing I do for me,' I explain.

'It's great that you have a job you love, but you still need things in your life that you do just for you. What about hobbies? You must have a hobby you enjoy.' Saffron raises an eyebrow and I have sudden image of her in a glittering pink leotard doing a perfect baton-twirling routine. I hide a smirk. Baton-twirling is exactly the kind of hobby Saffron would do.

'Look at my life.' I throw my hands in the air. 'I don't have time for hobbies. What do you do?'

'Oh,' Saffron smiles. 'I love hiking, especially geocashing; following co-ordinates and finding little treasures.' Not baton-twirling then. 'And I love escape rooms,' she continues, her eyes lighting up. 'Have you ever done one? They are so much fun.'

I shake my head. 'Not exactly a child-friendly hobby, is it? Would you want to be locked in a room with my children?'

'They do family-friendly ones,' she sing-songs, like she's giving me a sales pitch.

'No,' I laugh. 'Not escape rooms.'

'That's OK. That's me and what I like. We're talking about you. What kinds of things did you used to do before you had children?'

'Erm . . .' I bite my lip. Child-free days feel another lifetime ago. How selfish I could be, how guilt-free. What did I do? 'I used to like swimming, I think. I used to go every weekend, both Saturday and Sunday, and swim at the leisure centre. I'd do length after length.' I smile, remembering the way my arms cut through the water and the achy feeling of my body after a long swim.

Josh used to come with me sometimes too, doing a few lengths and then goofing around, pretending to be a shark and grabbing my ankle. Acting like we were teenagers again, until the time the lifeguard told us off for kissing and I was so mortified I didn't go back for weeks.

I've not thought about swimming just for me for a long time. Swimming is now lessons and family time and teaching the children to swim. It's chaotic and exhausting and I'm always freezing because the last thing I get to do in the water anymore is actually swim.

'That's a great hobby. When was the last time you went swimming?'

'Alone?'

She nods.

'When I was pregnant with Olly.'

'Why did you stop when Olly was born?'

I shrug. 'I guess it felt too selfish to do something just for me. I didn't have my own time during the week, and weekends were about family time and then clubs for Olly. By the time he started at pre-school, the twins were on the way and life became even more full-on.'

Saffron raises her perfectly laminated eyebrows. 'Are you telling me you can't give yourself an hour in an entire weekend to do something for you?'

'When you put it like that, I guess I can.' My tone is reluctant. Saffron is making it all sound so simple, but it isn't. I sigh, wondering how Josh would feel about me deserting him for a few hours. 'Josh is away right now anyway so I can't.'

'But he's back next weekend, isn't he? You can go then.'

'I can . . .'

'I sense a "but" coming.'

'It's just, Josh is going to be exhausted and jet-lagged, and he'll probably have work to do, so I don't think he'll be up for looking after the kids while I go out.'

'They're his kids too, Becca. And he's been away for weeks, leaving you here to do everything. You deserve a break and he should want to give that to you. He should want to spend time with his children.'

'Oh, he does,' I'm quick to reply. 'He really does, it's just he likes me around too, for when it gets too much, you know? You've seen what it's like. It's a mad house.'

'One,' she says, with a single clap. 'We're working on that and have already made great progress. And two, you manage on your own.'

'Do I?' I make a face.

'Yes you do, Becca. Give yourself some credit, OK? You are carrying the load for your family, Becca. You need to look after yourself.'

I give a reluctant nod. 'I do.'

Saffron fixes me with a look and I huff a laugh. 'I will,' I correct.

'So, swimming,' she says. 'What else?'

'Dancing,' I say suddenly. 'God, I used to love dancing. And before you start trying to organise a night out for me, don't bother.'

'Why?'

A heat burns through my body. 'I . . . I don't exactly have a great circle of friends right now.'

'Why? You're so lovely.' Saffron's words seem so genuine, so nice, that it hurts to hear it, as much as if she'd told me I'm an awful person.

You are awful. Tell her!

I explain to Saffron about the mum friends I made and lost, and the friends from my design course who are a million miles away from where I am right now, who I don't keep in contact with as much as I should because deep down I'm jealous that they still have their careers and it doesn't feel like I do.

146

I pretend on Instagram that my life is perfect, that everything is balanced – my family, my design work. My feed screams, 'Look at me having it all.' But it's all a lie and if I spend time with those old friends, I worry they'll see through me.

Far from seeming disappointed, a smile lights up on Saffron's face and I have a sinking feeling I'm not going to like what's coming. 'But dancing is great. You don't need anyone else. You just need music. In fact . . .' Saffron reaches for her phone. 'It's something you can do with the kids around.'

Her eyes fix on her phone screen and as she taps away, my gaze stray to the back door wondering if it's too late to escape what's coming.

Saffron places the phone on the counter between us, pushing the volume to max as the Spice Girls' 'Who Do You Think You Are' blares out. I bark a laugh at the song choice. 'Seriously?'

'Come on,' Saffron grins, standing up and shimmying her hips as the beat of the music starts. 'This is a great song.'

'It was. In the 90s, when it first came out.'

'You need to start doing things for you,' she calls over the music as she twirls around before pulling me to my feet. Show me your moves.'

I laugh, but what have I got to lose? It's clear I'm not getting out of this. My hips sway, side to side, then my shoulders.

Olly, Matilda and Ben appear from the living room. I laugh at the three matching expressions of curiosity. 'What's going on?' Matilda asks, looking from me to Saffron.

'We're dancing,' Saffron calls back. 'Let's show Mum our moves.'

Saffron waves her hands in the air, shaking and shimmying like she's moving down a catwalk and strikes a pose as she reaches the back door. Matilda's face turns from curious to excited. She looks like she's going to burst with joy as she copies Saffron, taking her turn to twirl and swirl, before placing her hands on her hips and jutting her chin in the air. Olly and Ben go next as Saffron claps them down the imaginary catwalk.

They goof around, changing their moves as they go. Ben tries some break-dancing, making us all laugh as he flops to the tiled floor like a constipated seal.

And then it's my turn and there's no getting out of it now. Saffron, Matilda, Olly and Ben start to clap. Ben is completely off the beat, which makes me laugh.

'Come on, Becca,' Saffron calls.

Whigfield starts singing her dee dee na na na. 'Your turn, Mummy,' Ben says.

'Go on, Mummy.' Olly jumps out of the line, races around the island and pushes me towards the catwalk just as the Spice Girls tell me to move it and make it. Prove it and shake it.

I look at their grinning faces, and I let the beat take hold of me, shaking my way down the length of the kitchen. At the end, I strike my pose and turn around and around. Matilda lifts her hands and I pick her up and we dance together.

Ben and Olly grab each other and begin attempting some kind of salsa/waltz. Tears of laughter stream down my face. My sides hurt, from moving, laughing, but when the Spice Girls end and Whigfield starts singing her 'dee dee na na na', it's impossible not to do the moves I remember from school discos and then drunken nights out.

Saffron comes to stand beside me and the children line up opposite, copying our moves until they're dancing along, jumping forward and to the side.

By the end of the song, we're all laughing and panting, out of breath.

'Another one,' Matilda yells.

Saffron gives me her 'You're up' look and I remember her guidance. Clear boundaries, plenty of warnings.

'Good idea,' I say. 'We'll do one more song together and then if you want to, the three of you can continue dancing in the living room.'

'Can we have a proper disco one night when Daddy is home?' Olly asks. 'With lights and party music.'

'And party drinks,' Matilda adds. She's been desperate to get her hands on some Fanta ever since a picnic at the school last year when she snuck away to the fizzy-drinks table for the older children.

'Yes, yes, yes,' Ben shouts, pointing his fingers in the air with every yes.

Saffron changes the song to the 'Macarena'. I roll my eyes.

'What?' she laughs. 'I love nineties music.'

'Were you even alive in the nineties?'

She grins. 'Just.'

When the song ends, I'm surprised to see Olly, Ben and Matilda run off to Olly's bedroom, full of plans to make disco invitations and signs.

'Will there be games?' Ben asks in the hall.

'Yes,' Olly nods, taking his role as organiser seriously. 'Musical bumps and musical statues. We'll need prizes.'

I stare after them, open-mouthed. Saffron flashes me a triumphant smile. 'Clear boundaries,' she says. 'Now, how do you feel after dancing?'

'Good.' A smile stretches across my face.

'Just good?'

'Great. Even with the questionable music choices.'

'Hey,' Saffron says in mock hurt.

The kitchen seems suddenly too quiet as I empty the dishwasher. As Saffron replies to emails, I pull up my Spotify playlists on my phone. It's Adele and Norah Jones and Mumford and Sons. Music I love to have on in the background as I pour over my designs, but nothing that makes me want to jump up and dance. I find an old Taylor Swift album I used to love and play it on the kitchen speaker. I'm not dancing now, but I like the beat and feel of the music moving through me.

I thought Saffron was crazy when she told me to dance, but I'd forgotten how much fun dancing is. I make a promise to myself that when Josh comes home for the weekend, I'm going to make myself go swimming. And we'll have our disco with party games and dancing.

Chapter 22

By dinner-time, the fuzzy joy I felt from dancing evaporates along with my energy levels.

'Olly, Ben and Matilda were not born fussy eaters,' Saffron says. 'You have made them that way. And now we are going to unmake them. There is no reason why you need to cook more than one dinner for the whole family each evening or eat the same dinner five nights of the week.'

She calls the children to the kitchen and with her three claps, she sets them at a chopping board each like it's the *MasterChef* kitchen. As they chop peppers and carrots for a stir fry I know they won't eat, I hover around them, wincing every time they pick up a knife.

'That's great,' Saffron says to Olly and he beams up at her with his wonkily chopped peppers. 'As long as you remember to check your fingers aren't in the way of the blade, you're good to slice.'

When the stir fry is almost ready and all three children are busy setting the table, Saffron pulls me to one side and I'm aware of the camera, just a metre away from where we're standing. It's a reminder that however nice Saffron is and however much she is helping, this is a business to her. 'You need to encourage the children more, Becca,' she says. 'It's nice when people tell you you're doing well, isn't it?'

I nod, feeling shitty. My cheeks burn.

'So, why don't you do that?'

'I don't know. I thought I did.' My tone is sulkier than I mean it to be.

She shakes her head. 'Our first meeting was on Monday. I was here all day yesterday and today. In all those hours, not once have you told them 'Well done' for something or praised them. Encouraging good behaviour with praise is far more effective than trying to stop bad behaviour by telling them off, OK?' She gives my arm a squeeze.

My mood plummets further and I fight the desire to cry again. 'I'm crap at this,' I whisper, catching a tear with my finger before it can fall.

'Hey, that's your internal voice talking. You are not crap. You need to stop telling yourself that. It's exactly the same thing, don't you see? You don't give yourself any encouragement either. That has to change and it has to change now.' She gives me a gentle shove towards the kitchen. 'Right now,' she whispers in my ear.

'Er . . . well done cooking dinner today, kids,' I say, pasting on a smile. 'That was some great chopping! I'll pop it in the pan and we can eat.'

And, to my surprise, they do. Sort of. A few enthusiastic chews before the food is pushed to one side here and there. Surprisingly, it's Ben who eats the most. My sweet boy, who claims to hate most foods happily crunches on red peppers and orange carrot, and the rice too. Matilda and Olly don't do quite as well, but what amazes me most is that none of them complain or cry or throw their cutlery on the floor. They don't even ask to watch TV.

'Great job eating your dinner.' The compliment feels stilted in my mouth, and I hate that Saffron is right, hate even more that it's taken her to make me realise that I never compliment my children. When did that stop? I used to clap and cheer at every first step, first word, every finger painting and trip to the potty.

I hold up my hand for a high-five and they all grin, especially Olly, who finishes the high-five by launching himself at me and hugging me tight. And then it's stickers for the reward charts and more cheers.

'I'm going to leave you now,' Saffron says, scooping up her bag from the floor. 'You've all made great progress today. Tomorrow we're going to be creating a bedtime routine.'

I'm about to tell her she might as well be suggesting we're going to learn advanced physics, but after watching Ben merrily eating a carrot, I'm starting to believe anything is possible when Saffron is with us.

'And, Becca,' she says as she reaches the front door, 'great job today. You've done really well.'

'Thanks. See you tomorrow.' I smile at her compliment and realise again that she's right, it does feel good to get praise.

When the kitchen is tidy and the children are playing in the garden, I make myself a gin and tonic and take a well-deserved sip. Today was not a massive failure. There is no doubt all three children are responding to Saffron's routine and structure. There have been fewer fights, fewer 'that's not fair' comments and stomping 'no's.

I gaze out of the window over the sink. The rain has stopped and there are cracks of bright blue among the grey clouds. Olly is kicking a ball around the garden and Ben and Matilda are running in and out of the clean clothes, now sodden and in need of another wash.

I slide my glass onto the counter and step barefoot onto the patio, breathing in that just-rained dewy freshness in the air. I unpeg the sodden washing from the line and it drops with a slap of wet material into the basket. As I turn back to the house, Matt appears from his back door, waving as he sees me.

'Hey,' he calls out, stepping over to the fence.

'Hi, Matt,' Olly shouts. 'Look at me. I'm going to be a footballer.'

'Hi, Olly,' Matt waves back. 'Hi, Matilda. Hi, Ben.' Matilda waves but Ben drops his gaze and carries on playing.

'Hi.' I step to the fence, dropping the basket to my feet. 'How's it going?'

He groans, running a hand through his hair and leaving it sticking up on one side. 'Terribly, but I'll live. I've realised it's one thing to run away from a place, but quite another to run away from your thoughts. My ex – Laura – wants to talk, but I don't know what there is to say.'

'It must be hard. I'm sorry.' I think of Josh then and the woman who answered the phone. I hate how my imagination, my insecurities, has taken that somewhere dark.

'I guess I can't stop going over the mistakes I made,' Matt continues.

'Hey,' I give him a reassuring smile. 'It's Laura that wanted to break up.'

'I'm starting to wonder if it's not quite as simple as that. I always get too wrapped up in the story I'm writing. Getting the first draft onto the page becomes this all-consuming beast. For weeks on end, I'll do nothing but write. It's not an easy thing to live with. I just don't know if I'll ever meet someone else, you know.'

'You will. Look at you; you're a catch.'

A smile lights up his face and he holds my gaze in a way that causes heat to crawl up my neck.

'Thanks,' he says, 'And sorry for being a grump. Pity party, table for one,' he says with a rueful smile.

154

'Don't be daft. It's fine. We're friends. I'd better get in. The glamour of re-washing the washing awaits,' I joke.

'Yeah, me too. Liam is coming over first thing to drag me out for a run.' Matt pushes away from the fence and we walk in parallel to our separate back doors. Just as I'm about to step inside, Matt calls my name. 'Oh, Becca?'

'Yeah?' I turn to face him.

'I totally forgot to ask,' he pauses, a mischievous smirk crossing his face. 'Do you think I could . . . swing it, shake it, too?' he says, and then twirls around in a dance.

I burst out laughing, my cheeks now flaming red. 'You heard the music?' I cringe and pull a face.

'Well,' he drops the pose and looks sheepish. 'I happened to be in the garden and the Spice Girls isn't the kind of music you hear every day anymore. Not unless you're at a very bad birthday party. So, I might have had a sneak peek over the fence. Just to make sure you hadn't been seriously injured.'

I give him a quizzical look.

'You know, they say if you fall and you're in trouble you should play 90s music at top volume as a sign you need help.'

'They say that, do they?' I grin.

'They do.' He gives an assertive nod. 'It actually reminded me,' he snorts a laugh, 'of the Year 9 talent show you did with . . . What was that girl's name?'

'Oh God. That was Julie . . . Julie something.'

He clicks his fingers. 'Julie Williams. You did—'

'A dance routine.' I groan as the memory surfaces. 'We didn't even practise. We just got up on stage and danced around. We came last. Even the boy who did the magic show where the white rat escaped across the school hall and almost gave Mrs Gardner a heart attack came before us.'

'Looks like you've still got the moves,' he says, copying my arm-waving shimmy as he struts into the house. I shake my head, but I'm laughing as I shove open the door to the utility room. I think about the school talent show as I sort the clothes and herd the children upstairs and into the bath and while I fold a pile of dry clothes – the never-ending cycle of washing. How brazen we were to get up on that stage and dance our hearts out. We didn't care what anyone thought of us. It reminds me of Matilda now I think about it. Her fierce way of doing everything just how she wants to. I can't believe Matt remembers that.

I haven't thought about school and the girl I was back then in years and now every time I see Matt he reminds me of who I used to be. I pull up Spotify and choose Kylie Minogue and before I know it, Matilda is with me, all clean and shiny faced, and we're dancing around my bedroom, giggling and shimmying as we fold (and in my case, refold) clean washing.

Just before bed, I text Josh goodnight. We haven't spoken since a snatched conversation five days ago. He never replied to my text about who the woman was who answered his phone. We haven't spoken at all, in fact, since then. I wish I knew what he was doing out there, what he was thinking. Is he missing us?

Chapter 23

Thursday dawns hot and sunny. I'm just stepping out of the shower when my phone pings. I grab it from the bed, hoping it's Josh texting. It's not, and that knowledge deflates something inside me.

Is he really so busy that he can't text me or call me?

He'll be home tomorrow night, I tell myself as I unlock my phone and see a message from my mum.

Hello darling, I'm having a wonderful time! Just wanted you to know that I'm so proud of you!! Bowls-club Jean shared a video of you and the kids from some nanny site and I found her on Instagram. I've watched them all! You're doing brilliantly. I knew you didn't want me to leave you this summer, but I wanted you to see you could do it on your own! Love you xxxx

I sit down on the bed and read Mum's message again. I smile, glad Mum can see how I'm doing, that she's proud of me. Of course, I'm not really doing it on my own though. Saffron is here. It's her magic, not mine.

Then another thought strikes me. Mum has seen Saffron's posts. I thought if my own Instagram handle wasn't tagged in Saffron's posts, no one would know it was me. There are millions of Instagrammers, millions of influencers. It didn't cross my mind that anyone I knew might follow The Toddler Tamer.

Another message dings on my phone. Jessica's name appears at the top of my WhatsApps. I steal myself for what is to come. Jessica, whose bedroom walls Olly scribbled over, and all those St Helena's mums, rarely get in touch, but when they do it's usually a subtle dig, a way of belittling me. I should've blocked them all after the last message a few months ago about a birthday party for a boy in Olly's class, and whether I wanted to contribute to the present. It was the first time I'd heard about the party, and from listening to the playground chat, it appeared the whole class were going. The whole class except Olly. And even though he didn't seem to know, or maybe didn't care, I raged for days about the injustice of it. That text had been nothing more than a 'ha-ha, you're not invited' poke, rather than an actual question.

One moment with a Sharpie, one sodding moment, and we're blacklisted for life. And I'm sure Jessica's boy gave Olly that pen and pointed him towards the wall. He might have set traps for the postman and blasted our neighbours with Nerf bullets, but Olly has never coloured on the walls at home. He'd seemed genuinely surprised at the horror on Jessica's face.

I should delete it without looking at it, but I don't. I'm too weak for that. I open the message and find three words:

Is this you?

The words are followed by a laughing emoji. Pasted below the question is a link to a tweet. I tap the screen and Twitter opens to the profile of a man I've never heard of.

I scan his tweet, trying to understand why Jessica has sent it to me. It reads:

That moment you hear the bin lorry and realise you've forgotten to put the bin out!

I scroll down, and that's when I see the meme accompanying the tweet. My body grows cold then hot – ice then fire. The heat burns my face. My mouth drops open.

It's me.

I am the meme.

My breath catches in my throat. My pulse races.

What the hell?

I tap the screen and watch in mounting horror at a three-second video of me stepping on that bastard piece of Lego yesterday when I was carrying Matilda to the reflection step. The clip is in slow motion, the camera zooming in as my face contorts and my lips move into an angry, teeth-baring 'No'.

The tweet has a thousand likes and over five hundred retweets. And this is just one tweet by one random man.

Oh God!

This can't be happening!

I'm a meme.

I open a new tweet and type 'Step on Lego' into the GIF search box, and there I am, number one next to a clip of a man on a running machine, running barefoot as someone pours an entire box of Lego onto the belt.

I watch the clip again. And then again. Then I swipe on to Instagram and Saffron's account. She's uploaded several of yesterday's videos. There's me and Matilda, back and forth to the reflection step, then all of us prepping dinner and us dancing too. You hear those people on reality shows always saying how they forget the cameras are there. I thought it was rubbish, but I really did forget.

The dancing video has over two hundred and fifty thousand likes. A quarter of a million people have watched me dance.

The humiliation hits me in waves – dancing and then the meme. Dancing again. I picture the mums huddled around a phone at the playground near school, watching and laughing at what a crap mother I am.

Everyone is laughing at you! Everyone can see how stupid you are!

You're a terrible mother.

My breathing comes fast. My pulse races. And by the time Saffron knocks on the door at exactly 9 a.m. I'm not just humiliated, I'm fuming. A red-hot rage.

'Morning,' she grins, all brisk and fresh as though it isn't already a billion degrees outside. Despite the shower, I'm already sticky with heat and annoyance.

'Look at this,' I say by way of greeting, thrusting my phone at her. 'Look what someone has done.'

She takes my phone in her hands and peers at the screen. I watch her face, waiting for that same moment of horror to dawn, but she is calm to the point of infuriating.

'Well?' I huff.

'It's a meme.' She gives a shrug, seeming utterly unfazed.

'Of me! It's a meme of me.' I snatch back my phone and shove it into my pocket.

Saffron looks at me then, and finally her face softens, sympathy. Pity. 'I can see that. I'm sorry you're upset about it.'

'Of course I'm upset. Someone has made me into a meme.'

'So?'

'So, it's completely humiliating. Every time, literally every time someone wants to use a GIF about something bad happening they'll find me, and it will be my face posted all over social media again and again and again. For ever. I'm completely ruined.'

She starts at that. 'Ruined how?'

'I told you. I've been humiliated.'

'By whom?' Saffron's calm, her questions, only serve to infuriate me further. How does she not see how awful this is?

'A mum from St Helena's sent it to me, which means they'll all have seen it by now. The entire school!'

Saffron turns away and closes the front door. 'I thought you didn't like any of the mums at the school. I didn't think you had any friends there.'

'I don't.'

'So, what does it matter what they think?' She asks, facing me again.

'It just does.'

She tilts her head to one side and folds her arms. 'Now you're sounding like my thirteen-year-old sister.'

I spin on my heels and storm into the kitchen, feeling every bit as unreasonable as Saffron is suggesting. All of a sudden, I can't decide if I like Saffron or hate her. There are times when I am under her spell, times when every word she speaks hammers home a truth I didn't even know about myself, but there are just as many times when I feel scolded and furious.

'It's embarrassing,' I say, jabbing my finger on the switch for the kettle.

'But there's nothing linking that meme to you, or to me for that matter. Even my followers don't know your name or your Instagram handle.'

I grit my teeth as I make our coffees. Just once, just one time, I would like to be the calm one, the rational one. The one who is right.

There's a shout from upstairs. 'I can see him,' Olly shouts with a whoop. I catch the rumble of an idling engine and my mood plummets again as the meme is shoved to the back of my mind and I steal myself for the battle I'm about to fight.

Chapter 24

'The postman is coming,' I tell Saffron, abandoning the coffee I'm making.

'And that's a problem, why?'

I'm already halfway across the kitchen as I turn to reply. 'Olly likes to shoot Nerf bullets at him. It's awful. Sometimes we don't get post for days. I'm sure he saves it up in his bag. It's a total nightmare.'

'What do you normally do about it?' Saffron asks.

'I take the guns away. It causes a massive argument.' I sigh, wishing I'd slept better last night. It was too hot in bed with the twins. I'm tired and angry and I feel in no way prepared to deal with Olly this morning.

'And every time you take the guns away, you argue and then eventually Olly gets the guns back and does it again?' Saffron tilts her head to the side and look at me like she's waiting for me to catch up.

I nod, seeing the futility in it.

'Is there a different approach you could take then?' she asks. 'Why does Olly shoot bullets at the postman?'

'I don't know. It's fun to him. A moving target.'

'Let's ask Olly, shall we?'

'Olly?' I call up the stairs. 'Saffron and I have something to ask you. Could you come down please?'

'In a minute,' he shouts back.

'Now please.'

There's a pause, a beat where I'm sure he's weighing it up, but using Saffron's name works its magic and a moment later Olly appears at the top of the stairs, a large blue plastic gun in his hand. 'What is it?' he asks, racing down to meet us in the hall.

Before I can answer, Saffron is flinging open the front door and waving a greeting at our disgruntled-looking postman, whose bushy black beard makes him look more like an Arctic explorer than a postman. His approach is slow, eyes narrowing as he sees the three of us crowding in the hall.

'Good morning,' Saffron says, her tone so bright and light that it sounds like she's about to break into song.

In contrast, the postman's 'Hello' is a short grunt filled with suspicion. I watch his face harden as he sets his eyes on Olly. Whatever Saffron is planning now, it's a terrible idea. She has no idea how much this man hates us. And who can blame him?

'Olly,' Saffron turns, beckoning him closer until he's wedged between us in the doorway. 'This is—' she waves a hand at the man and he coughs before he speaks.

'Nick.'

'Nick, this is Olly.'

'I know who he is.' His gaze his hard and I have the sudden urge to slam the door shut in that skittish, irrational way I do when it's dark outside and I have to call the cat in and, even though it's been open all day and no axe murderer has wandered in, I'm suddenly convinced that someone is about to fly through the doorway and get me, and my heart skips a beat and I barely let Rex scoot past before I'm slamming the door and locking it.

'I'm Saffron, and this,' she points to me, 'is Becca.'

I lift my hand in a little wave before feeling stupid and dropping it again.

'We were all just saying how we'd love to get to know you better.'

'I wasn't,' Olly says, looking curiously between us. The desire to laugh bubbles up inside of me. What the hell is Saffron up to? 'I was about to shoot him.'

There's a pause, stony and awkward, but Saffron glides right through it, sweetness and nice. 'What do you like to do in your free time, Nick?'

There's a pause before he replies. 'Fishing mostly. I deliver my post in the morning and then I like to sit by the river in the afternoon. It's peaceful. More peaceful than delivering post.' He glares at Olly.

Olly shifts a little and I think he's going to run away, but he stands his ground, the plastic gun still gripped in both hands.

'I can imagine.' Saffron gives him a sympathetic look. 'Becca has been trying to get Olly to stop shooting bullets at you for some time now.'

'She's not doing a great job then.' The retort comes fast and, even though it's true, it still cuts deep.

'No,' Saffron agrees. 'But we're fixing that today, and the first step is for Olly to meet you. What else can you tell Olly about yourself? Have you always been a postman?'

'No. I just took the job so I could fit my fishing in. I was in the Navy for twenty years.'

'On boats?' Olly asks, shuffling forwards a little.

Nick gives a stiff nod. 'Ships. Very big battleships. We went all over the world.'

'Did you see any killer whales?' Olly asks.

'I did, as it happens.' Nick smiles for the first time. 'I saw a mum and her calf off the coast of Norway. They're a lot bigger than you think from seeing them on TV. The mum was the size of two double decker buses.'

'Cool,' Olly says, grinning.

'So, Olly,' Saffron says. 'Perhaps you could think of another question to ask Nick tomorrow when he brings the post. You and your mum could answer the door and I'm sure Nick will answer it for you.'

Nick flashes me a 'who the bloody hell is this woman?' look and I give my best 'it's easier just to go with it' shrug.

'OK,' Olly says eagerly. 'I'm going to think of a really cool question to ask.' And with that, he races upstairs.

'Thank you,' I say to Nick. 'And I'm sorry about the shooting.'

He nods and hands the post to Saffron before turning to leave.

Saffron closes the door with a satisfied smile

'How did you know to do that with Nick?' I ask.

Saffron gives a wide smile. 'Olly saw the postman as a moving target, and now he sees Nick who used to be in the Navy. He's not going to shoot Nick. I saw it in a nineties hostage film, I think. First rule of being a hostage: humanise yourself to your captor.'

I laugh. 'So, it's not just cheesy pop you like from the nineties, then?'

She smiles and shakes her head.

'But what about the Amazon delivery men? We can't befriend all of them, can we?'

'Probably not, especially at the rate you order on Amazon.' She gives me a wicked grin.

'Hey,' I cry in mock hurt. 'In case you haven't noticed, I don't get out much.'

Saffron gives me a playful nudge. 'We're changing that. One thing at a time. Today, we're going to do crafts.'

'Crafts?' I groan, thinking of the mess. 'What kind of crafts?'

'We're going to make some targets for Olly. I'm thinking ugly aliens,' she says, before rummaging in her bag and pulling out a packet of googly eyes.

'Do you seriously carry those around with you everywhere?' I ask.

Saffron winks at me. 'You'd be surprised at their uses. Sometimes,' she says, lowering her voice and leaning in, 'when no one is looking, I add a set of eyes to the milk bottles in the supermarket.'

I've no idea if Saffron is joking, but I can't help but laugh at her conspiratorial whisper.

'Then,' she says, adding the hand clap I've become all too familiar with, 'we're going to keep working on behaviour before we tackle bedtimes. You have zero routine, Becca. How do you expect the children to know it's time to prepare for bed and calm down if you don't create a calming environment?'

'I . . .' There is no answer. 'I don't know.'

Saffron purses her lips and waits for me to say more. Clearly, she's missed her calling as an interrogator. I have a sudden image of her sitting across the table from a master criminal with her 'butter wouldn't melt' smile as the criminal sobs into his hands and begs for mercy. 'Olly was a really good sleeper at first,' I say, filling the silence. 'So, I guess we didn't really need a routine for him. He used to just fall asleep about seven thirty and that was that. But then the twins arrived. Two babies, both of whom hated sleeping anywhere but on me. It was hard on Olly. He was used to having me all to himself, and the twins took every drop of energy I had.' I shrug, as though the next part is obvious. 'Olly started getting out of bed and coming to see me, playing up, wanting attention. Bedtimes became chaos. I was juggling feeding twins with trying to put Olly back to bed. It was easier to let him play and wear himself out. It's never got any easier.' I hate the sound of my excuses. I hate that I wasn't a good enough mother to create the soothing 'bath, story, bed' routine everyone else seemed to nail, but there are no words to describe how hard it was when the twins were babies, how no matter what I did, it wasn't enough.

I lean against the wall and bury my face in my hands.

'Repeat after me,' Saffron says. 'I'm a good mum.'

I lift my head and snort.

'I can see what's going on inside your head. You're beating yourself up, aren't you?'

I give a reluctant nod.

'It's just like we talked about yesterday. Repeat after me, 'I'm a good mother'.

'I'm a good mother,' I say.

'And again.'

'I'm a good mother. I'm a good mother. I'm good mother.'

Saffron nods, satisfied. 'You've had it tough,' she continues. 'You're a single parent, trying to—'

'I'm not a single parent.' My voice is sharper than I intend in my speed to correct her.

She raises a perfect eyebrow. 'Where was Josh while you were trying to get two babies and a young child to sleep?'

'He wasn't home in time from the office.'

'So, what does he do when he gets home to make your life easier?'

I think for a moment, raking through thoughts and memories, searching for something. Anything. 'He's tired from working long hours,' I say eventually. 'He's a good dad, though. Honestly, he loves the children and they love him. He just doesn't have much time.'

'I see this a lot, Becca. One parent is absent so much that when they are there, the kids are delighted to have five minutes of playtime with them, while the other parent picks up the slack. The parent who isn't there much gets let off the hook from doing anything more.

'If Josh was able to be part of this process, I would be sitting you both down right now and looking at the household tasks you each do, the burdens you both carry. I'd be looking at how we could make them more even. But he's not here. You're doing this alone and you're an incredibly capable woman, a great mother.'

'If I'm so great, why are you here?' I throw the question at her. It's stupid and doesn't need an answer but Saffron replies anyway.

She smiles. 'Everyone needs a little bit of help sometimes. Isn't that allowed? You have to believe in yourself, Becca. As I was saying, you're a great mother and you have three amazing children, who in the last few days have really responded to the structure you're giving them. I know you are going to nail the bedtime routine. Come on,' she says, clapping her hands. 'Let's get this day started.'

Chapter 25

The day disappears in a flurry of crafts, stints on the reflection steps, and pep talks from Saffron. Olly throws some glue at Ben and gives Matilda a run for her money on how many times he can dash off. Even when Saffron steps in, he runs off giggling, until I'm frazzled and teary.

Then Matilda refuses to tidy up again and it's her turn on the reflection step. This time, I tell her the mess will wait for her and only when it's tidy will she be able to join Ben and Olly in the paddling pool. I'm gobsmacked when it works and she does her time without complaint. It's a tiny victory in a day of failing.

Ben is last, and I'm sure he throws his fork on the floor and refuses to pick it up just so he can have a go. He seems almost smug as I march him to the bottom step of the stairs.

'One warning and then the step,' Saffron reminds me. 'You must follow through. Warning after warning just teaches them that their actions have no consequences, that you are too weak to deal with them. Are you weak, Becca? Will you let a four-year-old get the better of you?'

I hiss a 'No', while crying a 'Yes' in my thoughts. Today feels even harder than yesterday. The children still aren't listening to me. It was easier when I didn't try to discipline them. I know that's unfair and not really true, but I still think it as I carry Ben back to the step for the tenth time.

And then, before I know it, it's bedtime.

'We've talked through the plan. You can do it,' Saffron says, giving me a 'you've got this' thumbs up as she moves the cameras upstairs.

I run through the steps in my head as the bath fills with water. Be kind, then firm, then don't speak at all if they continue to get up. Routine, routine, routine. Bath and a story for the twins while Olly gets an extra fifteen minutes to play. Then a story for Olly. It all sounds so simple, but the children love their extra play at night. I can't see them giving it up without a fight.

But, to my surprise, Ben, Matilda and Olly accept the new routine without so much as a whine. The stories calm them down and as I close Olly's door and listen to the silence of the house, I turn to Saffron and give her a thumbs up.

'Oh my God,' I whisper. 'It's worked.' I speak too soon. The thud of footsteps comes before I've made it to the top of the stairs.

It's Olly. Always the ringleader. I hear the knock, a tap, tap, tap on the wall between his room and the twins'. The little monkey. I march into his room, mustering my firmest voice. 'Get back into bed, Olly. It's time to go to sleep.'

'But I'm not tired,' he says, matter of fact. 'I want to play. It's still sunny outside.'

There's a tapping sound from the twins' room, followed by voices and a giggle. This is just a game to them. The realisation sucks the last of my energy and if it wasn't for Saffron and that sodding camera, all those viewers judging me, I'd slink down to the kitchen and let the chaos reign.

Saffron's voice rings in my head. 'Don't you want some down-time, to have the evenings to yourself?'

I do. I really, really do. I want to sleep in my bed without being kicked in the back by whichever child has slipped in beside me. I want to watch adult TV shows under a blanket with Rex on my lap. And it's the right thing, too. It's not just about what I want. The children are always so tired, so grouchy. They need more sleep than they're getting.

'It's time for bed now, Olly. Good night,' I say as Olly reluctantly climbs back into bed.

'When is Daddy back?' he asks, snuggling under his duvet.

'Tomorrow night but not until very late so you'll see him on Saturday morning.'

'Are we still having our disco?'

'Yes, on Saturday,' I reply.

'What music will we listen to?'

I'm about to answer when I catch myself. The questions are a delaying tactic and I walked straight into it. 'We can talk about it tomorrow,' I say, stepping to the door. 'Goodnight, Olly.'

The moment his door is closed, Ben appears in the hall. He's snivelling, tears rolling down his face. 'I . . . I can't sleep. I'm scared.'

My heart melts at the sight of him and I almost scoop him into my arms and hug him tight, but I feel Saffron glaring at me. 'Do not give in' that look is saying, and so I crouch down to Ben's level and reassure him that there's nothing to be scared of, that I'll be right downstairs. I tell him that if he sleeps in his own bed tonight, all night, he'll get a sticker on his reward chart.

He nods and I walk him back to his bed and tuck him in. Matilda is miraculously still in bed but she's sitting up with a heap of Barbies on her lap, playing in the soft glow of the night light. I scoop up the dolls and place them in the toy box. 'It's time for sleep.'

On it goes. An hour of back and forth, Olly then Matilda, Olly then Ben, then Matilda, then Ben, then Olly. Each time I silently guide them back to bed, convinced I'll still be here at 2 a.m., but then something seems to click and when I close the door on Ben and Matilda's room at eight fifteen, there really is silence. I hold my breath, not daring to move, not daring to believe it's finally worked.

I tiptoe down to the kitchen and Saffron gives me a big hug. 'Well done,' she says, beaming at me. 'I knew you could do it.'

'I can't believe it. It's not even eight thirty,' I gasp.

'Tomorrow you'll do it in half the time and by the end of the week, it will be seven.'

'It's unbelievable. Seriously? What do I do now?'

Saffron smiles and scoops up her bag. 'Whatever you like.'

There's a niggle of sadness as she turns to leave. I might not always like what Saffron has to say, but I like her company and suddenly I don't want her to leave, I don't want to be alone. I'm about to ask her if she fancies a glass of wine when she gets there first. 'Have a lovely evening,' she says. 'Do something for you, OK?'

'I will. You too.' My reply is bright but inside I feel a crushing loneliness.

At the door, she turns to me and her eyes lock with mine. 'You'll be fine, Becca.'

I swallow back a lump and nod my head. 'I know.'

The moment she's gone, I wander around downstairs, puffing cushions and trying to tidy a room that is already tidy. Not only have I got the evening to myself, but now the children tidy up after themselves, there is nothing for me to do.

I drop on the sofa and pick up my phone. My finger hovers over Instagram before I change my mind. I don't want to see other people's lives tonight, and I don't want to risk seeing another meme of myself. I'm about to turn on the TV when there's a light knock at the door.

I leap up, expecting Saffron again but to my surprise, Matt is on the doorstep, wearing a white t-shirt and an apologetic smile. 'Becca,' he makes a face. 'You wouldn't happen to have any rice, would you?'

'Sure,' I smile. 'Come in.' I wave him into the hallway, glad for the distraction.

'You're a life saver.'

'It's no problem.'

Matt follows me into the kitchen and leans against the counter as I open a cupboard. 'Here you go.'

'Thanks. I can return most of this in a second. I only need a cup. I thought I'd make myself a curry and got all the ingredients, but I forgot rice.' He rolls his eyes and pulls a face.

I laugh. 'It's fine. No rush.'

He hesitates then, pushing his glasses closer to his eyes. 'You don't happen to be hungry, do you?' He carries on before I can reply. 'It's just, I've made enough for a small army and, well, actually, I could do with picking someone's brain about an idea I've had.'

His face is pleading and so I smile and say 'yes'. The pasta I had with the kids was hours ago and, to my surprise, my stomach rumbles in agreement.

'It will have to be here though, if that's OK?' I point to the ceiling. 'They're asleep.' I still can't believe it, but it's true.

'Great.' Matt breathes a heavy sigh as though he's been holding his breath. 'Umm, right. I'll be back in twenty minutes.' He pats the bag of rice.

'I'll do that,' I nod at the bag in his hands.

'Really? Great,' he says again. 'I'll be back in a minute, and I'll try and find a few more words than "great",' he adds, and I laugh again.

Matt appears at the back door a few minutes later with a saucepan in his hands. There's a pack of naan bread tucked under one arm and a six pack of beers under the other. He looks frighteningly close to dropping the lot, so I rush forwards and take the beer and the naans. 'Thanks,' he says and I try not to jump with surprise as he kisses my cheek, pausing ever so slightly too long.

For the briefest of moments, I think of Josh all those miles away in the arms of another woman. How easy would it be for me to do the same? I shut the thought down. Matt is just being friendly, and I'm married. I won't let my imagination read more into this and ruin the one and only friendship I seem to have in my life right now.

'This smells . . . great,' I say.

'Beer?' he asks.

I nod. 'Thanks.'

The beer is cold and refreshing. I haven't had a beer for years and as I take my second sip I wonder why I ever stopped drinking it.

We lay the food out across the island, Matt scooping two portions of a thick, creamy curry onto our plates. I follow with the rice, and then we have another beer each and we chat about his day and the book he's writing, then move on to the recent Olympics and politics. It's the first adult conversation I've had for weeks, months even, that doesn't revolve around the children.

'What did you want to pick my brains about?' I ask when the food is finished and the beers are all gone and we're drinking white wine again.

'Oh. Actually, it was the comics. I—'

174

'Do you need them back? They're upstairs. I can grab them. We've read them every night this week. Olly and Ben laughed their heads off when the bully got caught in his tutu.'

Matt grins. 'Well, that's good to hear.' He pauses, fiddling with the label on the wine bottle. 'The thing is, and I'm aware this is going to sound a bit stalkerish and nutty, but seeing you has awakened something inside me. It's like I've got all these memories rushing around my head that I thought I'd forgotten. And ideas too. Book ideas I used to have for children's books, and they're all back. They're all I can think about. Every time I sit down to write my crime book, I find it's the other books I want to write.'

'Don't go blaming me for missing your deadline,' I laugh, feeling the heady whoosh of a little too much alcohol after a long day.

'I won't,' he grins, running a hand through his hair. 'I've a got a call with my agent tomorrow. I'm going to pitch her one of my old ideas.' Matt's face is alight with excitement. He looks happy, alive.

'That's sounds amazing,' I say. 'I think you'd be brilliant at that. Honestly, Olly loved your writing. He thought it was so funny.'

'Phew! That's exactly what I wanted to ask you about. I thought, if you said they were rubbish, then I would cancel the meeting, bury the ideas and carry on with my crime books.' He says it like he's committing himself to a life of misery.

'No, don't. You have to write children's books for all the kids like Olly who struggle to find stories they enjoy. With lots of pictures.'

'I will then. I want them to be part comic, part chapter based.' He leaps up then, excited, like he's going to start right this second and I realise that he probably is. 'I'll dedicate the first one to Olly.'

'I'm glad you're happy,' I say and I am, but there's a part of me that's jealous too. I know that feeling – the buzz of an idea - that is coursing through Matt's body right now. It's addictive and exciting and I miss it.

'Thank you,' Matt says with a grin

'You don't have to stay. If you want to go and write, I mean. I get it.'

'No, I want to be here,' he says 'Come on. Show me those dance moves again.'

Before I can stop him, Matt is shutting the kitchen door and pulling out his phone. The pumping beat of a Jess Glynne song thrums around the kitchen.

Matt starts shimmying and then he's got his imaginary fishing line out and is pretending to catch me on it.

I throw my head back and laugh. 'Oh no,' I say. 'This is your happy mood, your dance. I'm not—'

'Yes, you are,' he sings, grabbing my hand.

The wine and beer and Matt's silliness takes hold of me and I give in and start to dance, hands in the air, twirling around, not caring that I look like a complete idiot. Matt's dancing too, jumping up and down beside me.

He grabs my hands and we jump together, giggling and silly, and then he jumps up as I move and our bodies bump together. We're still dancing but it's slower. Matt's hands are no longer in mine, but around my body and he's pulling me close and I can't hear the music above the rush of my pulse drumming in my ears

My body aches in that electric, longing way that I had completely forgotten was possible. Matt moves closer and there's a part of me – a part I'm not proud of – that wants to keep moving down this path we've stumbled onto. But already I'm pulling away, wriggling out of his arms, because a bigger part of me doesn't want this.

I don't know what's going on with me and Josh right now. I don't know if he's happier away from us. If he's seeing another woman or if it really is that his work means more to him than we do, but whatever it is, this thing now with Matt in my kitchen isn't the answer.

'Matt,' I say as the song ends.

'Don't say anything.' He shakes his head. 'I'm sorry. Too much wine and excitement. I'm an idiot and I'm sorry.'

'It's OK, it's just . . .'

'We're friends,' he says, before I can find the words. 'Good friends and that's all I want. I promise. I just had a stupid moment there when my teenage self realised he was dancing alone with Rebecca Double Trouble.'

I huff a laugh. 'I'm really not that person anymore.'

'That's not the first time you've said that, and I want to get to the bottom of it, but right now, I think I should go home to bed. I've got a lot of mortifying embarrassment to wake up to tomorrow.'

I laugh again at that and I'm grateful for his jokes easing the tension between us. I busy myself with tidying up as Matt collects his things. He says a cheery goodbye at the back door and I go to bed and hope our friendship can survive what happened tonight.

Chapter 26

I realise, the moment I wake up, why I stopped drinking beer. The hangover! Not to mention my bloated stomach. Eugh! I look four months pregnant and my mouth feels as though I've been licking Rex's bottom. Although, considering she slept on my pillow last night, maybe I did.

Rex stretches out, nuzzling her head against my hand. I run a hand over her sleek fur. It's unusual for her to sleep with me. And when I turn over and take in Josh's empty side, I realise why – no Ben. No Matilda. No arms flung at me in the middle of the night; no little feet kicking the small of my back.

I can't wait to tell Saffron. I grab my phone to check the time and gasp. It's nearly 7 a.m.. Not only have Olly, Ben and Matilda all slept in their own beds, but they've slept for a whole extra hour. After going to bed hours earlier than usual. I can't believe it!

The joy I feel almost wipes away the cringing embarrassment of my almost-kiss with Matt last night. Gah! Maybe if we pretend it didn't happen we can go back to how it was.

And then there's the disappointment at my empty phone screen. No missed call or 'looking forward to seeing you' message from Josh. We've barely spoken for four weeks. I don't know how it's going to be, seeing him. I'm torn. Half excited, half something else. He's not back until late tonight and is leaving again on Sunday evening. He'll be jet-lagged and exhausted. A niggling part of me wonders if there's any point to him coming home, but I push it away as Ben and Matilda bounce into the room, quickly followed Olly. They are the point, and if last night is anything to go by, then Josh and I might get some much-needed alone time too.

It takes double the normal amount of toothpaste, three coffees and a slice of toast to shift the fuzzy effects of last night's alcohol. Beer then wine feel fine, my arse!

I groan when Saffron arrives at 9 a.m. on the dot and drags us all out of the house. 'You've made such great progress in the house, but you need to be able to discipline the children when you're out and about too. You can't lock yourselves away all the time.'

I mumble something about there being a reason we don't go out, but Saffron claps her hands and off we trek. I was hoping for the park, but it's the supermarket Saffron wants to go to.

We walk through the huge automatic door and I feel a blast of air conditioning on my bare arms.

'What are we getting?' Matilda asks.

'Um . . . just some fruit.' We don't need anything. A huge delivery arrived yesterday ready for the weekend, but I can see why Saffron wanted to come here. It's a test.

One you're going to fail!

No, I'm not. I can do this, I tell myself.

Olly, Ben and Matilda dance around my legs as we make our way to the fruits, narrowly dodging the bakery section and the fresh doughnut display. I'm about to give myself a pat on the back when we inadvertently wander into the toy aisle. There is surely a special section of hell reserved for the person who thought it would be a good idea to put toys in supermarkets.

I pick up my pace but it's no use. Matilda gasps at the glowing neon pink display of plastic tat. Her eyes widen and I watch her step almost hypnotically towards the Barbie dolls. 'Can I get one, Mummy? Please? Please, please, please.'

My insides knot but I shake my head. 'No, baby. We're just buying fruit.'

'Please, please, please.' The final please is louder than the rest and delivered with a stamp of her foot. A woman with a toddler sitting happily in the trolley looks my way.

You're a terrible mother. Everyone thinks it!

A helplessness sweeps over me and I feel myself waver. Maybe I should buy them each a toy. We've hardly had much excitement this week. But Saffron is by my side before I can cave. 'If you buy them something now, then you'll be buying them something every time.'

I nod. I hate that she's always right.

'No, Matilda,' I say again. 'We are only getting fruit today. We can make frozen smoothies later.'

'I hate you,' Matilda shouts.

Her words hit like her punch and, before I can react, she's gone, ducking past me and sprinting towards the end of the aisle.

'Matilda.' My shout is ignored. I turn to Ben and Olly. 'Stay here with Saffron.' I don't wait for a reply before dashing after Matilda. At the end of the aisle, I collide with a trolley, the metal clipping my hip.

'Watch out,' someone grumbles, but I'm not listening.

I look left, then right, searching for a flash of green sun dress, but I can't see her.

My breath seems to catch in my lungs and all I can I think is, 'What if something bad happens?'. On a whim and in a panic, I spin right and down towards the bakery aisle, and there she is, chatting away to someone as though it's the most normal thing in the world.

'Mummy, look who I found,' Matilda says, her outburst forgotten.

I rush forwards, scooping Matilda into my arms. 'Matilda, don't ever run away from me again,' I gasp. 'I was so worried.'

Matilda must catch the emotion in my voice because her face crumbles and tears fill her eyes. 'Sorry, Mummy,' she says, burying her head in my neck and, finally, I breathe again.

It's only then that I look up and find the smiling face of Mrs Young.

'Hello, Becca. How are you?'

'Oh, Mrs Young, hello.' I smile but inside I wish the earth would swallow me up. The last time I saw Mrs Young, Ben was flying off the end of her banister, and now she's found me with Matilda running free in a supermarket.

'Your little girl was just telling me about the Barbie she wants,' Mrs Young says, with a sympathetic look.

'It's got pink highlights,' Matilda sniffles.

'I was just telling her that sometimes we have to wait for things. Isn't that right, Becca?'

I nod. 'Yes, it is. Thank you for catching her. I'd better go back to Olly and Ben.' I add a wave and turn quickly away before my cheeks flame any darker.

'Please don't run away again, Matilda. If you'd hurt yourself, I wouldn't have been there to help you.'

She's quiet, but her little hands tighten around my neck. This is why we don't go out much. This, right here. I swallow back the emotion threatening to leak out of me and head back to the toy section in search of Saffron, Ben and Olly.

They are standing exactly where I left them, playing a game of I spy.

'You're back,' Saffron says, with a smile for me.

'I just wanted the Barbie really badly,' Matilda says. 'But Mrs Young says I need to wait.'

'Mrs Young is right,' Saffron says.

'I've actually had an idea, though,' I say, hesitating, wondering if it's stupid.

Saffron gives me an encouraging nod. 'What's that?'

'Well, we haven't thought of a prize for when the reward charts are filled yet. So maybe you could all choose a small toy today and I'll take a photo of it on my phone and when your chart is filled, we can come back and get it.'

The children jump and cheer, and Ben and Olly scatter along the aisle, looking with feverish excitement at each toy.

'That's a great idea,' Saffron says. 'And you're letting Matilda know that you've listened to her.'

'And what if I see something next time?' Matilda eyes me suspiciously as I place her gently back on the floor.

'Then we can take another photo to remember it, and you can save up your pocket money or wait for your birthday or Christmas.'

As soon as we're back in the car I'm ready to go home, but Saffron shakes her head and directs us to a soft-play centre I've not been to since the twins were babies. Olly had been four at the time and thought it would be a fun game to steal children's shoes from beneath the tables and hide them in the ball pit. I knew nothing about it until an angry dad came to tell me, by which time Olly had blocked himself in the curly slide, and Matilda and Ben were wailing for a feed.

The place is just as I remember – a windowless warehouse with uncomfortable metal chairs. But, to the children, it is a paradise of brightly coloured slides and climbing and play, and so I try not to mind the sticky tables and watery coffee.

Olly, Ben and Matilda kick off their shoes the second we're through the door and disappear, leaving Saffron and I to find a table.

'Where do you live?' I ask as I place two coffees down in front of us and realise I know nothing about Saffron.

'South London – Bexley Heath. I'm still with my mum and dad, and my brothers and sisters.'

'That sounds pretty full-on.'

She laughs. 'Yeah, it is sometimes but I tried moving out last year. I rented a studio flat, twenty minutes down the road from home, and I hated it. When you've lived in a house like mine all your life, silence feels very strange. I missed all the chat and banter and being squashed at the edge of the sofa when we all watch TV together.'

Saffron's confession surprises me. 'I pictured you in a flat, I think. All pink.'

She laughs. 'I do like pink. I'll move out one day. I just . . .' she shrugs. 'I want to live with someone.'

'Like, friends?'

Her smile falters. 'Or someone special.' She sighs. 'I don't have either in my life very much right now. It's not like I work in an office with loads of other people my age.'

'Have you tried the online dating sites?'

'Constantly,' she says, with an eye roll. 'You hear really awful things about online dating and some of it is true, but there are a lot of genuine people out there too. I've had a few nice dates, but most of the time if I tell a guy what I do, they run for the hills. They think because I work with children, I must want them.'

'And don't you?' I ask. 'God, sorry, that's so rude of me. I just assumed you did, but it's none of my business. I used to hate it when people asked me that.'

She laughs. 'It's fine. We're friends. You can ask me. And yes, I think I do one day, but I'm in no rush. I know better than most how full-on parenting is and I want to enjoy my life with someone for a long time before I think I'll be ready.' Saffron sighs.

'I guess it's not exactly a career that's likely to lead to love either.'

'No,' she laughs. 'But I love what I do. I set up The Toddler Tamer because I knew I could help families, and there is no better feeling in the world to me than watching families grow closer. And I'm so lucky to have a big family. I'm never lonely.'

Something in the expression on Saffron's face makes me wonder if that last statement is true, but I don't push it.

When it's time to leave, Saffron tells me to call the children over and warn them that they have only five minutes left. They nod before racing away at full speed.

'Giving them a warning of a change of activity allows them time to finish what they're doing and process the change. And they don't feel like they're being dragged away while they're in the middle of a game.'

After Matilda's supermarket sprint, I'm not expecting the warning to work, but it does, and when I call them back five minutes later, they come willingly; red-faced and sweaty, grinning and out of breath.

'We played hide and seek,' Ben tells me as he pulls on his shoes.

'You all played really nicely. Well done,' I say.

'Can we come back next week?' Matilda asks.

I nod. 'Sounds like a plan.'

'How long until Daddy gets home?' Olly asks.

'Not until very late tonight,' I remind him. 'You'll see

him when you wake up tomorrow. Shall we go home and have some lunch? Then we could paint him a welcome-home poster in the garden.'

They all nod and we start to walk out. I can't believe it. No fuss. No screams. Saffron gives me a thumbs up and I realise that this was all me. The warning and the praise. I even suggested crafts. Go me!

It won't last.

Maybe not, but right now, it's good.

We're by the door when Saffron spots a poster and calls the children over. 'Hey, Olly, Ben, Matilda, look at this.' She taps a printed A4 sheet advertising a toy sale for the following week, raising money for the hospital.

'What is it?' Ben asks

'It's a second-hand toy sale,' Saffron explains. 'People donate the toys they don't play with anymore and they're sold to other children, and the money they make goes to getting new things for the children's ward at the hospital.'

'Are we going to get new toys, then?' Matilda asks, her eyes lighting up.

'We should give our old ones,' Olly replies, looking from Saffron to me.

Saffron's face lights up. 'Exactly. I noticed you three have a lot of toys. Wouldn't it be good to know that the ones you're not playing with have new homes, and that you've helped raise money for other children who are stuck in hospital and can't come to places like this to play?'

All three children give solemn nods and carry on walking to the car park. A toy sort out. Now Saffron really has gone mad. We've still got a ton of baby toys in the toy boxes. I've tried before to get rid of things, but Ben and Matilda have screamed and screamed, desperate to keep everything.

The afternoon turns into the evening and at seven fifteen I tuck Olly into bed and kiss him goodnight.

'Daddy will be here when I wake up?' he asks, already sleepy.

'Yes, but you have to go to sleep first or you can't wake up tomorrow and see him.'

He nods and snuggles down in the covers, and I'm overwhelmed with the love I feel for this wonderful boy. I kiss his forehead and tell him I love him.

'Love you too,' he mumbles.

Saffron grins at me as I tiptoe downstairs. She turns off her camera and holds out her hand for a high-five, and even though it's ridiculously cheesy, I high-five her back.

'You did it,' she grins.

'You did it,' I reply. 'I never would have believed this was possible. It's seven thirty. They have never gone to bed this early before.'

'You were brilliant tonight. You did everything right. And now you have the evening to yourself and you've got Josh coming home too. I bet he won't believe the change here.'

I laugh and shake my head. 'He'll think he's walked into the wrong house.' There's a buzz of excitement in me now at the thought of Josh coming home. I'm no longer thinking about how little we've spoken over the past few weeks. Instead, I'm thinking of how much I want to see him, kiss him, hug him; but, more than that, I want him to see how different things are now, how hard we've all worked. I want him to be proud of us. Of me.

Saffron waves goodbye and then it's just me in this quiet, quiet house.

Chapter 27

Rex saunters into the kitchen, eyeing the room with a suspicious glare.

'It's weird, isn't it?' I say.

She rubs against my legs and purrs. 'I'm glad to see you approve of the bedtime routine,' I say to Rex, to myself, to the empty kitchen. 'I can do anything I want.'

I pick up my phone, before dropping it again like it's on fire. Instagram was my go-to place, but I don't want to see the videos Saffron has uploaded or stumble across another meme someone has made of me.

But it's more than that, I realise. The calmer my life is – the closer it looks to the photos I post – the less need I feel to post validating photos or scroll through other people's accounts.

A loneliness threatens to engulf me. I stand by the window and watch the sun stretching across the lawn. I think of going outside and sitting in its warmth, but I see Matt at the top of his garden, a drink in one hand, a book in the other, and something stops me.

I know we'll be fine. We'll have one awkward conversation and brush last night's moment of madness under the rug, but I'm not ready for that tonight. Instead, I step into the living room and scan the book shelf in the corner.

All the books are organised in size order, with the pages facing outwards. It looked amazing in the photograph I took for my Instagram feed last month, but it's ridiculous now when I'm actually looking for a book to read. I used to love reading. Horror was my favourite. The gorier the better. Now it's all snails and whales and three little pigs. I'm about to move all the books around when I catch the familiar scrape of a key in the lock of the front door.

I check the time. It's only 9 p.m.. Too early for Josh to be home, and yet the front door is opening and he's standing in the doorway, looking dishevelled and tired but smiling too.

'Hi,' he grins, his voice loud and I can't stop myself shushing him.

It's not the greeting I'd planned after nearly a month apart and not the one he expects either. His smile falters and he steps forward, his foot kicking against the door.

'Don't slam the—' I hiss just as the door crashes shut with a reverberating thud.

I freeze, holding my breath and listening for the tell-tale sound of chatter and footsteps, but all is quiet.

'What's going on?' he asks. 'Are you playing hide and seek?' And before I shake my head, he's dropping his bag and calling out in a loud sing-song voice. 'Olly, Ben, Matilda?'

'Sshh!' I hiss again and this time the smile on Josh's face drops completely. 'They're asleep,' I explain.

'What?' The one word is said with a comical surprise and he looks at me as though I've just announced the children have taken a trip to the moon.

I beckon him into the kitchen before closing the door. 'The kids are asleep,' I say again.

'Asleep?' He glances at the clock. 'It's not even nine.'

'I know.' I grin triumphantly, waiting for his disbelief to morph into praise. 'And hello, by the way. It's good to see you,' I add. And it is. Even with the whisper of

188

tension I can already feel between us, it's good to see him. I lean forward and we kiss. It's brief and I pretend I can't tell Josh's mind is elsewhere.

He drops onto one of the stools, loosening his tie and kicking off his shoes. He looks terrible. The skin under his eyes is dark, and sagging a little, as though he hasn't slept for a week. His lips are dry and there's more grey around his temples than when I saw him last. 'I've literally just legged it through Customs and across London,' he says, with a long exhale. 'I've rushed to get back here so I could spend time with the children tonight. I've missed them. Why did you put them to bed early on the one night I'm coming home?'

His words slice through me. The tension bubbles and when I speak my tone is cutting. 'I didn't put the children to bed early. I put them to bed at their bedtime which is 7 p.m. now.'

'Since when?'

'Since this week when I cracked the bedtime routine, thanks to Saffron's help.'

'Who's Saffron?' He rubs his hands over his face and I already sense him zoning out.

'The nanny I told you about in one of my emails. Well, she's not actually a nanny. She's more like a witch.' I laugh.

'A witch?' He frowns and then stands, stepping over to the back door and staring out into the garden.

'Or a fairy godmother. She's been helping me with the kids' behaviour while you've been away.'

'Right.' He nods and I can tell he is holding back a barbed comment.

'Josh, you didn't tell me you were coming home early. The flight you said you'd be on doesn't land until 10 p.m.. I wasn't expecting you home until midnight.'

'I got an earlier flight so I could spend more time with the kids. Although, clearly, that was pointless.'

The anger I've been fighting to keep at bay froths to the surface. 'If you'd have called me or texted me to let me know, I'd have kept them up,' I fire back, wondering if it's true. Their bedtime routine is so new, but already it feels so precious. They've been noticeably happier today; fewer tantrums, fewer tears. I'm sure getting eleven hours of sleep instead of seven or eight hours has something to do with it.

'Right.' He sighs and heads to the fridge, pouring himself a glass of wine.

I know Josh well enough to know that 'Right' is his signal to change the subject.

He's already bored of you. You should leave it!

I grit my teeth against the voice. No, I tell myself. I'm not leaving this.

'Maybe if you'd have texted me at all this week, you might have thought to mention your earlier flight. Obviously, you've been far too busy to bother talking to your wife or children this week.'

'I have been too busy, as it happens,' he says, before walking out of the kitchen. A moment later, I hear him carrying his suitcase up the stairs. I let him go and sink on to the living-room sofa, trying to distract myself by watching a crime drama, but I can't keep up with the constant twists when my head is full of Josh. I'm teetering on a fence between anger and sadness, unsure which way I'm going to fall.

It's half an hour before Josh appears in the doorway. His hair is damp and he's wearing an old t-shirt and a pair of shorts.

'I'm sorry,' he says. 'The whole flight home I was thinking about how great it was going to be to surprise you and the kids by coming home early. I didn't handle it well.'

My anger softens. 'I'm sorry too. I thought you'd be pleased the kids are in a better routine.'

'I am,' he says, stepping forwards. 'It's amazing.'

'And I'm still awake. You know – your wife?'

He smiles, sitting down beside me and taking my hand. 'I know. And you look beautiful tonight. Let me just check on the roses and then I'm all yours.' He moves to stand but I grip his hand and pull him back.

'Are you seeing someone else?' The question is out before I can stop it and I hate myself for asking, hate how pathetic I sound, but I have to ask.

'What?' He huffs a laugh of surprise.

'A woman answered your phone when I rang last week,' I add.

'What time was it?'

'It was evening here. About eight, I think.'

'So middle of the afternoon New York time. It must have been Rachel. She's the team secretary.'

'And she answers mobiles too?'

'Sometimes. When I'm in meetings and we're waiting on calls from London, I leave my mobile on my desk. That's all it is, Becca. Rachel is twenty-one. She's sweet, but she's just a kid.'

'What about—'

Josh pulls me towards him, his lips finding mine, and we kiss for a long time, desire awakening inside me. 'There's no one else but you,' he says, voice low and filled with intent. 'Come to bed, Mrs Harris,' he whispers.

'What about your roses?'

'They can wait. This can't.'

I smile and let him pull me to my feet and lead me upstairs, wishing I couldn't feel a lingering tension still hanging between us.

Chapter 28

The children are ecstatic to see Josh on Saturday morning. They sprint into our bedroom, diving on the bed and elbowing out the last of our sleep. I slip out of bed and make us both coffee as he cuddles and talks and tickles and listens to a month's worth of little voices and all that's happened.

'So, what I'm getting here is that you all love Saffron and she has magic powers,' Josh laughs.

Matilda gives a high-pitched giggle. 'Yes.'

'Can she fly?' He gives a comical frown.

'No,' comes Olly's reply, outraged at the suggestion.

'Can she turn invisible?'

'No,' Ben shouts.

'So, what does she do?'

Olly thinks of this a moment. 'She makes boring stuff fun and she makes Mummy happy.'

I bark a laugh of surprise at Olly's explanation. Saffron has made me cry, she's made me furious, she's made me grumpy. The very last thing I've been this week is happy. And yet I smile because maybe there is something in it. I've been laughing more and playing with the children in a way I never felt I had time for before.

When Josh suggests pancakes for breakfast, I ask if he minds if I go for a swim. He raises his eyebrows as though surprised at the question but in the next second

192

he's nodding. 'Of course. That sounds great. Go and have some time to yourself.'

He shoos me away with a wave of his hand and a grin as he tips Ben and Matilda upside down on the bed. I don't need to be told twice. Unearthing my swimming costume and goggles from the back of a forgotten drawer, I'm out the house and halfway to the pool in minutes.

It's only as I'm parking the car and striding into the leisure centre that a knot of anxiety parks itself in my stomach. It feels like so much has changed in the house since Josh left. I didn't tell him about the reflection step or any of the other rules and routines Saffron has put in place since he went away.

But the thrill of being responsible for no one but myself for the first time in weeks soon takes over and by the time I'm slipping into the cool pool and cutting through the water, all I'm thinking about is moving my body and how good it feels to be swimming again.

The freedom is blissful and I enjoy every second of the ninety minutes I'm out of the house. I'm even smiling as I park the car on the drive, wishing I could bottle this feeling up, tuck it behind the gin bottle in the top cupboard and swig sneaky gulps whenever it all feels too much.

At the very least, I'd have liked to have kept my happy glow for longer than it took me to turn the key in the lock and open the front door. The obliteration of my peace is instant.

Mess.

Everywhere.

Hot Wheels cars and blankets and Lego and Barbie dolls cover the floor. There are piles of Matilda's clothes on the stairs as though she's tried on every outfit she owns in the time I've been out.

A month ago, walking into this chaos would have been familiar, expected, but that only makes it worse. It's a savage reminder of how far we've all come with Saffron's help, and how little it takes to slip back.

I step into the kitchen and fight back frustrated tears as I survey the gloop of pancake batter spattering the sides and dripping down the cupboards. Used pots litter the counters. It's like the unit in *The Great British Bake Off* when a panicking contestant has made three batches of failed scones.

The tears dry in my eyes. My frustration turns bitter and sharp. Of course, it's me who'll be expected to clean up. It's like Saffron said. Josh has been away so much that all he has to do is be here to be a hero in the children's eyes.

The thought is followed by another, quick on its heels. This never would have happened if I'd stayed at home this morning. And that thought alone makes me want to scream. I should be able to leave the house for two sodding hours without coming back to this.

There's a trail of wet footprints on the floor and I follow them out to the garden where Matilda, Ben and Olly are taking it in turns to jump into the paddling pool. I notice the newly cut lawn and the weeded borders, and wish it made up in some small part for the mess of the house, but it doesn't. I'm too angry to appreciate it.

'Mummy!' Matilda calls joyfully. 'Watch this,' she says before attempting a cartwheel that leaves her plonked on her bottom in the water and giggling furiously.

'Very good, baby,' I say, my voice too high, too strung out. 'Where's Daddy?'

'He had to do something,' Olly replies. 'He's coming back in a minute to play jumping in the pool with us. He promised.'

'What have you been doing this morning?' I ask.

'Gardening.' Ben makes a face.

'I helped,' Olly says with a proud smile.

'I didn't,' Matilda sing-songs.

'I didn't either,' Ben adds.

'I'll just go find Daddy. Back in a minute,' I say, before turning away, the anger hammering along with the beat of my pulse. I pick my way through the mess in the hall because I know exactly where I'll find Josh. I collect teddies and discarded clothes as I climb the stairs, dumping them on Matilda's bed before heading to the study. Sure enough, Josh is sat hunched over his laptop, peering at the screen. He turns towards me and yawns.

'Hey,' he says rubbing at his left shoulder. 'Did you have a nice time?'

'I did until I came back to the house and found it looks like a bomb has gone off. What the hell happened?' My voice is hard and there's that tension again between us, a knot of resentment I don't know how to begin unpicking.

'What's the problem?' he asks, seeming genuinely perplexed. 'We made pancakes and did some gardening. I spent time with the kids. That's what you wanted, wasn't it?'

'Me? Don't act like you've done me a favour, Josh. They are your children too. Last night you said you wanted to spend time with them.'

'I didn't mean it like that,' he sighs and rubs at his eyes. 'Of course I want to spend time with them. I just meant that you wanted to go swimming too and I was happy for you to go.'

'Oh, were you? Oh, thank you so much.' My voice drips with sarcasm. 'How nice of you to let me out the house for a few hours after weeks without a break. I'm so grateful.'

'Becca,' Josh sighs. 'What's going on here? I don't understand what you're upset about.'

'I'm upset because I leave the house for two hours and now, instead of us being able to spend time together as a family, the rest of the day is going to be about tidying up. The children are supposed to clean up themselves before they can play anything else.'

'That's new,' he says with a surprised smile.

'Yes.'

'You're right. I should've tidied the kitchen. I'll do it, OK? It said it was going to rain this afternoon and I wanted to do some gardening while it was dry. I've been looking forward to it for ages.'

'Except now you've shut yourself away in here again.'

'I was just checking my emails quickly. I've said I'll play in the paddling pool with them now.'

'You can't.' I shake my head and sigh, biting back the desire to rage and cry. 'The children need to clean up their toys.'

'Can't it wait? I promised.'

'No, it can't,' I snap. I bite the inside of my lip. Am I being unfair? I have a sudden longing for Saffron to be here, pulling me to one side and telling me what to do. Josh hasn't seen the children for weeks. What harm will it do if I let them off from tidying this one time?

I can picture Saffron's raised eyebrow. 'So, when Dad is home, the rules don't apply?' she'd say, or something like it, clapping her hands and hurrying us along, making cleaning the mess fun for all of us in a way that I've never mastered.

'Fine,' Josh replies, his tone as bitter as mine. 'If they're tidying up then I might as well finish doing this.'

'So, you're leaving me to be the bad guy who has to tell them to clean?'

He sighs again. There is tension in his face as though every part of him is willing me to go away. A sadness threatens to engulf me. 'Becca, come on. I've got horrendous jet lag and I'm exhausted. What does it matter who tells them to tidy up?'

'Fine,' I turn on my heels and storm back to the garden. Then I take three long, deep breaths before I talk to the children. This is not their fault. This anger is not at them.

'Kids,' I say. 'It's time to tidy up.' And before I can stop myself, I find I'm clapping just like Saffron. 'You can play again in the paddling pool later.'

'But, Mummy,' Ben whines. 'Daddy is coming.'

'I've just spoken to Daddy and he agrees with me that you can all play together once your toys are put away.'

'I'm not going to do it,' Olly says, defiant. 'I didn't play with any of those toys. I'm going to wait for Daddy.'

Matilda and Ben look first to Olly and then to me. I see them weighing things up, choosing their side. They sidle up to Olly. 'Us too,' Matilda says before jumping in the paddling pool again.

It's not you they respect. It's Saffron. Without her, you're still a failure.

A fresh dart of anger pulses through me. The desire to shout is almost overwhelming. Instead, I take a breath and, forcing my voice to be calm, I give them a warning. 'We can't have the disco tonight when the floor is covered with toys. So, we are going to be tidying today. The sooner you do it, the sooner you'll be back out here, playing with Daddy.'

There's a pause and I sense the twins waiting for Olly.

'Olly,' I say. 'I could really do with your detective work in the kitchen. I know you didn't get any of the toys out but you did help with the pancakes. And there are lots of drops of pancake batter that need to be found and cleaned up.'

He nods at that. 'OK, Mummy.'

Matilda's face falls so fast that at any other time I'd have laughed at the comedy of it. She was clearly hoping for a bigger standoff.

I wait another beat and then Ben nods. 'I'm going to be the fastest tidier you've ever seen,' he declares, racing towards the house.

'Make sure everything gets put away in the right place, though,' I call after him, feeling something lift inside me. I can do this. I can get the children to listen to me.

'Can we listen to some music while we tidy?' Olly asks.

'Good idea.' I find a nineties pop playlist that Saffron would approve of and hand Olly a cloth. As we get to work, my anger dissolves, leaving only the tension humming away inside me.

Josh and I have been married for nine years. I thought we were solid, happy. But last night I found myself asking him if he was having an affair and today all we've done is bicker after weeks of being apart, of barely being in contact. Something feels off. And it's not a recent thing either. But, without the children causing constant mayhem, it's easier to see, or harder to ignore perhaps.

Chapter 29

I place the last bowl of crisps on the table and survey the feast the children have helped to make. It's the perfect party food of triangle sandwiches and sausage rolls, pineapple and cheese sticks, wobbly green jelly in the shape of a space rocket and cups of pre-made squash.

There are two fillet steaks marinating in the fridge for me and Josh to eat later. I'm still pissy and hurt at Josh over our argument this morning, but I also know that I didn't explain the new rules to him. We've lived in chaos for years. How could I expect him to know that things have changed? And so, I make an effort to push the anger aside. This is our one night with Josh before he flies back to New York and I want it to be fun.

'This is pretty epic,' Josh says, appearing in the kitchen, wearing shorts and a Hawaiian shirt he got on holiday in Spain a few years ago and hasn't warn since.

'We may have gone overboard,' I smile. 'The children have been so excited about this disco and having you home.'

'I like the look of overboard,' he says, smiling at my outfit. My eyes are drawn down to the red dress I'm wearing. Matilda's choice. There's still a grass stain on the side from her jaunt in the garden as Captain Hook, but I'm surprised how well it fits and how good it makes me feel, wearing it. I've teamed it with gold sparkly heels that I know Matilda will steal the second she gets the chance.

'Thanks.' I grin, enjoying the compliment, the feeling of being seen by Josh that is so rare. 'You don't look too bad yourself.'

'A small miracle, considering how tired I feel. My body clock is completely out of whack. Shall I put some tunes on to keep me awake?'

'Good idea.' I follow Josh through to the living room. The curtains are drawn against the sun. It's only five thirty and the light is still blazing through the windows. I switch on the flashing fairy lights I dug out from the Christmas box in the loft. It looks more tacky-grotto than disco but I know the children will love it.

As soon as the music starts, the children race downstairs, lining up, one after the other: Olly first, then Matilda, then Ben. Olly is wearing his favourite green dinosaur t-shirt and an old pair of orange swim shorts. Matilda is wearing a Cinderella dressing-up dress and Ben is in his astronaut glow-in-the dark pjs.

Josh steps forward, holding out his hand. 'Tickets. You must show your tickets. No ticket, no entry.'

'Daddy, it's our disco,' Olly admonishes, but he holds out his ticket anyway and skips into the living room. Ben and Matilda wave their tickets at Josh as though he really might not let them in without them, and then Josh turns to me.

'Got a ticket?' he asks.

I laugh at his deadpan expression. 'Er . . .' My eyes dart to Olly. He howls with laughter.

'Mummy, where is the ticket we gave you?' Matilda asks in her best head-teacher voice, her hands on her hips.

'I don't know.' I make a face. 'I think I might have lost it.'

'Well, I'll let you off this time,' Josh says. 'But only because I was hoping you might be here tonight,' he adds, as though we're not husband and wife, standing in our living room, but two strangers at an actual disco. 'Do you think . . . if you're not too busy later . . . will you dance with me?'

I laugh. 'Alright then. Unless someone better comes along.'

He gives me a mock hurt look, hand grasping his chest as though I've wounded him.

The hour flies by in silly dances and party games. The children have wrapped up their own prizes for each game, and I win a pink teddy bear that Matilda snatches back straight away, and we all laugh when Josh wins one of Olly's socks.

'It's not even clean,' Josh declares, sniffing the sock and pretending to faint in a way that sends the children into hysterics.

We break for party food before more dancing. I put on Whigfield's 'Saturday Night' and the children scream in delight when Josh joins in with the moves too. I'm about to end on the 'Superman' song when Josh takes my phone and selects 'Stay Another Day' by E17.

'You have to end a disco with a slow song,' he tells the children, before taking my hand and pulling me into his arms. 'This was the song that was playing in the pub the night I first met your mother.'

'It's a Christmas song,' I say.

'It's the song that always makes me think of you.'

Josh holds me close and we shuffle our feet from side to side in the classic school-disco way. At the end, we kiss and the children yell and shout, cheers and protests all in one go.

There are groans when I open the curtains and turn off the fairy lights, but no tantrums, and even Josh is impressed.

'Right, I will put these rascals to bed,' he says.

'You, Mrs Harris, can get our dinner ready.'

'Don't forget—'

'I know. You've already briefed me. Firm voice,' he says, lowering his voice and croaking, sounding more like an East End gangster than a determined parent.

In the kitchen, I swap disco music for Adele and sing quietly along as I cook the dinner. When it's ready and keeping warm in the oven, I tiptoe upstairs to get Josh. I imagine him distracted by an email, but when I open the bedroom door, I find Olly, Ben and Matilda nestled on my bed with Josh in the middle, reading them a Julia Donaldson book they've heard a hundred times before. It's a sweet scene and a few weeks ago I would've posted a photo on Instagram, but instead a niggle of frustration rises up. All my hard work this week has counted for nothing if Josh can't support it.

'It's past bedtime,' I say, fighting to keep my voice cheerful. I don't want another fight tonight. I want delicious food, laughter, romance.

'They said they weren't tired,' he says with a sheepish grin.

'Of course they did, but that's not the point. It's bedtime. We talked about this. Our dinner is ready.' I swallow my anger. It's only the first week of a proper bedtime routine, I remind myself. And even though it's important, even though I wanted to show Josh how well I've been doing, how well the kids have been doing, this, this time together for them, is so much more important. 'Daddy will finish reading you the story and then it's time to go to sleep.'

Ben's face lights up. He opens his mouth to ask something but I get there first. 'In your own beds.' He sinks back against the pillow, snuggling further into the crook of Josh's arm.

I sit at the edge of the bed as Josh takes his time, doing all the different voices.

'One more?' Matilda asks. 'Please.'

'Oh no,' I say before Josh can cave again. 'It's time for sleep.'

Josh kisses them each goodnight and heads downstairs, and it's me who stays and tucks them in, who tells Matilda she can't play quietly in her bed, and guides Olly back to his room when he remembers an idea he has to tell me about.

When I finally make it downstairs, Josh is snoring softly on the sofa and the sumptuous dinner is cool and unappetising.

I slip outside with a glass of wine and sit in the evening sun, fighting back tears. I don't know why I'm upset. It's only a dinner, and yet it's not. It's this whole weekend. It's been a disaster. For every moment of fun and laughter there have been ten more when I've felt frustrated or angry, when Josh and I have bickered or outright argued.

It's an hour before Josh emerges from the house, looking groggy and confused. 'Sorry,' he mumbles. 'I ruined dinner.'

'It's OK,' I lie.

'We could do it now.'

I nod and get up.

Josh lights a candle as I reheat the dinner. The steak is rubbery and the chips taste stale already. Neither of us eats much or talks much. I can tell by Josh's yawns that he's desperate to go to bed.

'Are you enjoying New York?' I ask, eager to rekindle the romance and fun we had at our disco. 'What's the city like?'

He makes a face. 'I've hardly noticed, to be honest. I can describe in detail the inside of my four-walled hotel room and the seventh-floor office, but that's about all I've seen.'

'But you've been going out for dinners, haven't you?'

'It's just food and dull shop talk with people I find either boring or loathsome.'

After dinner, we go to bed and make love. There is none of the passion of last night, but we go through the motions, ticking a box. The thought sticks in my mind as Josh falls asleep and I lie awake. It isn't just the sex. Our whole relationship feels like one huge effort of going through the motions, of moments of joy spattered among arguments and tension. I turn onto my side and feel utterly lost.

On Sunday morning, Josh takes the children to the park while I make a picnic lunch for us to eat in the garden. They come back red-faced and bouncing with excitement. 'I made a friend,' Olly announces with the same vigour as if he'd had a lottery win.

'That's great,' I reply.

'So did we,' Matilda says.

'Charlie is eight like me and Isabelle is four like them. And Daddy made a daddy friend too.'

I look to Josh and he smiles in agreement. 'I had a very nice chat with an electrician called Richard. We bonded over our shared desire to spend more time gardening.'

'I'm hungry,' Ben says.

'I've made us a picnic to have in the garden, and then I've got something fun for us to do.'

'What is it?' Olly asks, jumping at my feet, paws out like a kangaroo. Ben and Matilda copy him, and then Josh, and suddenly we're all bouncing up and down.

'You'll see. Lunch first. Hop along.'

When our picnic is over, Josh steps away to pack his suitcase and I send the children inside for ten minutes while I set up the buckets and sponges. I smile to myself, already picturing the fun we're about to have.

'OK,' I shout in through the back door. 'You can all come out now.'

There's a cheer and a clatter of toys, and I gasp as I realise they're tidying away their game before coming out. Victory!

'What are we doing?' Olly asks, eyeing the two buckets I've placed either side of the paddling pool.

'We're having a water fight.'

The children stare at me agog, their gaze moving from me to the buckets and back again.

'Really?' Olly asks.

'Yes,' I laugh. 'Why is that so hard to believe?'

'You never let us throw water.'

'In the bath, I don't. But we're outside now, and we're going to have rules.' I feel a sudden urge to clap my hands as I speak. Bloody Saffron and her clapping.

'We each get a bucket and a sponge. There are two teams. Olly and me will be one team, and Daddy and the twins will be on the other. You're only allowed to throw the wet sponge at someone on the opposite team and you have to stay on your own side of the paddling pool when throwing them.'

'Yessssss,' Olly hisses, before running to a bucket and picking up a sponge, plonking it into the bucket. 'It's freezing!' he laughs.

'How do I get my sponge back when I've thrown it?' Ben asks.

'You can run to the other side to get it,' I explain. 'But you have to be on your side to throw it and no one can throw one at you while you're on the wrong side . . .'

I'm turning back to Olly to make sure he understands when I catch sight of Josh in the corner of my vision. Olly has seen him too and gleefully grabs at the wet sponge, throwing it across the lawn to where Josh is standing. It's only as it's flying through the air that I realise Josh is wearing his suit. Confusion and horror draw on Josh's face as he catches sight of the sponge and tries to duck. He's too slow and the sponge clips the top of his shoulder before landing on the patio with a resounding splat.

'Hit,' Olly cries out, dancing around his bucket.

'Olly!' Josh's voice is angry, cutting through the excitement, a pin to a balloon. 'Don't do that!'

Olly's face crumples. His joy hardens before my eyes. 'Mummy said I could.' His voice is just as furious as Josh's but carries the weight of his tears too as they fall down his cheeks. He kicks the bucket, spilling the water across the lawn before running inside.

'It's OK,' I call out to Olly, but he's gone.

I round on Josh. 'He was just playing,' I hiss. 'We're having a water fight. I told you earlier.'

'No, you didn't.' He pulls off his jacket and brushes at the wet patch. 'I've got to wear this on the flight tonight.'

'It will dry,' I snap.

'Not in the two minutes before my taxi arrives.' Josh's entire body is tense, his jaw set.

'What do you mean? It's only one o'clock. Why are you leaving now?'

'My flight is at six,' he says, as though pointing out the obvious.

'Oh.' I step back, feeling wrong-footed again. How does he always do this to me? 'You didn't tell me that. I thought you were leaving at six.'

He shakes his head. Looking miserable and still angry.

'It's just water,' I say again. 'I told Olly we were having a water fight. He thought you were on the opposite team.'

Josh sighs. Defeated. 'I know. I'll go get Olly.'

A few minutes later, we're at the door again, waving Josh away. It's been a roller coaster of a weekend. The disco was so much fun, and the picnic, but it feels tainted by our arguments and the cloud Josh has left under. I turn to look at the children. Three sad faces stare back at me. Olly still has tears staining his face and Matilda is one wrong word away from a screaming tantrum.

'What about that water fight, then?' I ask, forcing a playfulness into my voice.

There is not the same whooping excitement as before, but we soon find the fun, the splat of a cold sponge lifting us all, and I try not to think about the relief I feel that Josh has left again, and what that means for our marriage, our family.

One week later

Chapter 30

I got cocky. That's the only way to describe the build-up to the school-uniform shop. Josh left for New York and the children I settled quickly into our routine. It was another week of Saffron by my side, of supermarket trips, days out, dinners at the table, tidying up and bed on time. I let my guard down. There was even a little part of me that felt smug as I pulled into the multistorey car park in town.

School-uniform shopping is a day to be dreaded, and one I've put off for as long as I dare, running the risk that they've sold out of the sizes I need. It's always chaotic. Three children all needing uniform from one shop – one shop! – where the uniform apparel is sold. One poky corner of a shop, twenty different schools, hundreds of parents all needing different colours and sizes of uniform at exactly the same time. It's a gauntlet for mothers – a middle-class supermarket sweep, minus the chirpiness of Dale Winton.

Last year, when all three children needed uniforms for the first time, my mum came with me. She took the children to the nearest park and I walked them, one by one, into the store, got them kitted out and dropped them back to my mum before collecting the next one. Weaving through town, breathless and sweaty, giant paper bags banging into my legs. It took four hours in total and by the end of it, I felt like I'd run a marathon.

'It's only a few minutes' walk,' I say as the twins walk by my side, Saffron a step behind, walking with Olly, ready with her moral support and guidance if I need it, which I really don't think I will. I've been acing our trips to the supermarket this week.

The sun is out, but there's a cool wind that prickles the hair on my arms and makes me wish I'd brought a cardigan. I lead us through the shaded pedestrianised high street, past the market stalls selling pancakes and hot dogs, phone covers and those weird colourful bubble pop-its that are all the rage this summer, all the way to the edge of town and Elliot's Department Store.

It's a three-storey building, all dark shelves, bleak lighting and inane instrumental soft rock playing from a hidden sound system. It's the kind of place that sells classic florals in the women's department and tweed jackets with leather elbow covers in the men's. It's the kind of store that has been around for over a hundred years and hasn't changed much in that time. It's hard to see, as we make our way through the empty make-up department and then the shoes, how this shop has stayed in business for so long. They don't even have a proper website, just a holding page with their opening hours on it and a promise of online orders coming soon, which has been there for at least five years.

And then, up the stairs and right into that poky corner where it seems every mother in a twenty-mile radius has congregated at nine forty-five on a Monday morning. My heart sinks with dismay at the long queue weaving across the second floor all the way into the women's lingerie section, or the big knicker room as Matilda calls it.

So much for thinking we'd be in and out. This, this right here, is how this stuffy old shop stays in business, by monopolising the school uniform of the local private schools and forcing us to stand in line, to wait our turn to be served. I grit my teeth against a rising tide of frustration. I can't even go to the rails myself and pick out what we need.

We join the back of the queue and I feel my confidence falter as I scan the faces of the other waiting mums. I shouldn't have left it this late in the summer. I can just imagine Jessica, Faye, Sarah and Lisa lining up together at eight forty-five on the second week of the summer holidays, ready and poised for when the store unlocks its doors. They'll have had bags packed with healthy snacks and a plan to brunch afterwards. Jessica would've done a list. She'd have made copies too, handing them to each of the women. Everything they'd need, right down to the branded PE socks. Cow!

'Mummy,' Ben says, tugging on my arm. 'I'm bored.'

'It won't be long,' I lie before shuffling us two inches forward. The line ahead hasn't moved but I bunch us closer to the family in front and hope the children won't notice.

'Mummy,' Ben says, whining now.

'Let's play I spy,' I say. 'You can go first.'

'Ben always goes first,' Olly huffs, kicking at the floor with his foot and sighing in full 'Kevin the teenager' mode.

I turn to look at Olly, surprised by his tone. He's changed so much over the last few weeks. He's taller, for one thing; his face has lost the fat of early childhood and there are hints of the man he will one day be. But it's his behaviour that has changed the most. He's so much more willing to help, even encouraging the twins when they start to flag. He's happier, laughing more, smiling. I am too, I think, and I know it's Saffron's influence on us, her order and rules that we are responding too.

Today though, a dark mood hangs over Olly, reminding me so much of Josh on a Sunday night, when thoughts of work take over his mind.

I spy carries us through lingerie and within throwing distance of the uniform department. There are three mums ahead of us and I'm itching to get to our turn. Ben and Matilda are dancing around me, playing a game of tag where my legs are home. Every few seconds, one of them throws themself at me and I'm almost knocked off my feet.

'Ben, Matilda, stand nicely please,' I say, voice firm, aware of Saffron's eyes on me. She's standing a little way off and I wish she'd stand beside me and chat or pull out something magic from her bag that the children will love, but she wants me to know I can do this alone. And I can, I think. I hope.

'What did we say we'd do after we get our uniforms, if you behave nicely?' I remind them.

'Go to the park,' the twins chorus, their feet stopping dead.

'Can we get an ice cream?' Matilda asks.

'Yes, we can.' I smile as she slips her warm little hand into mine and I allow myself a tiny pat on the back, a moment of glee that they've listened to me. And then we're at the front of the line and an assistant steps up to us. She's young – a teenager – with jet black hair and a bored expression on her face. 'Can I help you?'

'I'd like uniform, please,' I say in my most cheerful voice, fighting back the sarcastic retort desperate to escape. Why else would I have stood in this line for an hour?

'Which school?' she asks.

'St Helena's. All three of them.' I wave my hand to Ben and then Matilda, and then Olly; except Olly is no longer by my side. 'Hang on,' I say to the assistant, before spinning around to Saffron.

She tilts her head, pointing to a display of coats with her eyes and I follow her gaze and spot Olly's white trainers poking out from behind the rail.

'If you're not ready, you can rejoin the queue in a minute,' the assistant says, and the mum behind me is already stepping forwards, dragging a little boy with neatly combed hair and a crisp blue shirt along beside her.

'We're ready,' she says. 'We won't be long, will we, Cyprus?' She turns back to the boy and, even though everything around me is unravelling, I can't help but raise an eyebrow. Cyprus? What kind of name is that?

'No,' I say as panic circles around me. 'We're ready now.'

'You're it,' Ben shouts to Matilda, and their game begins again.

There's a shuffling in the queue behind me. Someone tuts. The impatience is rippling around us, but we've been queueing for so long and there is no way I'm missing my slot.

'Come this way,' the assistant says, waving the woman and her son around us. Something snaps inside me. It's the way the assistant is looking past me, ignoring me now. It's the taxi driver all over again, and Josh and his dumping me at the side of the road. It's every waiter I never told that the food was cold or inedible, every hairdresser I lied to that my hair cut was lovely when it wasn't. It's every time I've allowed myself to be pushed aside or ignored.

'No.' I sidestep the woman and her son, blocking their path. 'Sorry,' I say in a tone that suggests otherwise. 'But no. We've queued for over an hour and we're ready now,' I say, before turning to the display of coats. 'Olly,' I call out. 'Come out now. Look, it's our turn.'

There's silence. I feel the eyes of the assistant and the woman and her son, and the mums in the line behind her, all staring at me.

He crawls out, head first, on all fours. His face is tight and angry, but he's listened and, in that moment, I feel pretty bad ass.

'Right,' I say with a tight smile. 'We'd like three uniforms and PE kits for St Helena's school please.'

The assistant nods and leads us to a counter.

'It,' Matilda says, as Ben throws himself into my legs, almost knocking me sideways.

'Ben, Matilda, stand still. This is your warning,' I say. 'Olly, would you come over here, please?'

He ignores me.

'Olly?'

'What?' he snaps.

'Would you come over here, please?' I repeat, knowing I should admonish his tone, but right now I just want to get through this and get out.

He makes a show of taking three long steps and standing beside me, arms folded tight across his chest.

'I don't want a new uniform. I—'

'But your old one is too small now,' I cut in. 'It won't take long. I promise.'

There is a moment when I think he's going to listen, to calm down, and then something flashes in his eyes. A darting look of defiance that I know all too well. He takes a step towards me and before I can move, stop, shout, his little hands have formed two tight firsts and he throws a punch at the top of Matilda's arm, sending her knocking into Ben, who falls back, hitting the floor with a thud.

All hell breaks loose around me. Any moment of bad ass, any sense that I've got this, evaporates with Ben's first piercing scream. I crouch down and scoop him up, hushing him in my arms.

The punch was a calculated move on Olly's part. Minimum input, maximum damage. Matilda's rage explodes. Her face burns red with almost comical speed. It's like a thermostat turning up inside her.

'Olly,' I say, my voice louder than I intend, angrier. 'You don't hit your sister,' I say, before trying again to soothe Ben.

Olly's eyes are fixed on Matilda and he laughs, an annoying 'ha, ha' finger pointing at Matilda's face. It's the final push and, before I can move, Matilda throws herself at Olly, animal-like. He dodges, then waves. Taunting again.

Saffron steps in then. Thank God. She takes Ben from me, cuddling him as though he's the most precious thing in the world.

I swoop up Matilda and calm her down too, fully aware of the assistant still standing by the counter and every single person in the store looking at me.

'Olly,' I say, 'you must not hit. You are going to sit on this spot here for two minutes and when you're done, you will apologise and then we will get your school uniform.'

'No,' he growls. 'I HATE SCHOOL.' Olly's scream echoes across the store. Everyone freezes. Ben stops crying. Even the annoying soft rock seems to have stopped. It's like we're all in a game of musical statutes.

I can't do it, I realise. I really am a crap mother.

Told you so.

The voice is taunting and I have nothing left within me to dispel it.

Chapter 31

I drop the bags in the corner of the kitchen. Two thousand, five hundred and sixty-six pounds on three school uniforms. At some point soon — an hour, a day, I don't know — that cost is going to sting, but I'm too numb, too broken to process it. I slump against the kitchen counter, dropping my head into my hands.

I have no idea how I got through it. How we didn't get kicked out of the store and told never to come back. Olly shouted and raged the whole time, refusing to try anything on. I put him on the reflection spot, as Saffron called it. Where he sat, cross-legged and angry, turning his back to me. I gave up trying to get him measured and bought the next size up in everything. The twins picked up on Olly's mood and were grouchy as they tried their uniforms on, Matilda grumbling about wanting to wear trousers, not the required knee-length, pleated skirt.

Everyone was staring, judging. And I could tell what they were thinking. Why doesn't she just go and come back another time? I wanted to, but Saffron was standing by my side and I had to prove to her, to myself and to Olly, that I would see it through, no matter how long it took.

The shop assistant no longer looked bored, but sympathetic, working as quickly as she could to get our order. When it was done, she patted my hand as she handed over the receipt. A small gesture to mark that we'd been through something together. I had to fight back the lump in my throat as Olly sobbed and hiccupped beside me.

The kettle purrs into life as Saffron bustles around the kitchen. From the living room, I catch the opening theme tune to *Scooby Doo*.

You failed!

You'll always fail.

'I won't,' I whisper to myself, not really meaning it.

'Becca,' Saffron says, placing a caring hand on my shoulder. 'You did well to persevere with the reflection spot. Well done.'

Tears swim in my eyes and I let them fall, dripping wet spots onto my arms. I feel shaky, spent. 'I don't know how it went so wrong. What did I do?'

'Becca,' Saffron says and I lift my head. 'You did really well,' she says again.

'But?' I urge her on.

'Why do you think Olly reacted like that in the store? Why doesn't he want a new uniform?' she asks.

'He was just being difficult. It wasn't the uniform, it was the shopping he hated.'

'It seemed like more than that. He tried to tell you something before he lashed out at Matilda, but you interrupted him.

'It's just Olly being Olly. All kids say that they hate school at some point.'

'Children don't hate school, Becca. Especially not at Olly's age. He was trying to tell you something, and he became frustrated when you didn't listen, which is why he lashed out.'

'It's a fantastic school,' I say, desperate now to make her understand. 'It's the best school in the whole county.

219

Parents send their kids from all over to go there. Some drive for an hour every single day. We live ten minutes away.'

'I'm not saying it isn't a good school. I'm not saying you should change anything. What I'm suggesting is that you listen to what he has to say and show him that you are listening. That you care about his feelings.'

'Of course I care,' I reply, sounding snappier than I intend to. 'Sorry,' I add.

'I know you care, and you know you care,' Saffron says, her voice infuriatingly calm. 'But does Olly know?'

'Yes.'

Saffron cocks an eyebrow.

'What should I do?' I say, wiping my eyes.

'Talk to him. Tell him you're ready to listen and that you want to understand why he is so angry about returning to school. There might be a simple explanation, something you can fix easily. First and foremost, listen. Show him you are hearing what he's saying. Then put a plan in place to address the issues he raises.'

I nod. 'When?'

'Now,' Saffron replies, stepping to the door and calling Olly into the kitchen.

A strange burst of nerves hits my stomach as Olly shuffles in from the living room. His eyes are still puffy from crying and he looks sheepish and downcast.

'It's OK,' I say, to myself as much as Olly.

'Pull up a stool, Olly.' Saffron points at the counter. 'Would you like a drink?'

He nods but there's an uncertainty to it.

A moment later, she places a glass of squash in front of him, including a cocktail umbrella and a paper straw that make Olly smile. 'Thank you,' he says.

'So.' Saffron sits down, resting her hands on the counter. 'Now that we've all calmed down, Mummy and I want to have a chat with you about what happened at the shop earlier. It's important to understand that you can be honest and that you're not going to get in any trouble. This is a chat about you and your feelings.' Saffron looks to me, her gaze insistent.

'That's right,' I smile, resisting the urge to pull Olly into my arms and hug him tight. 'So, what happened today?' I ask. 'Why did you get so upset?'

Olly shrugs.

'Come on, Olly,' I urge.

'Don't know.' He says, folding his arms.

'Olly,' Saffron says. 'If you don't talk to Mummy, she can't help you.'

'Please,' I add. 'I don't like to think of you being unhappy. What made you so upset about getting your school uniform?'

'I hate that school.' His voice is a soft mumble and I lean forward to catch the words.

'Why?' Saffron asks.

'The boys are mean. They don't like me because I don't want to play football with them. They always do things and then tell the teacher it was me so I get in trouble.'

'Like what?' I ask.

'Taking Mr Bubbles out of the water. They did it at break and put him on my chair. I was only trying to put it back when Mrs Harwich came in. And Billy, Sebastian and Leo said they saw me take Mr Bubbles out of the water. I tried to tell them that I didn't, but no one believed me.'

I remember the call from Mrs Harwich. 'There's been an upset,' she said, explaining the situation. 'It's not so much what he did, but that he continues to lie about it.

We really try to be a trusting school, and this behaviour isn't acceptable.'

My cheeks grow red at the memory. How I promised to talk to Olly. How I accepted what she told me, without waiting to hear Olly's side, believing her over my own child.

'I'm sorry that happened,' I say. 'It's not nice when people aren't nice to you. I can talk to the school,' I say. 'I can make sure they know what's going on.'

'It's more than just them,' Olly says. His voice is stronger. He's fired up now. 'I don't like it there. All they want us to do is sports and music. We never do any science, and I really love science and I don't like PE. It's boring. I always get told off for not running fast enough, but I'm trying my best.' Fat tears plop plop onto the counter. The sight of them breaks my heart a little.

'Oh, baby,' I say. 'Don't cry. We can fix this. I'll talk to Mrs Harwich.'

Olly climbs onto my lap and sobs into my arms. 'I don't like it there, Mummy,' he says. 'Ben and Matilda hate it too. Last year, Molly in 2B moved to a different school. I want to try a different school.'

I hold him tight and run my hand over the back of his hair. 'It will be OK. We'll talk to the school. I'm sure they'll be able to help us. Is that OK?'

He nods, hiccupping in my arms, his hot hands clinging to my neck. 'But if . . .' He hiccups again. 'If they can't help us and I still don't like it . . .,' he pauses, giving a shuddering sob, 'can we go to a different school? My new friend, Charlie goes to a different school. We can try that one.' There is so much hope in his voice that even though I can't possibly imagine ever sending the children to a different school, I nod.

'But we need to talk to the teachers first. We need to try and sort things out.'

He sits back, wiping his eyes with the backs of his hands. 'Can I watch *Scooby Doo* again now?'

'Yes, baby. Off you go.'

He gives me a tight squeeze and slides from my lap, and it's only when he's gone that I feel the weight of exhaustion pulling me down once more.

'I had no idea what was going on with the boys in his class,' I say. 'I mean, he's mentioned that he doesn't like them, but I didn't pay much attention to that.'

'And now you've listened, how do you feel?'

'Like a terrible mother.' I scrape my hands through my hair and force myself to look at Saffron. Her face is the picture of sympathy.

'How many times, Becca?'

'What?'

'How many times do I need to tell you that you're a good mother before you believe me? Your confidence is still at rock bottom and I think it's really affected every part of your life, not just being a mother.'

I nod. She's right. 'Thank you.'

'For what?'

'For making me see that I need to listen more.' I bite my lip, fighting back more tears, and it's a relief when Saffron leaves for the day and I pour myself a glass of wine and wish I didn't feel so shitty.

'I'm a good mum,' I say to the empty kitchen that night. 'I'm a good mum. I'm a good mum.'

I wait for a wizard to appear, a fairy godmother to grant me a wish and make everything better, but nothing changes.

Chapter 32

'Becca.' Matt's voice calls from the garden. I look up from the sink and spot him, leaning on the fence, waving me outside.

I smile, ignoring the lingering awkwardness. We've barely seen each other since the night of the curry and dancing. I'm sure Matt's been avoiding me. There's been the occasional wave and brief chats over the fence when the kids are playing outside, but it's not been the same and I've found myself missing our friendship.

'Hi,' I say as I reach the fence.

'Becca,' he says, his face filled with schoolboy excitement. 'First of all, I'm sorry about the other night. I'd had too much to drink and—'

I hold up my hand to stop him. 'It's fine. Honestly. Can we just forget it happened and go back to being friends?'

His smile widens. 'Yes, that's exactly what I was going to say.' And then he pauses, and the silence stretches out, and I find myself wondering if we'll ever make it back to how it was.

'You look very happy about something,' I say eventually.

'I am and it's all thanks to you.' His hand appears from below the fence and he holds out a beautiful bouquet. A mix of red and yellow roses and huge blue daisy-like flowers, sprigs of lavender and fern.

'Wow,' I say, taking the bouquet in my arms. 'You didn't need to buy me flowers. What are they for?'

'So,' he says with a breathless gasp, 'I had the meeting with my agent and editor, and pitched them the children's book series I've been thinking about since I came here. They were really keen and I threw myself into it. I've barely moved from my chair. Look . . .' he turns around. 'Is my bum completely flat, or what?'

I laugh and try not to stare at his perfectly round bottom. At least I know he isn't avoiding me now.

Matt spins back. 'I sent my editor some opening chapters this morning, along with some outlines of future books, and she loves them. We're going to push back the crime book until next year, giving me loads of time to write my first children's book.'

'That's so brilliant,' I grin. 'So, that would explain why I haven't seen much of you for the last week.'

He gives me a sheepish smile. 'Sorry.'

'Don't be. I'm so pleased for you.'

Matt shifts his feet, his gaze moving back to the house.

'Go on,' I laugh. 'Get back to work.'

He grins, and all but runs inside.

In the kitchen, I find my favourite blue glass vase and take my time to arrange the flowers, slotting in one and then another, and moving them to the front and back. I lose myself to the task, my thoughts returning to Saffron's comment about listening, about how important it is to listen and to show you're listening. It sounds so simple, and yet I never listened to Olly's complaints about school, and I certainly never showed him I was listening. Why not? My jaw clenches as I think about all the times I've been posting on Instagram, or faffing around the house, cleaning, tidying, trying to get that perfect photo, and one of the kids has asked for something or told me something, and I've just not heard them. I constantly berate Josh for checking his emails, but am really any better when it comes to social media?

I open up Instagram and scroll listlessly through my feed. What pleasure do I find in losing myself in other people's lives? Fake lives too. I only have to look at my own photos to know how far from reality they stray.

Somewhere along the way, I told myself that this is the world we live in, that everyone does it, but that's not true. I've been telling myself that my business needs to be on Instagram, that I need to keep my 10K followers by posting imaginative photos and interesting content for Rebecca Harris Interiors, and yet the steady flow of work I had before the summer all came from the little advert I put in the shop window in the village, then word of mouth after that. I have a website if people want to find me online. I don't need Instagram.

I swallow hard, take a long gulp of wine, then I press my finger onto the app until it shakes on the screen. I press delete. It disappears immediately, leaving me a little bereft but determined too.

Now what?

I think of Olly again. How I should've listened. And then I think of Josh. Our weekend of trying and failing and trying again. Of all the weekends, the months, the years. When was the last time we talked? Properly talked. Not just the day-to-day monotony of our lives. The 'This Saturday, Olly has a swim badge to complete,' or 'Can you grab some milk on the way home?', 'Where are my cufflinks?', 'Is Matilda too old to be sucking her thumb?'

We used to talk all the time. Josh used to call me on his lunch break and we'd chat for ten minutes, then again after work for longer. Even when we were first married and living together, he'd still call just see how my day was going and tell me something about his. After Olly was born, my days were exactly the same. Feed, nappy, crying, sleep. Repeat. I stopped answering his lunchtime calls, telling him I was too busy, but it wasn't that. It was because I didn't have anything interesting to say. I wish I'd kept picking up.

But it's not just talking that we're failing at, it's listening too. I unlock my phone again and call Josh. It rings seven times before cutting to voicemail.

I stare at my phone for a long time, willing Josh to call me back and knowing he won't. It's four o'clock in New York. I picture him at his desk or in a meeting. Other images come uninvited. The woman from the funeral with the glossy hair. The secretary he mentioned. A young, pert New Yorker showing Josh the city, knowing him well enough to answer his mobile.

He's having an affair! It's so obvious.

No! I shove the images away. I close my eyes, despair, frustration, a wrenching loneliness. It's all there. But how can we listen to each other when we don't talk?

I open Josh's name on WhatsApp and flick through our two-, three-, four-worded messages back and forth. And then I stare at the voice note icon. All I need to do is hold it down and speak.

He won't listen.

He won't care.

'Yes, he will.'

I drop onto the sofa and press the voice icon. There has to be a start, an olive branch, a change. Our marriage might be alright on the surface, but beneath it? I don't know if it's rotten or just gone completely.

'Hey,' I say, feeling more than a little ridiculous, talking to myself. 'I know you're busy right now and I'll be asleep

227

by the time you're finished for the day, but I thought . . . I thought I could record a voice note to you now and you can listen to it when you're free.'

I take a breath. Now I'm doing it, I don't know what to say. 'You wouldn't believe how quiet the house is. It's so weird with the children in bed. I don't think I realised how exhausting it was having them awake so late. I thought it would tire them out so they'd sleep later, but the weird thing is, now they're asleep by seven thirty, they don't wake up until seven. I didn't realise how much they needed that sleep, and how important it was to have some time in the evening without them. I think you did, though. I think you were frustrated that they didn't have a proper bedtime. I'm sorry about that. Letting them stay up was the easy thing to do, but when they were around me all the time, it meant I wasn't alone in the evening to realise how lonely I am. And I am lonely.' I sigh but I keep going.

'Saffron talked to me today about Olly. She thinks he's frustrated a lot of the time because we − I − don't take the time to properly listen to him. She made me sit down with him and talk about school and what he thinks about it. It really helped me to understand him better. And it got me thinking about us and how we don't listen to each other either, do we? How can we when we barely talk? We're in this marriage together, raising this family together, and yet most of the time I feel alone . . . I feel lost.' That word again. I swallow hard. It's the first time I've said it out loud.

'I don't even know what that means, just that I'm not sure who I am anymore. There's a new neighbour who's rented Greg and Glynis's house for the summer. It was someone I went to school with. It was so weird bumping into him. He reminded me of who I used to be. God, that sounds like I'm going to start dressing and acting like a teenager again, doesn't it? I'm not! It's more that I used to have this total certainty back then of who I was and who I wanted to be.

'Being a mother . . . it's amazing. I wouldn't change it for the world, but it's taken something from me, a sense of self that I don't know how to get back. My interior design business helps, but I know you think it's just a hobby. A little game to keep me entertained. Sometimes it feels like you see my life as being one big holiday, where I can do whatever I like, while you're the only one working and sacrificing. And that's not true. Every day, I sacrifice another piece of myself just to get up and do the same shit over and over again.

'I feel like an ungrateful bitch for saying all this. And I'm not. I am grateful. We've got a beautiful home and three beautiful, healthy children. We've got this amazing life here . . . but . . . I . . . I still feel so fucking lost.'

Tears blur my vision. I move my finger away and the voice note pings its way around the world in an instant. I don't know if Josh will listen to it, properly listen. I don't know if he'll reply or call me, or anything, but as I climb the stairs to bed, I feel better, lighter. It's a start.

Chapter 33

I wake to bright sunshine streaming through the curtains and the sound of Ben and Matilda chatting softly in their bedroom. There's padding of feet and more talking. Whispers that are as loud as shouts. Giggles.

I smile, picturing Ben slipping into Matilda's bed to play and talk.

My phone is on the bedside table and I pick it up, remembering with a wave of anxiety that I deleted Instagram last night. The void it's left behind feels ridiculously huge this morning. But when I see a reply from Josh on my home screen, all thoughts of social media are forgotten.

I turn onto my back and open the message. It's a voice note. A reply. My smile widens.

'Hey, Becca,' he says, his voice deep and quiet. I close my eyes and I can almost believe he's lying next to me. 'It's midnight here. I've just got back to my hotel room after a tedious client dinner at some stupid high-rise restaurant that revolves while you're eating. I went to the toilet at one point and when I came out again, the table had moved. It was ridiculous and swanky, but all I wanted to do was drink a pint of water, grab a hot dog from a street vendor and go to bed.'

He pauses, and I hear him gulping back a drink. 'I really liked your voice note. I liked hearing your voice. I've listened to it three times now. I . . . I didn't realise you felt lost, Becca. I thought you were happy. Seriously,' he pauses for a moment and there's a rustle of covers. 'I thought you had everything you wanted – the house, the car, the family. I guess you're right, we haven't been doing a very good job of talking lately.

'For what it's worth, I'm sorry if I made you feel like I didn't believe in your business. I guess my jokes landed a bit flat there. The truth is, I was worried you were taking on too much when you already felt so stretched from the kids. I didn't want you to feel like you had to build up some amazing business to prove anything to anyone, because it wasn't like we needed the money. I didn't stop to think about it from your point of view. I won't make jokes anymore. I'm proud of you for setting up your own business and doing what you love. I'm actually pretty jealous.'

I start at that. Jealous. Why on earth is Josh jealous of me?

'I know you're wondering why,' he continues, and I smile again. 'It's because you're following your dream and you're so passionate about it. You get to do what you love. That must feel amazing.

'I wish I was there with you right now. With you and the kids. I wish I didn't have to spend all this time away from you. I don't just mean New York. I mean all of it. The long days, the working at weekends. I wish there was another way.

'Do you want to hear something crazy? I feel lost too. Completely, in fact. But it's late and my alarm is going to go off in just under five hours and I need to sleep. Good night, Becca. I love you.'

I listen to the message again, and the rise and fall of Josh's voice, before I reply.

'Hey, sleepy head,' I say. 'I hope you got some sleep last night. Thanks for your note. I can't believe you feel

231

lost too! I thought you were a proper grown-up – you know, someone who has their life together, rather than just pretending at this adulting. Is it New York that's making you feel that way? You're over halfway now and then you're home with us again, everything how it was.'

My insides knot at my words. Back how it was, but it won't be, because even though things aren't perfect and I'm still learning every minute of every day with Saffron, how to be a better a parent, we've changed. The children have changed; I've changed. Even just bedtimes have made a huge difference. I think forward to school starting and those days to myself, then the evenings too – empty space stretching out before me. The Becca of July would have craved that time, but when I think of it now, all I see is the loneliness.

'God, we're really crap at talking, aren't we?' I continue. 'I've just woken up and I'm alone in my bed. I know it's the best thing for them and for us, but I miss the early-morning cuddles. I really think one of the reasons I let things get so out of control was because when everything is so chaotic, I don't have time to stop and think, or realise how lonely I am.

'Saffron is coming over again today. I wish you could meet her. She can be . . . pretty forthright. There's no hiding at the back of the class. But she's also really kind and perceptive, and she's taught me a lot about how to be a better parent. We're having a toy clear-out today. Can you believe it? The children are really excited to be having a big tidy-up.

'She's really helping me, too. She thinks I've lost my confidence. I don't know where it's gone.' I bite my lip. 'That's not true. I think . . . I think I found motherhood so much harder than I thought I would, so much harder than everyone else seemed to find it. It's like, from the moment Olly was born, everywhere I looked, there were mums who knew exactly what they were doing. Mums who'd paired off in their groups, friendship coming to them as easily as the night feeds and nappy changing and knowing exactly what every cry and wail meant. I know that's probably not how it was, but that's how it looked to me.

'I went from being a designer – being good at my job, loving every day, knowing exactly what I was doing – to being a mother, and feeling like a failure overnight.'

The sound of a door crashing open drags me back to the present.

'The monsters are awake. I'd better go. Love you.'

He won't listen. He won't understand. He's going to think you're crazy. Bet the girls in his office don't talk about losing their confidence and feeling lonely.

'Shut up,' I say to the empty room, throwing my phone on the bed and kicking off the covers. The air is warm and sticky with the start of another heatwave. I dress quickly, slipping on a summer dress I've not worn for years. It's blue and light and floaty, and I don't even care that it's short and shows off the pasty white of my legs.

By midmorning there are piles of toys everywhere – kitchen, bedrooms, living room, hall. I'm kneeling on the living-room rug, working my way through the wall of toy boxes. Olly is running between us with a clipboard. He sorted his toys out first, donating some old Spider-Man figurines. Now Saffron has given him the task of making lists of all the things we're donating and he's taking the job very seriously.

'Matilda is giving five teddies to the toy sale.' He runs out of the room and then back again a moment later. 'Make that four,' he says, with a shake of his head.

'I love Gertrude too much,' comes Matilda's defiant shout from upstairs.

'That's OK,' I call out as Olly disappears again and my phone buzzes with a message. Another voice note from Josh. I stand up and stretch out my back before stepping into the garden to listen.

The air is thick with heat, the sun fierce. I sit in the shade and open the message.

'Hey, Becca,' Josh says, sounding brighter than he did last night. 'I'm eating breakfast right now. Excuse the munching. I ordered room service. My hotel room is so corporate, I might as well be sleeping in an office. It's so depressing. But at least I get a few extra minutes on my own before I have to leave for the actual office.

'I liked waking up to your voice. The confidence thing is . . . I don't know how to say it, but yeah. I think you're right. I think you have lost your confidence and I wish I could make you see that you are still the amazing, brilliant woman you were when I met you, and you are an amazing mum. The children and I are lucky to have you.

'I've been thinking about how we argued at the weekend because you thought I was having an affair with Rachel because she answered my phone. You do that a lot, you know? Think the worst of me. I think it could be connected to your confidence. It makes me sad that you think so little of me that you always assume I'm cheating on you, or don't want to spend time with you. I know I'm out of the house so much and I'm home so late, I could be doing anything but, Becca, I'm only ever working or coming home to you.' He sighs. 'I'd better go.'

There's a pause when I think he's hung up, but then he speaks again. 'Fuck, I hate this. I hate everything about it. I hate how our clients are all money-grabbing bastards,

234

and the bosses don't give a shit if you work yourself half to death, just as long as you meet your monthly figures.

'I don't know how I even ended up in this job. It was never what I wanted to do. It's not just being here, away from you and the kids, that makes me feel lost. It's this job. I hate it.

'Look, I need to go. I like doing this though. Send me a note later. Love you.'

The message ends, and I'm left staring at my phone. I feel boosted by his compliments, his reassurance that he loves me, but I'm surprised too. There was a sadness to his voice I've not heard before.

I look down at my phone, wondering how to reply, when I notice two other messages have come through. The first is Mum.

Hello Darling, just to say that you are doing brilliantly!!!
I can see it's hard but you're really making progress. You've
cracked bedtimes!! Looking forward to having the kids for
a sleepover in September. Love you xx

A sleepover? Wow! Mum has never offered before and I've never asked. How could I, when I knew how badly the children behaved at night? It's another reminder of how different things are now. I smile, already thinking of a hotel break, just me and Josh, as I open up the second message, surprised to see Lisa's name on my screen.

Hi Becca, how are you? I know we've not spoken properly
for ages, but I wanted to tell you that I think what you're
doing with the kids is really brave. I've been watching The
Toddler Tamer videos and learning loads too.

I know we were never close in the friendship group and
I'm sorry about how it ended. (I'm not really part of that

group anymore either.) I guess I found it scary how much you had your life together. Your house was always so tidy and your life so perfect. Anyway, I wanted to say well done! And also, if you fancy a coffee sometime, let me know. xx

I stare at the message for a long time and then I laugh at the stupidity of it all. I never felt like those women understood me or even liked me, and yet how could they, when they only saw the Instagram version. I'll reply to Lisa later and maybe we will meet for that coffee one day, after the summer is over.

I've always thought it was the chaos of three children that kept me isolated from other mums, but maybe it was me. The thought rolls around my mind as I step back inside.

Chapter 34

Josh and I continue our voice notes throughout the week. It feels like one long conversation, a heart-to-heart we should've had over a glass of wine late into the evening instead of via WhatsApp and three thousand miles apart. But we're talking, and I no longer lie awake at night, torturing myself with thoughts that Josh wanted to be in New York this summer, or has a mistress tucked away somewhere.

The heatwave is in full swing now. The sun glaringly bright and scorching in an azure clear sky. It's relentless. Day after day of heat. The plants are wilting, the grass turning a dusty yellow. Even Saffron has donned a light maxi dress. Her hair is still immaculate in its bun and her make-up perfect, but it's nice to see a softer side to her. She still thinks I'm holding back on something, not giving it my all. I don't know what else she wants from me. I'm trying so hard.

Matt has taken to popping in most days, teasing me about my dance moves, and Saffron about her music choices. Sometimes I catch him looking at Saffron as though he's trying to figure something out. It makes me wonder if he likes her. Then, other times, he barely says more than hello and I think I'm wrong.

Yesterday, Matt dropped by with a pack of ice creams for the kids and the opening chapter of his children's book, asking if we would read it. Olly took the job very seriously and even wrote a review for Matt, which made him laugh. 'From now on,' he said, 'I want all my edits to come with stick-men drawings.'

Matt's still bouncing with energy and it's a welcome relief from trying to sift through the mess Josh and I have found ourselves in.

At night, when the air is muggy and unbreathable, and I can't sleep, when I have no Instagram to scroll through, I listen to the voice notes, one after the other after the other, and wonder if we're making progress, if we're really listening to each other or just pasting over the cracks of our relationship in a different way.

I roll over in bed and check the time. It's 1 a.m.. I wonder about calling Josh. It's 8 p.m. in New York. Something holds me back. I don't know if these voice notes are helping, but we're finally talking to each other and, as ludicrous as it sounds, I'm not sure speaking on the phone is going to help right now. We're both lost and I don't know how we'll find ourselves, let alone each other.

Instead, I open our message feed and listen to the notes again. Me, then Josh, then me, then Josh. Then me again:

'Hey,' my voice is soft, quiet. I recorded it in the garden after putting the kids to sleep. 'You're right. I shouldn't always assume the worst. There's a part of me that wonders why you wouldn't have an affair. I mean, you're handsome, and still have a killer body – although, I don't know how, considering how many biscuits you eat every day. You're smart and funny when you want to be. You're a catch, Josh. And you work in an office with beautiful women every day. Why would you want to come home to me?

'I think part of it is how we met. Knowing I was the other woman. I think it's left an insecurity there. I'll try harder not to always jump to conclusions. I do trust you.'

Josh's reply had come that night: 'Oh, Becca, you were never the other woman. You were the only woman. Tania and I had been dating on and off for a year when I met you. We hadn't been on holiday together; I hadn't met her friends or family. We went on dates now and again. That was it. The relationship was going nowhere. When I saw you across the bar in that red dress you wore to our disco the other day, everything about you blew me away. Even before I plucked up the courage to talk to you, I knew I would never see Tania again. I felt more for a complete stranger standing on the other side of the room than I ever did for her. I called her the next day and told her it was over. There was no cheating, no agonising over which woman I loved. It was always you, Becca. I wish I could find a way to make you see what I see in you.' He pauses and, in the silence, I hear the sound of traffic moving around him, a car horn blasting, an engine idling.

'I know I'm a crap husband,' he says, after a moment. 'A crap dad. It eats at me how little I see of you all. I wish I could quit right now and come back.'

I recorded my message the second I heard his. 'You're not a crap dad or a crap husband. You're just busy and you work hard and that doesn't leave much of you for us. I try to understand. I know I was hard on you at the weekend. It's stupid to still be angry about it, but I don't think I'm quite over being dumped in west London and being given two days' notice on the New York trip. I don't even know if it's you I'm angry at or myself for being such a push-over. I'm sick of feeling like a doormat, Josh.

'You keep things hidden from me too much and then you drop these bombshells on me, like early this year when you waited until I was about to book us a holiday to Majorca in the summer, when I'd spent weeks researching

239

the best resorts and prices, and I was literally standing at my computer with a credit card in my hand, and that's when you tell me you've not had the time off approved because of a big merger coming up. And New York. You knew about that for weeks and didn't tell me. How? I don't understand how you could keep it from me, or why you do it. It's like you don't trust me to handle what you've got to say. Sometimes I feel like we're on different planets.'

'Becca,' Josh said in his next voice note, his tone apologetic. 'You have every right to be angry with me. You're right. I keep things from you. I don't mean to. I don't even know why I do it. The New York trip was eating me up. It's just . . . You were so happy about my one day off a week, and being able to work in the summer holidays and get a break, and I felt terrible. I knew I was letting you down and I knew you'd be upset and so I just . . . God, I'm a coward, but I couldn't upset you like that. Even though by the time I had to tell you, it was so much worse. I'm so sorry. I'll try harder. No, that's pathetic, isn't it? I will tell you things as soon as they come up.

'In fact, I'm going to start right now. They want to extend my trip by another few weeks. I'll be back mid-September. And there's talk of another New York trip in December. Just a few weeks this time. I'll be home for Christmas, of course. God knows why they like me out here. I'm so grumpy and miserable. I think they think I'm joking when I say things that aren't jokes. The other day, I told this finance guy that his spreadsheets were an abomination. The guy clapped me on the back and said he loved my British dry wit. I wasn't joking.' The street sounds fade and I picture Josh stepping into a building. 'I'd better go. I love you.'

New York in December? His words hit me hard. He'll miss Ben and Matilda's first nativity. He'll miss Olly's choir concert. He'll miss decorating the tree and seeing the kids sit on Santa's knee at the village Christmas Fair. I want to rant into a voice note. I want to tell him that there are only a finite number of magical Christmases, of infectious excitement, of the delight on our children's faces, their wholehearted belief in Santa.

But I bite it back. It will only make Josh feel worse, and, besides, he missed all this stuff last year when he was only working in the London office. The thought causes a despair to sweep over me. I didn't realise how much I was looking forward to him coming home either. And now it's not weeks away but nearly another month.

Josh left me another voice note before I'd found the words to reply. 'I can't sleep,' he says with a long sigh. 'I've missed hearing your voice today. I really am sorry about being back here in December, Becca. I really don't want to. I'm so unhappy here.

'I was thinking in the shower just now about our honeymoon in Italy. Remember that winery where we stopped for lunch and got completely plastered? We ended up getting a room for the night. It had that huge walk-in shower and we took one together. My shower is a bit like that. It made me think of you and us, and how much I miss you. Good night, Mrs Harris. Please message me back.'

I did, of course. How could I not? His sadness seeped out of the phone and into my thoughts, and I didn't feel angry about his second trip to New York. I just felt desperately sad. I thought the voice notes were helping us, and yet, all they've done is shone a light on the cracks in our marriage, in our lives.

So much has changed this summer. Saffron's time with us is almost at an end. There have been points when I thought I'd never be able to go it alone, but deep down I know I'll be fine without her. Seeing how well the children have responded has boosted something inside and while it's going to take time to get my confidence back, I feel stronger now than I have done in a very long time. I don't hear that voice in my head as much now, and when I do, it's easier to ignore.

But with Saffron leaving and the twins starting school, and Josh still away, it feels like we're at a tipping point, a moment when something will need to change in our lives. I don't know what that thing is, only that it's looming and I don't know yet if it's going to be good or bad.

Chapter 35

It was nearly dawn by the time I fell into a listless sleep, and by morning my head is a fog of Josh and voice notes, the kids, and the things I need to do today. I scoop up the basket of folded washing from the utility room, thinking how fast the days are passing. I don't feel like I'm the same person who cried all those weeks ago at the thought of an entire summer of just me and the children. Now, we're racing towards the new school term. Only two weeks to go. And even though I'm looking forward to going to back to work, there is a big part of me that will miss the days we've spent together.

I sidestep a row of Hot Wheels cars Ben is playing with in the hall, and then Rex, who is sat, tail flicking on the bottom step. Rex is gazing up at something on the stairs and I look up to see a pigeon. A very big, very grey pigeon, sat in the middle of my stairs.

I scream. Startled not scared. The pigeon coos, hopping up a step. Rex's tail flicks menacingly and she draws her body into a crouch, ready to pounce.

'What is it, Mummy?' Olly appears from living room, Matilda behind him.

'It's fine. It's just a pigeon. Rex must have brought it into the house. I just need to shoo it back out.' I say with more calm than I feel as I place the washing basket on the floor.

'Oh, I saw that,' Ben says with a nod, like we're admiring a piece of artwork.

'What do you mean?' I risk moving my gaze from the pigeon to Ben.

'Rex brought it in and left it on the stairs. I was going to tell you but then I forgot.'

I snort a laugh. Trust Ben to forget to mention a giant bloody bird in the house. The noise startles the pigeon, who flaps its wings before hopping up another step.

I lurch back and Matilda gives a little scream.

'It's fine. It's completely fine,' I tell the children, tell myself more like. It's only a bird.

There's a knock at the door. The three efficient taps that tell me it's Saffron. Thank goodness. She can help me. Olly springs forward and throws it open.

'Morning,' Saffron sings, stepping into the hallway and shutting the front door. 'How is everyone?' Her gaze moves to each of us in turn and I can see the question forming on her face before she asks. 'What's going on?' She's smiling but uncertain too.

'Rex has bought a pigeon into the house,' Olly says, pointing to the stairs. 'Mummy got scared and screamed.'

'I wasn't scared. I was surprised,' I retort. It's only a bird for God's sake. It's clearly more terrified of us than we are of it. Even so, I'm grateful for Saffron's presence. I have no doubt she'll take over any second, pulling something out of that bag of hers that will help. Is a net too much to ask? And the children and I can charge into the garden and wait until it's all over.

Except Saffron doesn't take charge. She doesn't do anything. She seems to have frozen. We're all looking at her expectantly, but her face has drained of colour and her panicked eyes are fixed on the pigeon as though at any moment it's going to grow ten foot tall and eat the lot of us.

'Are you OK?' I ask.

Her eyes dart to mine. She gives a small shake of her head before pressing herself against the wall, as though she might be able slip right through it.

'I have a phobia.' Her words are a gasped whisper. Every part of her appears petrified.

'Really?' I ask.

'It's called ornithophobia.' The look on her face is a mix of terror and pleading, and I feel a wave of sympathy for her before realising that there is only one person who is going to get this pigeon out of the house – me.

'OK,' I say. 'Don't worry. I've got this.'

You haven't!

'I've got this,' I repeat.

'Mummy,' Olly says. 'What's or-nee-phobia mean?' he asks, saying the word slowly, as though trying it on for size.

'It means Saffron is very scared of birds. She's going to wait outside while I catch it.'

'I'll help,' Matilda says, throwing her Barbie to the floor. I love her fierceness, but the Barbie clattering on the wood scares the pigeon who flaps its wings again and hops up another step. It's almost at the top of the stairs now.

Saffron yelps at the flapping before giving a furtive shake of her head and sinking to the floor. 'Can't move,' she whispers, tucking her head into her hands.

I take a breath. 'Right,' I say in a low voice. 'Kids, we need to stay calm so we don't scare the pigeon any more than it is already. Ben, I need you to take Rex and shut her in the utility room for a minute, then I want you to come back and sit with Saffron. Make sure she's OK. And tell her when it's safe to look.

'I think the pigeon is injured or stunned, otherwise it would be flying,' I continue. 'What I need is . . .' I cast my eyes at the washing pile, before looking to Olly. 'Can you go into the garden and get the two towels that are sitting on the table?'

Olly nods, scooting away.

'What about me?' Matilda asks.

I lift the washing out of the basket and place the pile on the floor, before handing the basket to Matilda. 'Can you hold this for me, please,' I say. 'We're going to try and trap the bird in the basket and carry it outside.

'Like how we catch spiders with a glass and a piece of paper?' she asks, stepping carefully forwards, and again I'm bowled over by her strength.

'Exactly.'

'Hurry up, please,' Saffron begs. There's a wobble to her voice I've never heard before.

Poor Saffron. I don't have a phobia and even I am more than a little freaked out about trying to catch this pigeon.

Olly appears and hot on his heels is Matt. Behind him is another man – he's got Matt's dark hair and cheeky smile, but he's smaller – a more compact version – and it can only be the little brother Matt has mentioned a few times. Matt and Olly both have a beach towel tied around their neck like a cape, one arm lofted in front of them.

'Matt has come to help,' Olly grins.

'And this is Liam.' Matt waves a hand at his brother.

'Hi,' I say. 'It's nice to meet you. We've er . . . just got a situation here.'

'I've come to the rescue,' Matt says doing a rather ridiculous superhero pose.

'I'm not sure how many people it takes to catch one bird, but if there's anything I can do, I'm happy to help,' Liam says, his eyes falling on Saffron and Ben.

'Liam, this is Saffron and Ben. They're not keen on birds. Perhaps you could keep them company and if the bird comes back this way . . .' I trail off. I don't know what I'm asking, but Liam gives a salute.

'On it,' he says, already striding to where Saffron and Ben are crouched.

I turn back to Matt. 'I'm not sure how that cape is going to help,' I say with a roll of my eyes.

'It's all about looking the part,' Matt replies.

'Fake it till you make it,' I grin.

'Exactly.'

In the corner, Saffron gives a whimper and I remember why we're all standing here.

'Where is the offending bird?' Matt asks.

Matilda points to the top step of the stairs where the pigeon is now sat, as frozen as Saffron.

'Wow,' Matt takes a step back. 'I was thinking sparrow. That's . . . That's as big as my mum's Yorkshire terrier.'

I give an exasperated sigh. 'Don't tell me – you want to sit in the corner too.'

'Noooo,' he shakes his head. 'Let's do this.'

Olly and Matt pull off their towels. I can tell by Olly's face that he's having second thoughts about bird-catching. I smile at him and nod to the where Saffron and Ben are sitting. 'Olly, would you mind helping Liam and Ben look after Saffron for us.'

Olly's face breaks out into a relieved smile and he scurries to the corner by the front door, dropping down on the other side of Saffron and patting her hand. I hand a towel to Matilda and take the wash basket from her, and slowly – very slowly – Matt, Matilda and I creep up the stairs.

'It's a bit like the *Scooby Doo* episode when Fred tried

to catch the swamp monster,' Matilda whispers, her little voice filled with excitement.

Matt snots a laugh and I give a huffed exhale. It's the nerves, I think. The absurdity of two grown adults and one four-year-old trying to catch a pigeon who has found its way into the house.

By the time we're halfway up the stairs, the three of us are shaking with silent hysterics. I risk a glance at Matt and see he's biting his lips, tears rolling down his face. My stomach cramps with the laughter I'm desperately trying to keep inside.

'Concentrate,' I hiss, but my attempt at stern comes out all wrong and we laugh even harder.

'Have you got it yet?' Saffron shouts from below us.

'Almost,' I say, voice soothing now. 'It's OK,' I coo to the pigeon. 'We're here to help you.'

Another step closer and I lift the basket, ready to trap it, but it senses the movement and hops with surprising speed onto the landing before disappearing around the corner.

'The pigeon is scared, Mummy,' Olly says from the step below me, clearly keen to join the fun now. 'It's going to keep moving away from you. You need to get it into a corner first, then it won't have anywhere to go.'

'Good idea,' I smile. 'Will you help me?'

Olly grins and hold up another towel. 'Ready.'

Ten minutes later, the pigeon, whom Matilda has now named Frank, for reasons only she knows, is backed into the corner of my bedroom and we've formed a wall around it, towels and basket lifted high. I'm convinced, as I drop the basket over the bird, that it will die of a heart attack long before we've managed to get it outside.

Olly whoops silently, jumping up and down, and suddenly our wall is toppling, and all four of us land in a heap on the floor, all tangled legs, laughter and relief.

We scramble up and I grin at the kids. 'Well done, guys. Let's get poor Frank into the garden, shall we?'

With some jiggling, we manoeuvre the basket so it's the right way up and cover it with a towel before Matt takes it from me to carry down the stairs.

Saffron whimpers as we reach the hallway, her perfect make-up gleaming with sweat.

'We've got it,' I tell her. 'Another second and it will be outside.'

'Is the pigeon going to die, Mummy?' Ben asks. He stands and follows the procession through the house.

'I hope not,' I reply. 'We'll put it in the garden for a minute and see if it flies off; otherwise we can find a rescue centre to look after it.' For some reason, it feels important that we don't let Frank die.

The moment Frank is on the grass, he hops to the other side of the lawn, and a second later, he flies away as though nothing happened.

The three children dance around, all wearing towels for capes. 'We did it, we did it,' they sing.

'Thanks for that,' I say, turning to Matt.

He laughs. 'I don't think I was much help. You had that covered.'

'You were great,' I insist.

'Next time I'll be on my game.'

I laugh and pull a face. 'Next time Frank comes to visit?'

He grins. 'Exactly. Right, I'd better check on Liam . . .' he nods towards the house.

'And Saffron,' I add.

We find them in the kitchen, Saffron sitting on one of the stools, Liam handing her a glass of water. They're talking very fast about something and it takes me a moment to figure out what it is.

'That one with an actor who plays a security guard,' Liam says.

'So easy. The cat lady was harder.'

'Have you tried the new spy—'

'The secret of the spy? No,' Saffron gasps. 'But I want to.'

'Me too.'

It's then that I notice Liam's t-shirt. It's black, and written in the middle, in white writing, is a list that reads: Eat, Sleep, Escape, Repeat, and suddenly I remember that Saffron loves escape rooms and by the look of Liam's t-shirt, so does he.

I feel a hand on my arm and look back. Matt is motioning me outside, and I step away and we sit on the patio instead.

'Is your brother single?' I ask.

Matt nods. 'He's always been pretty shy. Never met the right one, I think.'

'He didn't seem shy just then.'

Matt looks thoughtful for a moment and then nods. 'It's funny because when I was talking to Saffron the other day, I was thinking about how nice she was and I did wonder if I should try to set her up with Liam, but I didn't want to interfere.'

'Oh,' I say, laughing at my mistake.

'What?' Matt asks.

'I thought you liked Saffron.'

'Me?' Matt shakes his head. 'I mean, she's lovely, but she deserves someone who is young and fun, and I'm way too old and way too grumpy.'

I laugh at that. 'True.'

'Hey,' he swipes my arm. 'Actually, I've been chatting to Laura a bit.'

'Your ex?'

He nods. 'Nothing definite, but we're talking. I think moving here and seeing how committed you are to your marriage, even when times are tough, has made me realise that relationships are an investment. It's not something to give up on when you hit a rough patch.'

'That's true.' I nod and think of Josh. It doesn't feel like either of us is giving up on our marriage, but I still don't know how we'll move forward either, or how long we'll last if we stay as we are.

I shut the thought down. There is too much going on right now to be thinking like that.

'Is it safe to come out?' Liam calls from the kitchen.

Matt and I shout 'Yes', and Liam appears with Saffron behind him.

'Thank goodness.' Saffron gives me a weak smile and collapses into one of the chairs, just as Olly, Matilda and Ben rush towards us.

'Well done, guys,' I say. 'You all did such a good job of helping to save Frank.' I hold out my hand and high-five them, Olly first, then Matilda.

'Did I help?' Ben asks, looking hopeful.

I wrap my arms around him, hugging him tight. 'Especially you. If you hadn't put Rex in the utility room, she might have tried to eat Frank.'

'You were OK too, Mummy,' Olly says, voice earnest.

'Oh, praise indeed from my eldest child,' I laugh. 'But I'll take it.'

'Can we use the washing basket, Mummy?' Olly asks.

'Sure. What for?'

'We're going to play bird-catching.' And with that, they race off, laughing and talking, and I turn my attention back to Saffron.

'Are you alright?' I ask.

She nods, her gaze flicking quickly to Liam and then back to me, before tucking a stray hair into her bun and regaining her composure a little. I think of Saffron, the Toddler Tamer – this woman who has her shit together, who is fierce and straight-talking, and who is always, always right – and then I think of the Saffron who lives at home with her parents and brothers and sisters, who is terrified of birds, who is looking for someone special to share her life with, and I realise how young Saffron is, how even though it may sometimes seem like she has everything worked out, she doesn't. I lean over and give her a hug.

'That was great praising just now,' she says a moment later.

'Thank you,' I reply.

'I mean it, Becca. You listened to Olly. You asked for help. You worked as a team. You praised each other.'

'I'm surprised you managed to see all of that from your crouch by the front door,' I tease.

'Ha ha,' she says, rolling her eyes and smiling too.

'Seriously though, are you OK? If you need to go home, just go. We're fine.'

Saffron's face lights up in a smile. 'You are, aren't you?'

I grin back. 'Thanks to you.'

Saffron fixes me with a stern look. 'Thanks to who?'

'Me,' I concede.

'Exactly. You did all the hard work. Which is why today is my last day for a week.'

Something sinks inside me. I knew it was coming. After my idiotic misunderstanding during Saffron's first visit, I actually sat and read the paperwork she gave me. 'DIY week?'

'Yes,' she smiles. 'Do It Yourself week. It's time to put all those fantastic techniques you've learned into practice on your own. I'll come back next week and we can talk about any slips or problems you've encountered. And I'm always one phone call away.'

Matt and Liam stand up to leave. There's a lingering moment when Liam doesn't move, and then he drops his gaze and waves goodbye.

'Oh no,' Matt says. 'You do not walk away from a woman as amazing as Saffron without getting her number, mate.' Matt slaps Liam on the back before pushing him forward.

Liam's cheeks flush pink but he looks at Saffron with a hopeful smile and she laughs. 'This is so unprofessional,' she says, shooting me an apologetic smile.

'It's fine,' I grin. 'Go for it.'

When numbers have been swapped, and Matt and Liam have gone, I make cups of tea, and Saffron and I sit in a companionable silence that makes me realise how much I'm going to miss Saffron. I think somewhere in these mad weeks, we have become friends. Saffron is sweet and funny, and she has an innate ability to see a whole situation, as though her view on everything is bird's-eye, while the rest of us have tunnel vision. She speaks her mind, and there have been times when it's been hard to hear, but looking back, she's always been honest and supportive.

I think of how I no longer wake up and dread the day ahead with the children. How much happier we all are, how creating boundaries and rules has somehow created more laughter in the house, more fun, more hugs, more everything. I think about how grateful I am for that.

Chapter 36

'Christ, it's nuts here,' Josh says in his latest voice note. 'Yesterday, I realised I'd gone all day without drinking anything. Not a single thing. There hadn't been time to grab so much as a sip of water. I feel like I don't sleep so much as pass out with exhaustion at the end of the day, then get up and do it all again.' He sighs heavily and I feel a pang of sympathy for him. 'Anyway, that's not why I'm leaving you this note. I've been thinking a lot. And . . . well, I don't want to say too much now, but I've got a surprise for you. For you and the kids. You'll get it at the weekend.'

I play the note to the children over breakfast and as they crunch on their cereal, they delight in guessing what the surprise could be.

'Chocolate,' Ben says. 'A humongous, gigantic bar of chocolate.'

'I think it's going to be a new Barbie,' Matilda says, with all the certainty of Olly telling me he doesn't need the instructions for a Lego set he's going to build, and me digging them out of the bin an hour later.

'It won't be a Barbie. They're rubbish,' Olly says. 'That wouldn't be a surprise for all of us, would it?'

'They are not rubbish.' Matilda huffs. 'You are rubbish.'

I fight a smile at Matilda's boldness and give her a warning. The moment is forgotten, and when Olly suggests the surprise will be a puppy, they all clap their hands and agree, leaving me wondering if letting them guess was such a great idea after all. Will they be disappointed at the weekend when a bouquet of flowers arrives instead of a fluffy ball of fur? Oh God, what have I let myself in for?

I let the children record a reply to Josh. It's all shouts and talking over each other, garbled excitement, before I step into the quiet of the garden to tell him I miss him.

The day unfolds in games of snakes and ladders, and playing in the paddling pool. After lunch, Olly disappears into his bedroom. 'I've got my own surprise. Don't come in,' he says, narrowing his eyes in an attempt to be stern. 'It's top secret.'

The hours pass and I leave a snack outside Olly's door, which disappears at some point. It's not until nearly dinner time that he appears in the kitchen, hair ruffled, but smiling.

'It's ready,' he says, grabbing my hand and slipping his fingers through mine. They're soft and warm and insistent as he drags me up the stairs and into his bedroom. 'It doesn't work every time,' he says, biting his lip.

'It doesn't matter. I can't wait to see it either way,' I encourage.

'Close your eyes,' he says and I do, before he guides me carefully into his bedroom. 'You can open your eyes.'

Before me is a gigantic mess. Toys and books and dominoes are stacked everywhere. There are Lego towers and Lego men balanced on rulers. It's chaos, and as I perch on the end of the bed, I wonder if there was a way to peek into Olly's mind, if this is the scene I would see.

'Ready?' Olly asks. His eyes are wide as he looks at me. He's nervous and I give him a reassuring smile and nod.

Olly pulls a single clear-and-blue marble from his pocket and presses it into my hand.

'Put it there,' he says, pointing to a piece of orange Hot Wheels track sloping down from his lamp onto his bedside table. And that is when I see that it isn't chaos at all, it's an intricate chain reaction, one thing leading to another and another.

'Like this?' I ask, placing the marble at the top of the run. He nods and I let it go.

Olly whispers a 'Come on' under his breath as the marble starts to roll down the orange piece of track. At the bottom, it hits a line of twenty or so dominoes that snake around his lamp and fall with a click, click, click. The final domino knocks into a Lego man in a space suit, who is pushed from the drawers, landing on a see-saw made with a ruler. The end flicks up and knocks a Hot Wheels car, sending it flying down a loop-the-loop and shooting through the air.

'This is where it goes wrong sometimes,' Olly says, clutching my hand.

When the car hits a stack of books on his drawer unit, Olly shouts a 'Yes', fist-pumping the air, and I grin, my eyes fixed on the books, which topple forwards, nudging into a Lego wall, which falls forwards and hits more dominoes. Click, click, click. The last domino hits a Lego Batman who is tied to a piece of string. He jumps from the drawers, swinging fall circle and coming back to the drawers where he hits Olly's yellow toy crane, which whirs into life. The end of the crane swings around with the Lego Batman attached at the end and smacks the light switch on the wall. The light above us turns on just as the Lego Batman drops to the floor and lands in his Bat car.

'Ta da!' Olly says, his smile wide, and I pull him onto my lap and squeeze him tight.

'Olly,' I gasp. 'That was amazing! Really, truly amazing. I'm so proud of you.'

'It took ages. I kept knocking the dominoes over and setting the whole thing off. It's called a Rube Goldberg machine and is about creating something complicated to do something simple.'

'It's brilliant. Where did you learn that?'

'I read it in my *Big Book of Knowledge*.' His face is alight, beaming. It's the happiest I think I've ever seen him.

'I wish I'd recorded it to show your dad. He'll be so amazed too.'

'Will he?' Olly looks uncertain for a moment and, for first time, I wonder how much it affects the children to have a father who is absent so much. I hold him tighter and kiss the top of his head. 'One hundred per cent, yes. We are both so proud of you, always. This is amazing.'

He hugs me back before jumping to his feet. 'I'm going to reset it and show Ben and Matilda, and you can record it.'

'Great idea.'

I step into the hall, half expecting to see Saffron smiling at me, giving me all of her 'present in the moment' pep talks and praise. I wish she was here. Or Josh. I wish someone was here to share this moment.

That evening, the heatwave burns itself out and plump purple clouds roll across the sky. I leave the children to get dressed into their pjs before hurrying outside to collect in the washing. I grab at shorts and t-shirts, and little pants and socks, as a deep rumble of thunder sounds in the distance. The air around me seems to change from hot to cold on a single gust of wind.

I pick up my pace, stuffing everything into the washing basket, pegs and all. The first drop of rain hits my head as the last of the socks are thrown into the basket. Before I can take a step towards the house, the downpour starts. Sheets of rain fall from the sky, soaking me and the washing in an instant. I start to run, one step, then another. Already the dry ground is waterlogged and my feet slip and squelch.

My foot slips and I stop running to steady myself. And then I see the futility of running. I'm already soaked to the skin. Drenched, bedraggled. I drop the washing basket, hold my hands out and tip my head up to the sky, laughing at how everything can change in the blink of an eye.

'Mummy,' Olly shouts over the gush of the rain. 'What are you doing?'

'I'm standing in the rain,' I yell back with a grin.

'Can we come out?' Matilda asks.

I look at their clean faces, neatly combed hair and fresh pjs. Then I laugh again and nod, and Olly and Matilda rush outside to join me.

Ben is hesitant, standing in the doorway. Desperate to run out but weary too.

'Is there a storm?' he asks.

'Not yet. Come on. It's fun.'

And it is. We dance around each other, skidding and slipping in the rain until we are all shivering and giggling. Matilda starts singing 'Let It Go' and we all join in. I pick them up one at a time and twirl them around until a rumble of thunder sounds in the distance.

'Come on, kids. We'd better get inside.'

We drip muddy footprints on the kitchen floor as I grab a stack of towels to dry us, before warming three cups of milk. For once, the mess doesn't bother me. It won't take long to clean up when the children are asleep. Besides, it's only me that will see it, and I realise I no longer miss Instagram and the constant feeling of needing to document my life in such a way that made it seem like we were something we weren't.

I laugh out loud as realisation dawns. We are now the family I've been pretending to the world that we are. It's taken me stopping painting a picture for the world – or my followers at least – to truly achieve it.

When the milk is drunk, I read the children a story before kissing them each good night.

We are almost the family I was trying to paint, I think, as I clean up the footprints and put the washing back in the machine. I love the children so much, I love how close we've become over the summer. And yet there is an emptiness. I no longer feel so lost, but I don't feel complete either.

Chapter 37

Friday dawns overcast. Flat and grey, but dry after a night of storms. The children are still buzzing with ideas for what Josh's surprise could be. We're all feeling a little stir crazy and so, after breakfast, we bundle out of the house, Olly wobbling on his bike and the twins on their scooters. We're only going to the village green and the little playground that sits there, but it feels somehow dangerous to be out like this, just me, no Saffron, no car to contain the children in. What will I do if one of them runs off?

I take a breath and quieten the voice of doubt.

They won't run off. And, if they do, I'll handle it, I tell myself.

'Don't go too far ahead,' I say, and Olly brakes slightly, sending a wave of relief through me. 'And stop at all the roads.'

We make it to the green without incident and I feel a rush of triumph, wishing Saffron was here to see it. Someone to talk to. But it's just me, and the loneliness of that realisation sinks through me. Do I want Saffron here because I need her help, or her company? The latter, I think, before rolling my eyes at how pathetic it is that I'd rather have a twenty-something know-it-all telling me all the things I'm doing wrong, just to have some company, than be on my own.

The park is quiet. There are two children playing on the swings. The older of the two is a boy around Olly's age, with shaggy blond hair, and the younger is a girl, wearing a blue silk Cinderella dress, long blonde hair blowing in the wind. Their mum is sat on the bench with a pushchair beside her, her nose buried in a book.

'Charlie,' Olly yells, swaying perilously on his bike as he tries to wave. 'Mum,' he says, just as loudly, 'It's my friend Charlie. Remember the one I told you about?'

I nod, smiling at his excitement.

'That's Isabelle too,' Matilda says, as she and Ben drop their scooters to the grass and charge towards the play area.

'Play nicely,' I call after them, my voice lost to the shouts of 'Hi' and 'Look at me' from all five children who immediately launch into a game of the floor is lava, leaping from one piece of play equipment to another. Every few minutes, one of them will drop their foot to the floor, causing wails of protest and screams of delight.

I record a voice note for Josh, telling him about the storm last night and dancing in the rain, rambling on about nothing really, but it's everything, too.

When I'm finished, I slip my phone into my pocket, remembering Saffron's advice about preparing the children to leave places. 'Ten more minutes,' I call out, glancing at the sky above me and clouds threatening rain.

'OK, Mummy,' Olly shouts back.

The woman from the bench looks up at me with a pleading smile. 'I don't suppose there's anything I can do to bribe you into staying a bit longer?' She has strawberry blonde hair, the same colour as her children, and freckles that brush across her nose. She's wearing Burgundy dungarees and a grey t-shirt. Bright purple Birkenstock flip flops have been discarded on the floor beside her and one bare foot is jiggling the pushchair. There's an upturned book on her lap, with a bright pink cover, and she's smiling as she looks at me.

'Don't judge me, will you?' she says, tapping the book, before I can reply. 'Reading is my only escape from the madness.'

I laugh. 'No judgement from me. Anything to escape, eh?'

'I think only mums of three or more children fully appreciate that sentiment. I'm Amanda, by the way.'

I smile my agreement. 'Becca. How old?' I ask, nodding to the pushchair, before sitting down beside her.

'Six months. He's not much of a sleeper though. Night time is party time according to Dylan. I'm hoping for another half an hour of sleep before the tornado which is my baby descends on us again. So, if I could bribe you into staying a while longer, because your children are the first thing that has stopped the "I'm bored" chant of the older two all summer. I think they met each other when my husband, Richard, brought them to the park a few weeks ago.'

'Yes. I've heard a lot about Charlie. How old is your son? He looks the same as age as Olly.'

'Charlie? They're eight. Charlie isn't a boy though.'

'Oh, sorry. I just assumed.' I look back at the child chasing Olly across the climbing frame. The blond hair is short, cropped around the ears. The outfit is boyish too. A Ninja Turtles t-shirt and blue trainers.

'Honestly, don't apologise. Charlie was born Charlotte, but by the time they could grab things, and make their own decisions, it was clear that Charlie didn't identify as a girl. They don't want to be a boy either. They just want to be them, and today that is Ninja Turtles and blue trainers. Tomorrow it could be a rah-rah skirt and football boots.'

'I can't imagine all parents would be as relaxed about it as you are.'

'We're the black sheep of the village, that's for sure. All the snooty mums here who shove their kids into St Helena's, or St Hell-ena's as I like to call it.' Amanda adds a posh accent and I laugh, before cringing because I am one of the snooty mums.

'Your kids go to the village school?' I ask.

Amanda nods. 'Yep. We all love it there.'

'Are they accepting of Charlie?'

A grin widens on Amanda's face. 'Yes. The head teacher is amazing. She adores Charlie and always uses the "they", "them" pronouns. All the teachers are brilliant too and the children just follow suit. It's a lovely small school, a big family really. What about you? Are you local?'

'Yes,' I nod. 'We're at the edge of the village, and also black sheep.'

'Really?' She leans forward, delighted by my confession. 'Why?'

I roll my eyes and laugh. 'My children are pretty wild. We used to be friends with some of the snooty mums but I got cast out after an incident with Olly and a Sharpie at a play date.' My cheeks burn with the memory of it. 'Think black pen and white walls.'

Amanda tips her head back and roars with laughter, and for the first time I laugh too as I share every gory detail. By the end of the story, we're both doubled over.

'Oh God,' Amanda sighs. 'I've laughed so hard my boobs have sprung a leak.' Amanda clutches at her chest with one hand and wipes her eyes with the other.

'Mum,' a voice calls from the playground and I turn around to see Charlie hanging from the railing. Up close, I can see the same spread of freckles on Charlie's face as on Amanda's. They give me a wide smile before turning to Amanda. 'Can Olly, Ben and Matilda come for lunch? I want to show Olly my dinosaur collection.'

Amanda raises a 'what do you think?' eyebrow at me.

'We've got no plans, but I don't want to impose. I could take your number and we can arrange something another time, if that's easier?'

'Mum doesn't have a phone,' Charlie says in the tone I know so well from Olly when he can't believe I don't know something.

'I do,' Amanda protests with a grin. 'I just can never find it. And, in answer to your question, you won't be imposing at all. Come for lunch. We only live there,' she adds, pointing to one of the Tudor cottages that border the green. 'You'd be doing me a favour actually. Your kids can entertain mine while I feed Dylan and get some sandwiches made.'

'I can make sandwiches,' I offer, remembering the juggling act of baby feeding, and how the women I thought were my friends watched me struggle, curious, pitying, but rarely offering to help.

'Even better,' Amanda says. 'Come on then, troops. Let's go.'

Charlie leads the way, with Olly following a step behind. I wheel Olly's bike with one hand and carry the twins' scooters with the other as Ben, Isabelle and Matilda hold hands and run to catch up with the older ones.

'Your kids seem totally normal to me, by the way,' Amanda says as we reach the edge of the green.

'Thanks.' A lump forms in my throat and I swallow it away, telling myself to get a grip. 'They are,' I add. 'Most of the time.'

'Kids are kids,' Amanda says with a shrug. 'Sometimes they do dick things, but so do adults.'

I burst out laughing. 'I think you might be the wisest person I've ever met.'

'If that's true then I'm sorry to say that you are in serious trouble.'

As we walk, Amanda tells me she used to run a livery for an estate in Suffolk. 'I miss the horses but not the snobs. I'm desperate to work with horses again and dream of owning my own stables, but I don't know if it will ever happen.'

Charlie takes the key from Amanda and opens the front door. The kids burst through, scattering their shoes across the floor before disappearing upstairs. I push the shoes to one side and help Amanda with the pushchair.

'I like to think of it as homely,' she says, scooping a gorgeous Dylan from his seat, his wide, sleepy eyes blinking in the change of scene. There are coat hooks behind the door, three deep with coats and school bags, and an over-flowing rack of shoes below it. 'But that's just code for a bit of a mess.'

'It's not at all,' I say. 'It's how a home should look.' I mean every word as I follow Amanda into a kitchen with colourful drawings and certificates covering the fridge, and homemade pottery bowls on the shelves, and I realise how sterile my own house must look in comparison.

'Right, you,' she says to Dylan as she drops into a chair. 'Milk time.' Amanda unhooks her top and a hungry Dylan nuzzles her chest. I feel a pang of nostalgia for the breast-feeding days. At the time, I moaned constantly about how much my nipples hurt, how I felt like a cow. I rushed through it, grateful to move onto bottles, and yet, looking at Amanda now – the bond she has with Dylan – I feel I missed out on something.

'I'm desperate to get him to take a bottle,' Amanda says, as though reading my mind. 'But he's a right fussy one. I'm going to be feeding him until he can hold a cup, and my boobs are down by my knees.' She laughs, before waving a hand at the kitchen. 'Ignore the colour scheme. I'm trying to decide what colour to paint the cupboards. I think this one,' she says, nodding her head to an off-white, stone-coloured door. What do you think?'

I look around at the kitchen. It's a square room with an L-shape of cupboards and a sink. There's a huge American-style fridge-freezer opposite the cupboards and a long table with benches along the sides and chairs at either end. The kitchen is tiled with rustic orange, dark blues, light grey and greens, like a farmhouse kitchen, I think. The cupboards are dusty white after being sanded, and one door has rows of colour swabs on it in white and navy, sage and stone.

'The navy on the bottom, the stone on the top,' I say, without a moment of hesitation. 'You've got both colours in the tiles and having the two colours will bring the kitchen together.'

I feel Amanda's eyes on me for a moment before she shifts Dylan to her other boob and looks back at the kitchen. 'Oh my God. You're right. That's exactly what it needs. I couldn't see it. I just kept thinking it needed one colour. You should be an interior designer.'

I laugh. 'I am.'

'That explains it then. You'd better watch out or I'll be dragging you around the rest of the house. It's a work in progress.'

A shout carries from upstairs. 'Mum,' Charlie calls down. 'How long until lunch?'

'Soon,' Amanda calls back.

'Let me make some sandwiches,' I say.

As Dylan continues to feed, Amanda gives me instructions on where to find the bread and the secret stash of

266

biscuits she hides from her husband. Ten minutes later, a picnic feast is piled on the table and four hungry children appear, Olly and Charlie first, then Ben and Matilda, who is now wearing a pink princess dress to match Isabelle's blue one.

'Mummy,' Olly says, tugging my arm and looking at me with serious eyes. 'Don't call Charlie he or she, OK? It's they or them.'

'I know, baby. Thank you. Hi, Charlie and Isabelle, I'm Becca.'

'Hi,' they chorus.

We're halfway through lunch when the front door bangs open and a man appears in the kitchen. He's tall – six foot three at least – and wearing dark blue overalls. He has a thick blond beard and a broad smile. 'Hello, troops,' he says.

'Daddy,' Charlie and Isabelle shout. He steps to the table and kisses the tops of their heads.

'Richard, this is my new friend Becca. She lives in the village and her kids go to the snooty school, but we won't hold it against her because she's just fixed our kitchen dilemma.'

Richard raises his eyebrows. 'Wow, at last. I thought we'd be living like this forever. Thank you, Becca. Entire months of agonising over with. It's nice to meet you.' His eyes drop to the table and I see recognition cross his face. 'It's Olly, right?' he says.

Olly nods, mouth full of food.

'And Ben and . . .' He clicks his fingers. 'Matilda. We met in the park with your daddy, Josh.'

They all nod as Richard turns back to me. 'I bonded with your husband over a love of gardening and a dream of wanting to spend more time outside.'

'Sounds about right,' I smile.

Now what's spare to eat?' He grabs a plate and piles up the remaining food, making sure to add an extra sandwich onto Amanda's plate too. 'Hey, where did these biscuits come from?'

'Never you mind,' Amanda laughs before turning to me. 'Richard is a plumber so if you ever spring a leak, you can call him, day or night.'

'It's not like any of us sleep in this house at the moment, is it?' he says, scooping Dylan into his arms with one hand and eating a sandwich with the other.

Richard makes us all cups of tea before heading back out the door, and Amanda I stay in the kitchen until long into the afternoon, Dylan at our feet, shuffling on his bottom with a toy train as the other children play upstairs.

'You must really miss, Josh,' Amanda says at one point. 'I don't think I could live without Richard. I see him at lunchtime most days and we speak on the phone at least twice, and he's home by five.'

'It's hard sometimes,' I say, feeling suddenly bereft and longing for a life I don't have, one I'll never have.

Chapter 38

On Saturday, we make robot costumes out of boxes and play in the garden. I take a photo of the three of them, boxed up and grinning, and print it straight away, sticking it on the fridge, before moving the reward charts to join it, happy to see just how many stickers Olly, Ben and Matilda have.

I stand back and gaze at my kitchen. Where I thought the personal touch would look messy, it actually adds a sense of happiness to the room, and I smile and think of Amanda, who texted me this morning to suggest another play at the park next week, which I readily accepted.

The day drags on and we are all jumpy by 3 p.m., listening for the doorbell and the surprise Josh has sent us. It's close to bedtime when we finally hear a noise. It's not the doorbell, it's a key in the lock and the door sliding open.

Olly jumps up, and delight lights up his face as races to the top of the stairs, shouting 'Daddy', before running down and throwing himself into Josh's arms. The twins follow, hopping and jumping, before all three of us are hugging Josh and he's smiling wide and kissing us all.

'Hey,' he says. 'I've missed you all so much.'

There's a split second of awkwardness, when the children step away and Josh moves towards me. We are still the same people we were before he left after his last visit, and yet we have exposed a part of ourselves to each other that has left a rawness between us.

He takes my hand and pulls me into his arms, hugging me tight. 'I've missed you,' he whispers in my ear.

'Me too,' I say, and I mean it. 'What are you doing here?'

'Surprise,' he says. 'I was missing you all so much, so here I am. Since I'm not officially back for three more weeks, I thought another visit was in order.'

'Daddy, daddy,' Matilda pulls at his arm. 'Will you read our story?'

'Of course.'

'Can I have a fireman's carry upstairs?' Ben asks, jumping up at Josh.

'Me too,' Matilda and Ben chirp.

'OK, OK. One at a time.'

He turns to me, kissing my cheek. 'There's more,' he smiles. 'Let me put the kids to bed. Fix us both a drink and I'll come down. I need to talk to you.' There's a buzz to Josh's expression, an excitement I've not seen for so many years. He looks younger, I realise, despite the tiredness. He looks like the man I met fifteen years ago, and I wonder fleetingly if he's been given a promotion.

Thirty minutes later, Josh appears in the doorway, tired but still buzzing with something. He's showered and his wet hair is pushed to one side and dripping onto his t-shirt.

'I can't believe how much they've changed this summer,' he says with a sad smile. 'You've worked some miracles with them.'

'Blood, sweat and tears rather than miracles, but thanks,' I grin. 'So, come on then,' I say, pushing a glass of gin and tonic towards him. 'What's really going on? How long are you back for?'

There's a pause, and finally he nods slowly. I swallow, feeling the weight of something in the air.

He takes my hand and guides me to the sofa in the living room. Then he strokes my cheek and leans forward. Our lips touch and we kiss for a long time. When he pulls away, that same energy is dancing in his eyes. 'I love you, Becca. I know I'm a crap husband and a crap dad—'

'You're not.'

'It's OK. I know I am. It's taken me a long time to realise this, but in talking to you over our voice notes, I've realised that I'm very, very unhappy.'

My throat tightens. He's leaving me. Oh God. A wave of emotion hits me hard. Tears brim in my eyes. 'We can work on us.'

He gives a huff, an almost laugh. 'It's not us, Becca. We, us, are rock solid, I hope.'

'Then what? Your job?' I ask, remembering the way his voice cracked when he'd talked about his job last week.

He nods.

'Is this about getting another job? There must be hundreds of hedge fund manager positions out there.'

'It's not the company,' he says. 'It's the work. I hate it. I don't even know how I found myself working in an office to start with. I keep asking myself how I went from studying agriculture at university to sitting at a desk for ten hours a day. And I think, after my degree, I was sick of being broke, and my friend started working in the city and it looked from my impoverished-student state like he was rich, and so I applied for a few jobs and I got one. It was only supposed to be for a few years. I was going to build up a nest egg and start my own business. Then I got a promotion and then I met you and fell in love, and then it was holidays and marriage and children and . . .'

'So, it's my fault you're unhappy?' I ask with a frown.

'No, Becca, No. You and the kids are the only thing in the world right now that makes me happy. It tears me apart that I'm not here, and when I am here, I know I'm not giving you everything.'

'So, what are you saying?'

'I'm saying . . . I want to quit my job. I want to start my own business.'

'Doing what?'

'Gardening, and eventually landscape design. I want to go back to university and study for a Master's in landscaping. Just picture it, Becca: you can design the inside of houses and I can do the outside. I'll be home every evening for dinner and to help with the kids. It won't be long days apart. I'll be here for all of it.'

My heart is racing in my chest. I can't believe Josh is saying this. 'But what about money?' I ask. 'The mortgage. The school fees.' Our life.

He gives a slow nod, squeezing my hands in his. 'We'd have to make some changes.'

'What kind of changes?' Panic flutters in my chest. I gaze around at my perfect living room. My beautiful home.

'We'd have to sell this house and buy something smaller. A do-er upper, for starters.'

My heart is racing, pounding in my thoughts. I can feel Josh's eyes on me, an eager puppy waiting to see how I react, but all I can think about is how we can't sell this house. It's my dream home. All the work I've put into it.

'And the children will have to leave St Helena's,' Josh continues, sounding a little less sure of himself. 'We'll have to send the Land Rover back and get something smaller.'

There are no words.

It feels like someone has turned out all the lights and I'm floundering in the dark.

Josh has lost it. The stress, the exhaustion, it's pushed him into some kind of midlife crisis. He can't seriously be asking me to throw our whole lives away.

'I've seen this house that could be perfect,' Josh is pushing on. He hasn't noticed my silence, my panic, and I want to scream at him to 'read the room', but I still can't talk. I can't believe he's doing this to me again – dumping something monumental on my lap and just expecting me to accept it. 'Let show you.'

The 'No' dances on my lips. Never. No. Nope. Not in a million years. But all I can do is shake my head.

Josh opens a property page on his phone and tilts the screen towards me. The house in the image is a white detached house surrounded by an overgrown garden. 'The house itself is smaller. But it has some decent land so there's room to build out eventually. The land will be so handy. I'd be able to keep all my tools and machinery there. And the kids will love having a big garden to play in.'

'Machinery?' My voice sounds distant. Josh wants to uproot our family, our entire lives to become a gardener? I can't wrap my head around it.

'I'll need a lot of kit. A sit-on lawn mower, a wood chipper. I've been running some numbers and if we sell this house and make some cutbacks, then we can afford to buy this house, or one like it, and live off the money from the sale for a year while my business builds up, and yours too, of course.'

'Mine?'

'Yes. Your interior design business. If I'm home more, then we can share childcare and you'll have more time to work. That's what you want, isn't it?' He looks at me then with so much hope, so much excitement that I feel crushed under the weight of what is to come.

'I . . .' My mind is spinning. 'I mean, this is quite a surprise, Josh. You've really sprung this on me.'

'Have I? But you've been listening to my voice notes, haven't you?'

'I knew you were unhappy, but I thought that was being in New York.'

'Well, it's not.' The atmosphere around us becomes charged. We're one wrong word away from an almighty row that I don't want, but I don't know what to say either.

'What about your job? You've not handed in your notice yet, have you?'

He shifts on the sofa and a space forms between us. 'No. I wanted to talk to you first and see out the rest of the New York trip. And leave after that. You don't seem happy. I thought you'd be happy.'

'Josh,' I cry out. 'You're blindsiding me again. You can't seriously be expecting an answer now? I need to think about this. We need to talk through what it means in more detail. This is our whole lives, our home, the children's future. You can't expect me to go along with it. I need time to think.'

'What's there to think about?' he asks, looking exasperated and desperately sad.

'Everything,' I snap as anger rises inside me. 'You're asking me to uproot our entire lives so you can become a gardener, which, by the way, is something you've never mentioned to me before.'

'I have.'

'You haven't. I know it's something you're passionate about, but I thought it was a hobby. This . . . I'm sorry, Josh. This feels like a midlife crisis.'

274

He leaps up and starts pacing the floor in front of me. 'So, your answer is no then, just like that? No consideration for me and my happiness?'

'Are you seriously asking me to give you an answer right this second?'

'Yes, I am. I don't see what there is to think about frankly.'

A hot rage burns through my blood. All I can think about is how Josh has dumped this on me. 'You're right. There is nothing to think about. The answer is no.'

'Fine.' He strides from the room, taking the stairs two at time. I watch him go, before stepping outside and sitting in the garden. I can't be in the same house as him right now. A quiet fury continues to hum through me.

I struggle to process what just happened. How did we go from happy and kissing to an argument that feels so final? How can he ask me to change everything, to up and leave his job, without talking to me first, without giving me the chance to even think about it? This is our life. This is what we've made. We're happy. He can't just expect me to throw that all away on a whim because, out of nowhere, he wants to be a gardener.

I flop onto the lounger and the fuming continues. He's being completely unreasonable. Dumping this massive change on me after promising that he wouldn't do that anymore. Then he has the audacity to be angry with me when I don't nod my head like the obeying little wife he wants me to be.

The sky is darkening by the time I step back into the house. I'm still angry, but the time to think has cleared my thoughts, and I see now that Josh has got carried away with the unhappiness of being in New York. He'll calm down. We can talk properly, and he'll see things from my point of view.

I want Josh to be happy. I hate it that he's not, that he loathes a job which takes him away from us for so many hours, but I'm sure there's a middle ground. A change, but nothing so drastic as selling the house and pulling the children out of St Helena's.

I reach our bedroom and expect to find him sitting on the end of the bed, contrite and ready to talk again. But the bedroom is empty. So is the study. I walk through the entire house. The kitchen, the living room, the den, Olly's room, the twins' room. The children are fast asleep. Olly buried under his covers, Ben in his foetal position and Matilda star-shaped and covers kicked to the floor.

Josh is nowhere.

I climb into bed, expecting him to come home in the early hours and pull me into his arms, but he doesn't.

Chapter 39

It's not until Olly comes bouncing into the bedroom at 7 a.m., lofting a note from Josh that I realise he's gone.

> To Olly Boy, Matilda-Moo and Ben-Boo,
>   I had to take an earlier flight back to New York. I'll see you in a few weeks!
>   Love you lots,
>   Daddy xxxxxxxxx

Tears sting at my eyes as I read the note, the realisation dawning that Josh has flown back to New York less than twelve hours after arriving home.

All morning, I rage at the injustice of his behaviour. He left because of our fight. Once again, he tried to dump a last-minute change on me, wrong-foot me into giving up my home, moving to some run-down dump so he can cut grass for the rest of his life. No. Not this time. I may not be Double Trouble anymore, that fierce girl, but I refuse to be a doormat either. This is the life we've built. This is our home, our family. I won't allow him to throw it away on a whim, a fucking midlife crisis. The selfish bastard. Why can't he buy a soft-top sports car like every other man in his forties who has a crisis of confidence about his career.

My anger throngs through me for the rest of the day. I'm snappish with the kids and they respond to it with their own fury, squabbling with each other, refusing to tidy away their toys. Very quickly, my distraction and short temper sets a raging war in the house, where alliances are made and broken between the children every few minutes.

Everything has fallen apart, like a giant house of cards that took weeks to build and seconds to fall. I wish Saffron was here and at the same time I'm glad she's not. It's humiliating how badly I'm failing.

Of course you're failing. You didn't seriously expect to cope without Saffron, did you?

When Ben scurries away from the reflection step for throwing his dinner on the floor, I let him go. It's a mistake, and things move from bad to worse.

'Matilda is a poo poo head, poo poo head, poo head. Matilda is—'

'Olly,' I shout to be heard over the singing and Matilda's angry wails. 'Stop that. It's bedtime.' This isn't true. Bedtime was hours ago. It's nearly nine o'clock. I'm tired, done in.

'No.' His voice is full of indignant outrage. It's the first time I've seen his face screwed up like this for weeks. Another reminder of how epically we've fallen from any semblance of routine today.

'STOP IT. STOP IT. STOP IT. STOP IT,' Matilda screams.

'NOOOOOO. You knocked over my Lego machine.'

'I didn't mean to,' she says with a hiccupping sob.

My head is pounding. I'm still so angry with Josh for blindsiding me and for leaving without saying goodbye, but I'm teary now too, shutting myself in the bathroom or hiding in the kitchen. Why hasn't Josh left me a voice note? Why hasn't he said sorry? He is the one in the wrong here, isn't he? I banish the doubt from my thoughts.

'Yes, you did. Now I'm going to kill one of your Barbies.' Olly runs from the hall and into Matilda's room. She screams, sprinting after him.

'Kids,' I say, my voice lost to their shouts. I chase after them, passing the bathroom and catching sight of Ben. My feet stop dead. Olly and Matilda's fight drops to the back of my mind as I see the carnage before me.

Ben is sitting in the middle of the tiled floor, wearing only his pants. And all around him is a gloopy white and pink mess. Horror sinks through me as I spot the empty bottles of shampoo and conditioner, bubble bath and tooth-paste littering the floor. My stomach knots at the sight of more mess on the sink and the walls, splatters of colour that make me want to scream.

'Ben,' I cry out, 'what's going on?'

'Matilda and Olly wouldn't stop fighting so I'm making a slide all by myself.' He looks at me, his face set. There is no glee or joy, just a hard determination, a blame that this is my fault.

It is!

Before I can say another word, he flops onto the floor, belly first and skids around.

'You need to—' My words stop at the sound of a thump from Matilda and Ben's bedroom. But it's the silence that follows that sends a chill to my core.

I run into the room and find Olly on the floor, clutching his head. Matilda is standing over him, red-faced but anxious. It's gone too far. My arrival pops the shocked silence and they both burst into noisy tears.

There is nothing to do but sink to the floor and pull them into my arms and hug them tight as my own tears fall.

'It's OK,' I say, as much to myself as to Olly and Matilda. 'It's not been a good day for anyone, has it?'

279

I feel their heads shaking from side to side against my body.

'Let's all say sorry to each other and read a story before bedtime. Tomorrow will be better.' I sigh, heavy, sad. I let the anger of Josh's visit go. We'll sort it out somehow when he comes home for good. Or maybe we won't, but what matters right now – what matters always – are the children. 'I'm sorry,' I say, kissing the top of their heads.

'Sorry,' Olly mumbles.

'I'm sorry too,' Matilda adds.

I pull them closer and then Ben is in the room. 'I'm sorry too,' he says, and before I can stop him, he steps forward, still dripping with the contents of the bathroom, and drops into the middle of my lap, hugging all three of us.

'Ewwwww,' Matilda says. 'You're slimy.'

'Gross,' Olly adds, but something in the air has changed as I look down at my soap-covered t-shirt, and I laugh.

The humour is contagious and a moment later we're all giggling and huffing at Ben and the mess.

'Come on,' I say. Let's run a bath and clean up.'

The children trail after me, Olly gawping at the state of the bathroom. They stand in the doorway as I scoop handfuls of wet, sticky soap into the bath and run the water. When it's run, all three climb in, delighted by the mountain of bubbles.

It's nearly ten by the time the children settle in bed.

A bone-aching tiredness pulls through me and I drop onto the top step of the stairs and lean against the wall. What a mess I've made of everything. Tonight, today, has been an epic fail, and it's all my fault. I didn't do a single thing right.

There's nagging feeling in my thoughts, like I've got something else wrong but I'm too tired to think about it now.

I miss Saffron. Even her nagging and her clapping. I'm really not sure I can do it without her.

Of course you can't!

That voice. I thought it was gone for good.

I'm half-wondering if it's too late to call Saffron and cry down the phone, when there's a light tap at the door. A single knuckle. Quiet but insistent.

My heart lifts. Josh. It has to be.

I race down the stairs and throw open the door, the smile already on my face.

Chapter 40

It's not Josh. It's not Saffron either. It's Matt. He's standing on the doorstep in jeans and a white polo shirt. His hair is a mop of curls, wayward and grown longer in the time he's been here.

My smile drops and I realise with a mounting humiliation that he'd have heard every scream and shout through the open windows 'I'm sorry,' I blurt out. 'They've gone to bed now so you'll have some peace.'

He shakes his head and gives me that sheepish smile of his. 'That's not why I'm here. I have noise-cancelling headphones. If I want silence, I've got it. I'm here because . . .' He trails off, holding up a bottle of white wine, condensation glistening on the glass. 'I thought you could do with a drink?'

I look from Matt to the bottle and the emotion pushes up and out, and I sob right there on the doorstep.

'Hey, hey, hey.' Matt steps forward, wrapping me in his arms. His body is firm and warm, and I cry against his t-shirt; great heaving sobs.

Matt rubs my back and lets me cry it out. Only when I calm down and pull away does he make a face. 'Not quite the reaction I was going for.'

I snort, half sob, half laugh. 'Sorry.'

'Stop saying sorry, OK? Everyone is allowed to have bad days. It's OK.'

I nod and wipe my hands across my face. I look down and realise my vest top is splattered with Ben's gloopfest in the bathroom. I'm a mess.

'You don't have to invite me. It's late. Just take this,' he says, pressing the wine bottle into my hands. 'I'm here if you need me.' Matt steps back.

'Thank you,' I say. 'I . . . I'm a bit of a mess, but if you want to come in, I could do with the company.'

A smile lights up his face. 'You got it.'

I open the door wide and he steps inside. There is no peck on the cheek or lingering looks. We are passed all that. Friends. That's all. And I'm glad he's here.

'You'll never guess what?' he says in a conspiratorial whisper.

'What?' I ask in the same voice as Matt follows me to the kitchen, where I scoop up two glasses before stepping into the garden.

'Liam and Saffron are on a first date tonight.'

'Really? That's brilliant. I hope he treats her nicely.'

Matt laughs. 'They're doing an escape room. I mean, if there is one way to find out what someone is really like, it's to be locked in a room with them. They'll either never talk again or get married.'

I huff a laugh and try not to think of the state of my own marriage.

The evening is cool now, a promise of autumn just around the corner. It's nights like this that usually fill me with a sense of excitement and relief. The children will be back at school soon. I'll have free time again. I'll be able to work, to breathe, and yet there is a shadow over everything. Josh's words are still spinning in my thoughts. The anger is still there, that feeling of being wrong-footed again, and yet when I think about that conversation, it's the hope in his eyes, the excitement, that lingers. I push the memory away and drop into one of the chairs.

Matt pours the wine, sliding a glass towards me.

'Thank you.' I take a long gulp of crisp white wine, savouring the taste and the feeling of my mind and my body unwinding, unravelling.

'Come on then. What's going on with you?' he asks.

Tears well in my eyes and I dab them away. 'Sorry. I'm a mess. I had a big fight with Josh.'

It takes a full glass of wine for me to talk Matt through everything that Josh said and my feelings on it. 'I just can't believe he's dumped this huge change on me and expects me to just agree,' I finish, reaching for the bottle and topping up both of our glasses.

I expect Matt to agree with me, all sympathy and 'How dare he?', but instead, he's quiet, thoughtful.

'What is it?' I ask.

'Look, you are completely within your rights to feel blindsided . . .'

'But?' I say with a niggling unease for what is to come.

'It's just . . . you and me, we get to do what we love, right? You with your designs and me with my writing.'

I nod.

'And not everyone gets that. Most people don't even have something they love. They go to work, and they come home and watch TV, or whatever, and they never feel this fire,' he clutches at his stomach. 'They never get to know what it's like to wake up and be excited that it's Monday again and a whole week of doing what they love is stretching out before them.

'But Josh does know what his thing is – it's gardening. And he's found a way that it could maybe work for him. I know it's hard because his decision involves you and the kids too, but kids are pretty resilient and, actually, having their dad around probably means a hell of a lot more to them than having a swanky car.'

'It's not just the car,' I say, huffing a little. 'I'm not being materialist. This is their education and their home.'

Matt nods. 'I know. But maybe there's another way.'

'Well, if there is, he didn't hang around to talk about it.'

'Yeah, that's true, but he came to you with his dream and it sounds a bit like . . . sorry, but it sounds like you kind of killed it.'

Matt's words sink in and I drop my head in my hands. In one breath, my anger at Josh is gone, replaced with sadness and confusion.

'Shit!' I say. 'Shit, shit, shit. Why am I so crap at this?'

'At what?'

I half-laugh, half-sob. 'At adulting.'

'Becca, you are not crap at being an adult. You are a rock star. I see you with Olly, Matilda and Ben. I see how much of yourself you give to them. Plus being a designer and everything else you do. You're a complete inspiration. It's you that's got me and Laura talking again. I really thought that when things get rocky, the best thing to do is walk away. But I see you trying—'

'And failing.'

'And then trying again, even when you fail,' Matt continues, shooting me a stern look that reminds me a little of Saffron. 'And it's made me realise that I never stick at things when they get tough, I never push past that point to see the other side.' He finishes his wine and places the glass on the table. 'And, on that note, I should probably get to bed. It's an early start for me tomorrow. I'm meeting Laura for lunch in London.'

'That's really great,' I say, unsure how I've managed to

inspire Matt, or even save his relationship, when my own looks to be in tatters.

'Thanks for talking this all through with me,' I say at the front door.

'Any time,' Matt grins, pushing his glasses closer to his eyes and waving goodbye.

Later, I stare at my reflection in the mirror and sigh. I'm washed out, puffy from crying. But maybe there's something else too. A steely glint. I think of what Matt said about our passions and how lucky we are to have something that drives us. I think of Josh and the weary way he climbs out of bed on a Monday morning. I think of how much I love him. And suddenly, the argument doesn't matter. I just want to hear his voice and tell him I love him, that whatever happens, we'll be OK.

Chapter 41

I find my phone on the coffee in the living room. I snatch it up as I drop onto the sofa. There's a message on my lock screen. Something leaps inside me. Josh has left me a voice note. I fumble to turn up the volume and press play.

'Hey,' he says, his voice deflated, deadpan. 'Look, I'm really sorry for what I said, and I'm sorry I left like I did. Forget everything, OK? Like you said, it's a midlife crisis or something,' he barks a laugh. It's hollow and nothing like his usual humour. 'I got carried away and I forgot my responsibilities. I shouldn't have dumped it all on you like that. It's not fair of me to ask you and the children to change your whole lives because of me.' He sighs deeply, and there is so much emptiness in his voice that it yanks at my heart. 'I'll finish up in New York and when I'm home, I'll look for another job in hedge funds, maybe. It's fine.'

Tears blur my vision. This is what I wanted. An apology, an acceptance that I was right and he was wrong, and yet there is no jubilation, no vindication. Only a deep wrenching sadness.

We're a family. Olly, Matilda, Ben, me and Josh. We're a unit. Families should be together. And we're not, because Josh is never here. It's more than that though. When one of us isn't happy, it affects all of us, and Josh's misery over the last year, longer I think, has affected us all.

I open WhatsApp again and scroll to the very first of Josh's voice notes, and this time I listen. Really listen to the sadness, the misery, how unhappy he is in his job and with his life.

The realisation hits me hard. My gaze travels across the living room. The yellow cushions. The Farrow & Ball walls, the silver heart ornament that sits on the book shelf. The light on the ceiling with its twisted silver hanging. All this stuff I've placed so much value on. My perfect kitchen, my perfect house, my perfect photos for Instagram. But it's all been fake.

I hear Saffron's voice in my thoughts. 'You're holding back.'

She was right, but I never stopped to question why. The answer is staring at me in every single perfectly placed ornament. I thought if I made my house perfect, if the children went to the very best school, if I made everything just as I thought it should be, then I'd be happy. Whole. Except, I haven't been. This summer, cutting out social media and becoming the parent I've always wanted to be, has been the first time in years that I can remember laughing every day, waking up without a feeling of dread at another day.

I tap play again on Josh's voice notes.

'I'm proud of you for setting up your own business and doing what you love. I'm actually pretty jealous . . . It was never what I wanted to do. It's not just being here, away from you and the kids, that makes me feel lost. It's this job. I hate it.'

The truth is all here. If only I'd listened. Josh didn't spring anything on me at the weekend. He's been feeling this way for a long time. I was just too lost myself to see it.

I open the search engine and find the property he showed me on Saturday, cringing at how quickly I dismissed it. It's run down and needs work. That's undeniable. But when I looked before, I was searching for perfection. Now I see potential. And that land, that garden. Josh is right, the children would love it. Here, they are boxed in on three sides by neat brown fences. With the paddling pool and the washing line, there is barely space to walk around, let alone run, to charge into adventures. I smile to myself at the thought of Olly and the twins playing in a big open space, building dens and climbing trees.

I stop thinking of myself as the children dominate my thoughts. I was adamant in my fury on Saturday that we could not upend their lives. A new home, a new school. I didn't think it would be fair to the children or me. But is that true?

Olly's little voice echoes in my head. 'I hate that school . . . can we go to a different school? My new friend, Charlie goes to a different school.'

Deep down, I know the twins don't like it there either. It was always me, what I thought was best. I think about Amanda's description of the village school. 'It's a lovely small school, a big family really.'

I know St Helena's is a top school. The best. But the best for who? For what? What do I want for the children's education? Pushing them to be people they don't want to be? Or happiness? Acceptance? Isn't that all I've ever wanted for them? How have I lost sight of this?

With shaking hands, I press my finger to the voice note. It takes me a moment to find the words. 'Josh, I'm sorry. I'm the one who was wrong. About everything. I thought . . . I thought if I could make our life perfect then we'd be the perfect family, but I don't even know what that means anymore. All I know is that I want you home more. The children do too. They miss you so much. We can't be happy if you're not happy. Nothing else matters but us, our little unit. This house, the school, cars, clothes, whatever. It's all meaningless if we're not together. Please finish in New York and come home and follow your dreams. We're with you all the way. I love you.'

I stare at the voice note, waiting to see if it's been read. The ticks stay grey and my heart sinks. I climb the stairs and slide into bed with my phone still clutched in my hands.

Chapter 42

I wake with a start and think immediately of Josh. I scramble around my covers for my phone and find it shoved under a pillow. He's replied. No voice note this time. Just one word. Whoop!

A grin spreads across my face and I know deep in my core that whatever challenges lie ahead of us, this feels right. Josh will be home in three weeks and we will figure this out.

Another message pings on my phone. It's Saffron.

Can't wait to see you all again today! It's been a quiet week without you. Can't wait to hear how you've got on. See you at three pm. S xx

I cringe a little, knowing I'll have to confess to yesterday's failure, but I'm looking forward to seeing her. Before then, though, it feels like there is lots to do, lots to change. I text Amanda:

Hey, strange question – but do you know if the village school has space in Charlie's class for Olly and in reception for Matilda and Ben? Thanks! xx

Her reply is instant and makes me smile:

OMG! Don't tell me you're thinking of moving? I knew you weren't one of the snooty ones!! Let me send a text to Mrs Bilner, the head teacher. I'll get back to you ASAP. SO EXCITING!!

Amanda's excitement is infection and I find I'm grinning as Matilda, Olly and Ben stumble sleepily into the bedroom to snuggle beside me.

Her next message comes a minute later.

Mrs Bilner says they have space!!! She's in school today and suggested you pop in this morning for a nose around. 10am? xx

Nerves leap and jerk in my stomach at how quickly it's been arranged. But it's an excited nervous. A good nervous. I reply with a 'YES' and 'Thanks' and three smiley face emojis, while marvelling at Amanda texting the head teacher. I've only met Olly's head teacher once in the four years he's been at St Helena's. The idea of having his personal number and texting at 7 a.m. during the school holidays is laughable. But that's the point, isn't it? St Helena's is a different world, and I'm just starting to realise that it's not a world we belong in.

'What are we doing today, Mummy?' Matilda asks, snuggling up against me.

'Well,' I grin and take a breath. 'I thought we could do some exploring this morning.'

'Yesss,' Olly says, as Ben asks, 'Where are we going?'

I sit up a little and take in my beautiful children. What a journey we've been on this summer, me I think, more than them. I take a breath, the nerves returning. I look at Olly. 'How would you all feel about having a look around the village primary school where Charlie and Isabelle go?'

Olly's mouth drops open. 'Why?' he asks and I can tell he's trying not to get excited.

'To see if you'd all like to go there. I'm not sure any of us actually like St Helena's that much, do we? So, maybe we should try a different school.'

292

Olly's face changes again – a bright light being switching on. 'Really?'

I nod. 'If you like it.'

All three children leap up, and they cheer and dance around me. Excited. Happy.

'Right then,' I say, when they've calmed down. 'That's lucky you agree, because we're going to meet the head teacher at 10 a.m. and look around the school. And,' I add, with another fluttering in my stomach, the same excitement as the children are feeling, dancing inside me. 'If we can, we're going to look at a new house today, too. One that Daddy has seen that he likes a lot.'

The children stop, their faces falling. Panic is a pinprick to my bubble of excitement.

'Where?' Olly asks, his bottom lip sticking out.

'Still in the village,' I smile. 'It's even closer to the green, and the playground and the school.'

'That means it's closer to Charlie's house too.' Olly grins back at me.

I nod. 'It needs some work, though. Daddy showed me photos of it at the weekend. But it's got a very big garden with lots of trees to climb.'

'Do me and Matilda have to have our own rooms?' Ben asks suddenly.

'Only if you want to.'

They shake their heads and cling to each other, and I say a silent prayer that they'll always be close.

'Why are we moving?' Matilda asks over breakfast, her words muffled in the crunch of cereal.

'Nothing has been decided yet, but Daddy would like to be home more which means getting a different job and making some changes.'

'Like Charlie's dad?' Olly asks.

'Yes. Just like that.'

There is more dancing as we finish breakfast. The children talk excitedly about how they want their new bedrooms decorated.

We walk to the village school in the warmth of the late August sun. It feels precious now, like the last throws of summer. We pass the green and veer off to the playground and the swings for a quick play while I call the estate agent and find we can visit the new house after the school tour. Nerves flutter, jittery inside me, but maybe that's OK.

The school is everything I could've hoped for. Bright blue gates and colourful painted fences surround the building and playground. Mrs Bilner is in her forties, with dark hair and a big smile. She's bubbly and kind, listening with interest to Olly, Ben and Matilda's excited babbling as she leads us on our tour.

'This will be your classroom, Ben and Matilda,' she says. 'You have your own outdoor space to play in during class.' She leads us outside and I gasp at the sight of a mud kitchen. 'Is that—'

Mrs Bilner laughs. 'We do love a bit of mess in Reception. And just through these doors is your classroom, Olly.' She leads us into a bright yellow room. Display boards covered with sugar paper and trimmed with gold await the children's work. Around the room are dinosaur prints with dinosaur names beside them. 'Mr Knowles is a big dinosaur fan, Olly. Do you like dinosaurs?'

He nods. 'And science.'

'That's my favourite subject too. I run a science club on a Wednesday lunchtime. We do some pretty cool things, if you wanted to come.'

'What about sports?' Olly asks.

'We like sports a lot. We know it's important to stay fit and healthy.'

'I'm not very good at sports.'

'Maybe you just haven't found the right sport for you, yet?' she says. 'We like to encourage all of our pupils to try their best and have fun.'

'But what if I don't do well?'

'Will you try your best and have fun?'

Olly shrugs. 'I do always try my best.'

'We'll be proud of you then.'

As Mrs Bilner leads us back to the main entrance and hands me a stack of forms to complete, I feel an overwhelming desire to hug her. Amanda was right. There is a family feel to this school. There are no pretensions, no airs or graces. I've only been here for twenty minutes, but I feel welcome, I feel part of something, I feel accepted, and I can tell by the pleading looks on the children's faces, that hopping giddiness, that they feel it too.

I'm doing the right thing, I tell myself with absolute certainty. I'm a good mother. I love my children.

Chapter 43

As we walk across the green, the children talk non-stop about the school, begging me to take them uniform shopping tomorrow and to return the unwanted St Helena's uniform. An optimism threads through my body at the house we're about to see.

But even I can't hide the lurching disappointment when we turn down an unmarked lane and find ourselves at a gate hanging from its hinges, wood rotten and scraping on the floor. At the end of the driveway is a square house that reminds me of one of Matilda's drawings of a house – a front door in the middle, two windows either side and two on the top, below a red roof.

'Is that it?' Olly asks, his voice still bouncing.

I nod, forcing a smile as a man steps from a small Vauxhall Corsa. He's wearing a tight suit with a skinny tie, a sharp goatee and too much gel in his hair. Everything about him screams estate agent. 'Mrs Harris?'

'Becca, please. Hi.'

'I'm Alfie from Court and Son Estate Agents. I'll show you around.' He's quick to usher us inside, and I don't blame him. The once-white walls are dirty grey, and there are scrapes and marks from a plant that has long stopped climbing. I try to picture a bushy wisteria growing around the house, purple blooms hanging over the front door, but all I see is dirt and neglect.

Inside is no better. Sunlight streams through the window, like a spotlight highlighting every peel of wallpaper hanging from the wall, every cobweb. There's a stink to place that makes Matilda hold her nose. It's the damp smell of clothes left in the washing machine for too long, but worse. Alfie leads us through a narrow hall, past a staircase and into a dining room. There's something strange about the carpet. It's squishy, like walking on a bed of dead worms. I look at my feet and wish I'd worn trainers instead of sandals.

'There was a leak last month,' Alfie says, following my gaze to the beige carpet. 'A water pipe burst and, with no one in the house at the time, it went unchecked for a while. It's all been fixed now, of course, but the carpets need time to dry.'

'They need to be replaced,' I say. 'May I?' I point at the corner and crouch down.

Alfie shrugs a reply and so I lift up the edge of the carpet. The under layer is sodden and falling apart, but to my surprise, beneath it all are sturdy floorboards, running in narrow strips across the room. With the right varnish, they would be beautiful. I tuck the carpet back into place and as Alfie leads us upstairs, something Saffron said to me in one of our many, many talks, sticks in my head.

'Our lives are not rooms that need to be perfected. There is no such thing as perfect. Life is about building the room from nothing.' She went on to talk about how it's grit and hard work and love that builds the rooms. Lots and lots of love. I remember that. And how she said it will never be finished. 'There will never be a point when you will stand back and say, it's done, it's perfect. Life is a continuous journey of building, setbacks, building again.' She told me to stop believing in perfection because it's making me feel like I'm failing when I'm not.

At the time, her words had made me cry, but right now they lift me up and I start to see the potential. The children run through the four bedrooms, shouting which one they want. They're good sizes, even the smallest one, which will one day be Ben or Matilda's. They won't want to share forever.

The bathroom is in better shape than I'd hoped. It's all white, and despite a layer of grime, it's not too old. There are handles by the toilet and the shower – a sign of the previous resident.

'Who owns the house?' I ask.

'A gentleman lived here for many years. He used to be a handyman, I believe, but became quite frail. His two children moved him into a care home last year and he sadly passed away soon after, so the house has sat empty for a while. They're now keen to sell and, off the record, I think they'd accept a fairly low offer.'

'Has there been much interest?'

He opens his mouth and I'm sure he's about to give me all the bullshit, but I narrow my eyes and he stops short, shaking his head. 'There's a new estate in the next village. People don't want do-er uppers anymore.'

'Can we see the garden, Mummy?' Olly asks, pulling on my sleeve as we step back to the ground floor.

Alfie jingles some keys before unlocking the back door and leading us out to the garden. There are piles of wood everywhere. An old, rusted roller leans against the house alongside a wheelbarrow that's missing its wheel. I wonder if that makes it just a barrow.

Matilda charges across the overgrown lawn, arms out, giving her best battle cry. Ben and Olly are quick to follow. They run and run until they reach the trees, and Olly reaches up and swings from a low-hanging branch.

'You don't get gardens like this with a new build,' Alfie says. 'There was some interest a few months ago from a building developer who wanted to knock the house down and build a small estate on the land, but the children of the old owner turned down the offer. Apparently, their dad would have come back to haunt them if they'd done that.' He barks a laugh, showing how stupid he thinks they were, but I see it. This is a lovely house. A lovely home. Or it will be, with some love and vision.

I think of weekends spent playing out here, and barbecues and camping. I think of a little summer house in the corner – a studio for me to work in. Of the way Josh smiles when he's in the garden.

'What do you think?' Alfie asks, as I watch the children explore the garden.

'I think I need to speak to my husband.'

Alfie grins, taking my answer as a good sign.

'Two more minutes,' I shout down the length of the garden. The warning is second nature now, and when I call the children to come, they do, rosy-cheeked and breathless.

'Can we knock for Charlie and Isabelle on the way back?' Matilda gasps. 'And ask them to lunch.'

I nod. 'Sounds like a good plan. You can tell them you'll be classmates too.'

The children skip ahead and I pull out my phone and call Josh. This can't wait three more weeks. I'm desperate to talk to him. But his phone goes straight to voicemail and I don't leave a message.

Chapter 44

Throughout the afternoon, my optimism fades – like the batteries in Olly's remote-control car – until all that is left is a dull worry. I wish Josh would call me back. The distance between us suddenly feels insurmountable. I can't wait three more minutes to see him, let alone three more weeks.

Saffron arrives at exactly 3 p.m.. The children abandon their game in the garden and run to the door to greet her, and I realise I won't be the only one who'll miss her. She's all smiles on the doorstep, holding out a large homemade chocolate cake covered in Smarties. 'To celebrate,' she says, grinning as the children skip around her feet.

'Can we have some now, Mummy?' Olly asks.

'I want that bit with the orange Smarties,' Ben says.

Matilda smiles. 'I want the biggest bit.'

I cut cake for all of us and as the children take their slices outside to eat, Saffron and I draw out the stools and sit at the island for the final time. Saffron's camera is sitting on the counter but I've long since given up caring. In fact, if these videos of me can help just one other family, then I'd readily do it all again, meme and all.

'I think cake might have been a tad premature.' I pull a face.

Saffron leans forward, her full attention focused on me. 'What happened?'

I sigh and even though I only meant to tell her about how I gave up on the kids last night, the whole story of Josh coming home and everything we said and everything that's happened tumbles out. By the time I finish, our cups of tea are empty and the children have come in to set up a leaving show of some kind in the living room for Saffron. There are giggles and bursts of music drifting into the kitchen.

Her smile is sympathetic. 'Let's start with the children. That's easy. You dropped the ball and last night was a tough evening. Where did you go wrong?'

'I let them walk all over me. I wasn't firm and I checked out. I didn't give them the attention they needed.'

'Right.' She nods. 'So, what happens next? Are you going to give up and let things be the way they used to be?'

'No. I can't go back to that.'

'So, you're going to . . .'

'Keeping trying. Keep being present.'

'Not just try. You're going to do it, Becca. I have faith in you. It's time you had faith in yourself.'

I nod.

'And as for Josh. It sounds like you have a plan and you're both committed to making it work. I don't know anything about relationships but my mum always says that things might not always be easy, but that doesn't mean they're not right.'

'Talking of relationships,' I say with a grin. 'How was the escape room last night? Did you manage to escape?'

She laughs. 'Matt told you about our date, right?'

I nod.

'It was good. Liam is . . . a nice guy. We were both pretty focused during the escape room but afterwards we went for a drink and we laughed a lot.'

'Sounds promising,' I say.

'Yes. I think it is.' There's a wistful look on Saffron's face which makes me laugh again.

'I know, it's sad, right? To be so dreamy after one date. But honestly, Becca, I have the worst love life ever. I'm basically a spinster at the age of twenty-four. A spinster who lives with her mum and dad. Liam is the first man that's ever made me want to go on a second date.'

Olly bursts into the kitchen then, wearing an old vampire Halloween costume as a cape. 'This way please, madams.' He bows before leading Saffron and me into the living room, where the children dance and sing, and Ben attempts a magic disappearing trick with a skittish Rex, who dives from the room as soon as she's unleashed. We end it with dancing, shaking our way through The Spice Girls and Taylor Swift.

When the music stops, I catch the ring of my phone from the kitchen and sprint towards the noise, answering with a breathless, 'Hello?', hoping it's Josh.

'Rebecca? It's Mrs Young.'

'Oh, hi. How are you?' I ask out of politeness, wishing I hadn't answered the call. 'I'm so sorry I've been meaning to drop off some money to replace the picture frame my son broke.'

'Don't worry about that, love. I know you're busy, but with the summer holidays almost over, I wanted to talk about when you're coming back to work for me?'

'To work?' I ask, sounding stupid, but unable to stop myself. 'For you?'

'Yes. Of course.'

'I . . . I thought you said you didn't want my services anymore. After Ben slid down your banister.'

She gives a tinkling laugh. 'Oh dear, I think you must have got the wrong end of the stick. When I said now

302

wasn't a good time, I didn't mean for me. I meant for you. I could see how busy you were going to be over the summer. I didn't want to be the reason you were juggling too much.

'I remember the holidays all too well. I put my Helen and George into a holiday camp every single day because I worked in local government. They hated it. I ruined their summer holidays. I didn't want to ruin yours as well. It may not seem it to you right now, but the summer holidays are precious gifts and one day, your children will be grown and there won't be these weeks together anymore.'

'I . . .' A lump forms in my throat. 'I don't know what to say. I thought when Ben slid down the banister—'

'Every child who comes to my house slides down that banister. They can't help it. Even my Stan used to do it sometimes when he was feeling sprightly. Now, will you come back and get my house in order for me?'

'Well, the children start school on Tuesday.'

'Right,' Mrs Young says and I can hear the smile in her voice. 'Let's say Thursday at 10 a.m.. You'll want a day to yourself, I'm sure, but I'd like a few rooms done before Christmas, if that's not too adventurous. I've got both kids and all the grandkids coming, and I want the house to feel fresh and full of life for them.'

'We can absolutely do that. Thursday is great. See you then.'

'Rebecca, before I forget, there's a lady at my dance class who wants to freshen up her dining room before Christmas. Is it OK if I give her your number?'

'Of course. That would be brilliant. Thank you.'

'Alright then. See you Thursday.'

I end the call and return to Saffron and the kids. 'Good news?' she asks.

'Yes. It turns out Mrs Young does still want me to redesign her house.'

'Of course she does.' Saffron says, before picking up her bag and looping it over her shoulder in the way I've seen her do so many times now. With a stab of sadness, I realise this is it. Saffron is leaving. The children fall silent and bunch around me, and I know they feel the finality of it too.

'Are you sure you don't want to come back next week?' I ask as she moves to the front door. 'Just to check in.'

Saffron smiles, but shakes her head. 'You don't need me anymore.'

'I do,' I plead, but of course, she's right. We don't need Saffron. I've totally got this.

'Really?' One eyebrow lifts.

'What if they start new things that you haven't shown me how to cope with?'

'It doesn't matter. You have the tools to cope with anything. You always have. It just takes confidence, belief in yourself as a person and as a mother.'

I nod and hug my arms around myself. I'll miss her presence, her championing, even her love of nineties pop.

Saffron steps forward and envelops me in a big hug. I catch the smell of strawberries and sweetness. She pulls away and smiles. 'This isn't the end of us.'

'It isn't?' I ask, surprised.

'I hope not. You are an amazing woman, Becca. I hope we can still be friends.'

'I'd like that. And, for the record, you're the amazing one here.'

'We both are,' she grins. 'So, if I invite you to come dancing with me one night, you'll come?' I have a sudden image of what a night out with Saffron might look like. The two of us, plus some other mums she's befriended along the way. Saffron leading us into a nineties disco, hands clapping as she dances around us. I can imagine her cajoling the entire place onto the dance floor. The thought makes me smile.

'I would love that,' I say.

'Yaaay!' Saffron does a little dance that makes us all laugh. 'Well, I'd best be off.'

'Where are you going next?'

'A family in north London. A widowed dad and a little boy.' She looks sad for a moment. 'They've had a tough time, but I know I can help them.'

'Good luck,' I say.

Saffron crouches down and beckons the children towards her. They step forward, as eager as hungry baby birds wanting to be fed.

I drink them in. My lovely children.

They've changed so much this summer. It's not just the height they've gained, but Olly, especially, is carrying himself differently. He seems not just older, but stronger in himself. Matilda is calmer. Still playful and full of mischief, but thoughtful too. Ben, my sweet Ben, now sleeps through the night, most nights, and when he does get up, it's one quick cuddle, one whisper of reassurance, and he's happy to go back to his bed.

They are closer to each other too. Olly and Ben sharing Nerf guns and cars, Matilda joining in with the garish pink of her toys. There are more games of Peter Pan and crocodiles, cushions thrown on the floor as rocks to jump on, than fights. They are happier. I am too.

'Olly,' Saffron says, crouching down to give him a tight hug before pulling back and looking at him. 'You are an amazing inventor. Don't stop inventing things and exploring,' she says, and he shakes his head, looking tearful. 'The world needs people like you.'

He steps back and I put my arm around him.

'Ben,' she says next, and they hug. 'Remember, you are braver than you think. Keep sliding,' she adds with a wink. He grins and moves away, and then Matilda is there, launching herself into Saffron's arms and almost toppling her over.

'Oh, Matilda,' she smiles. 'You have so much courage. You are your own person. You know what you want. And I think,' she says, dropping her voice to a whisper, 'that your mum used to be a lot like you, but she lost her way a bit.'

'You found her again,' Matilda says.

Saffron smiles. 'She found herself. I just gave her a nudge.'

'I won't lose myself,' Matilda says, patting her body like she's checking she's still there.

'I know you won't.' They hug again and then Saffron is waving from the open doorway. 'This is always the hardest part,' she says, and I can see from the emotion on her face that she means it. 'Goodbye, Harris family. Good luck with your exciting new adventure.'

We wave her off as she climbs into her little pink Fiat 500. As I close the door, I feel the mood around us plummet.

'Right,' I say, and I give my hands a clap, mimicking Saffron and making Olly laugh. 'We have two options. We can sit on the sofa feeling sorry for ourselves and watch a Disney film. Or we can make the most of the last of the sunshine and have a water fight.'

'Water fight,' they shout, jumping up and down, and I laugh. 'Go get your swim things on. I'll prepare for battle.'

I really will miss Saffron, I think, as I fill the buckets with water. But she's right. I trust myself now in a way I haven't done since before Olly was born. I don't know quite how or when my confidence got knocked so far off kilter, but it's back and I won't let it go again.

Chapter 45

'Noooo,' I shout, crumbling to the ground as Ben and Matilda tug at my legs. Olly steps over me, smiling like a manic villain in one of his cartoons. He hoists the super-soaker water pistol into his hands and I scream. 'Don't you dare!'

'I dare,' he giggles.

'Do it!' Matilda says, the mastermind behind my takedown.

'Only if Mummy wants to,' Ben adds, his hands loosening around my foot.

I cover my face with my hands, ready for the burst of cold water to hit, but it doesn't. There's a pause and then Olly is jumping up and down. 'Daddy,' he shouts and I twist around to see Josh standing in the garden in a crumpled suit, a suitcase still in his hands.

'What's going on here, then?' Josh asks.

'We're having a water fight,' Matilda replies.

'Guys,' I say, getting to my feet. 'Daddy is wearing his suit and is very tired so let's not drag him into the water fun, OK?'

'What if Daddy wants to join in?' Josh says, smiling at me. 'What if Daddy thinks you all look far too dry to be having a water fight?' In the next moment, he's dropped his case and the hose is in his hands and he's running down the garden, spraying us all.

Olly screams with delight and charges at Josh with his gun, while Ben and Matilda hide behind my legs.

'How about we get Mummy?' Josh calls out. Olly turns to look at me, villainous once more, and I break into a run.

'No!' I call out, feeling the sprinkling of water on my shoulder. But then Josh is scooping me into his arms and carrying me across the garden.

'Not so fast, Mrs Harris,' he says, heading straight for the paddling pool.

'You wouldn't!' I cry out, too happy to see him, to feel the warmth of his body against me, to really care what happens next.

'Wouldn't I?' He winks. 'What do you think, kids? Shall I drop Mummy in?'

'Yesssss,' they chorus and then I'm dropping into the cold water. It's biting and I yelp, splashing a handful of water at Josh.

But before Josh can step away, Olly, Ben and Matilda are there, pushing and shoving until he topples in beside me and they follow, jumping in to splash and dance, and Josh leans over, pulling me into his arms and kissing me.

'I can't believe you're here,' I say. 'I thought I wouldn't see you for three more weeks.'

'I left the second I heard your note. I just walked out of the meeting I was in, grabbed my stuff and got on the first flight I could.'

'So, that's it. You're quitting?'

He gives a rueful smile. 'I pretty much have to now. After leaving like that, I'm pretty sure my career is over anyway.'

'Good,' I reply. 'You won't be able to go back to it then.'

'Are you sure?' Josh asks, serious now. 'I can't ask you to give up everything you love.'

'You're not. What I love is you and the kids. Everything that matters is in this paddling pool.'

'There's a lot going on in this paddling pool,' Josh says. Alarm registers on his face as he nods towards something brown floating in the water that looks like . . . it can't be. Oh God. It is.

'Kids,' I shout. 'Everyone out.'

We scramble out and wrap the children in towels and send them inside to get dried.

'False alarm,' Josh calls. 'It was just a pine cone.'

I laugh. 'Thank goodness.'

Josh steps towards me, hesitant again. 'The school—'

'I've already moved them. It's not just the money. They weren't happy at St Helena's. I was so fixated on getting them to the perfect school, I didn't stop to think who it was perfect for. The village school is a much better fit for them. You're going to love it.'

'And the house?'

'I went to see the one you showed me today.'

'You did?' Josh's face lights up.

'It needs a lot of work, but . . .'

Before I can say another word, Josh scoops me into his arms and we kiss again. It's familiar and sweet and hot. A rush of desire burns through my body.

'I want this new adventure as much as you do,' I say when we pull away.

'I love you, Rebecca Harris,' he says before we kiss again.

One year later

Chapter 46

Voice note from Josh:

'I just had to tell you I love you. It doesn't feel like enough for everything you've done for me. I'm so happy now, Becca. I know things are tight, but we're getting there and that's because of you. Thank you.

'I've been thinking about our wedding day today. Not the bit where I got a bit tipsy and you took advantage of me, Mrs Harris, but the moment you stepped into that room in your dress. You floored me, you know? And what I don't tell you enough is that every time you walk into a room, you floor me all over again.'

Voice note from me:

'You idiot! I only saw you in the kitchen an hour ago. I'm looking out of my studio window right now and I can see you at the end of the garden. Don't forget we promised we'd collect the kids together today.'

Voice note from Josh:

'I haven't forgotten. School pick-up and play in the park. Charlie and Isabelle for play and tea. I'm doing a BBQ. I'll collect the meat on my way back from quoting the Sullivans for their new garden renovation.'

Voice note from me:

'Great. Now leave me in peace. I've got to get these curtains finished by tomorrow and you're a distraction, Joshua Harris.'

Voice note from Josh:

'So that's a no to having lunch with me?'

Voice note from me:

'Oh go on then. I'll see you in a minute.'

Acknowledgements

If you've come this far then my first thank you is to you, dear reader, for reading Becca's story. I loved writing all the fun and mishaps she and the children found themselves in. It's not all based on my own experiences, but I will say that the pigeon story actually happened to me. And there have been plenty of times that I've wished for a Saffron in my life to quiet the inner voice.

My second thank you is to Rhea Kurien who is not only a champion of books and authors but is also kind and amazing! Thank you also to Sanah Ahmed and all the Orion Dash team for giving Becca, Olly, Ben and Matilda's story a home.

To my amazing agent, Tanera Simons, and her eagle-eyed assistant, Laura Heathfield for your fantastic editorial advice and for supporting me and my books always! I'm so grateful for all you've done and continue to do for me!

Thank you to all the bloggers, reviewers and early readers who put so much work into supporting and shouting about our books. You guys are the best!

I'm lucky to have a great group of friends around me both in real life and online, who have supported me through the highs and lows of writing, and I'm very grateful to all of them. Special mention to Laura Pearson, Nikki Smith and Zoe Lea for being the best author pals EVER! To Chris McDonald for his Nanowrimo group and support, and to Carol, Sarah, Catherine and Kathryn for being lovely.

Every so often, I get a little stuck and jump on Facebook to ask for help. So I must mention Martin Lee for his shrinking chocolate bar analogy and to Tracey De Biasi for coming up with the name of The Toddler Tamer!!! To Sarah Bennet, Helen Edwards and everyone else who comments and supports, thank you!!

To my daughter Lottie, I'm sorry I couldn't fit guinea pigs into this story, but I did manage a Jessie cat instead. I hope you like this book as much as the last one. Thank you to you and Tommy for all of your support, for listening to me prattle on about my stories and being such fantastic champions of my books.

And finally an apology. In the acknowledgements of *Just The Six Of Us*, I meant to write "And last but not least, to Tommy and Andy for all of your support!!" But what I actually wrote about my husband of over fourteen years and my amazing son, was "And last but least . . ." which caused lots of laughter in our house but was a typo, I promise. And so finally to Tommy and Andy for your love and support, thank you. It means the world!

Don't miss Laurie Ellingham's fun, uplifting and heartwarming blended family romcom...

'Warm, funny and relatable, JUST THE SIX OF US is a big hug of a book' Emma Cooper

When Jenny and Dan meet, sparks fly and they can't get enough of each other. What they can get enough of? Sneaking around and hiding their relationship from their kids...

Divorced, single, and ready for another shot at love in their forties, what they didn't count on is how hard second chances can be.

When Jenny gets some unexpected news, suddenly navigating exes and step-children becomes even more important...

9 781398 717244